THE FLAME TREE

THE ROYAL POINCIANA EDITION

BOOKS BY THEODORE PRATT

NOVELS: *The Flame Tree* · *The Barefoot Mailman* · *Miss Dilly Says No* · *Mr. Winkle Goes to War* · *Valley Boy* · *Mercy Island* · *Big Blow* · *Mr. Limpet* · *Thunder Mountain* · *Mr. Thurtle's Trolley* · *Not Without the Wedding* · *Spring From Downward*

MYSTERIES: *Murder Goes Fishing* · *Murder Goes in a Trailer* · *Murder Goes to the Dogs* · *Murder Goes to the World's Fair*

SHORT STORIES: *Perils in Provence and Other Ticklish Places*

THE FLAME TREE

THEODORE PRATT

Florida Classics Library
P.O. Box 1657 Port Salerno, Florida 34992

Florida Classics Library

AUTHOR'S NOTE

THIS BOOK carries on the story of the southeast Florida coast begun in my previous novel, *The Barefoot Mailman*, which tells how the mail was once transported weekly between Palm Beach and Miami by a carrier who walked barefoot along the only road, the beach. While in no sense a sequel, a few characters from *The Barefoot Mailman* appear as minor figures in *The Flame Tree*, for the period of both novels nearly touch. Henry M. Flagler, the Florida empire-builder, his third wife, Mary Lily, and Colonel Edward R. Bradley, the proprietor of the Beach Club, the famed gambling place, also appear briefly, the only characters meant to represent real people.

Very few liberties have been taken with the actual happenings during the opening up of Florida around the turn of the century. What changes from fact do appear have been made deliberately for the sake of writing a story instead of a history. The early days of the famous Royal Poinciana hotel at Palm Beach are pictured as closely to the way they were actually as could be accomplished by several years of intense research.

The "Ponce," as the huge hostelry was fondly known, was the most magnificent of the grand hotels of all time. It was singular in both spirit and physical appearance. It was the largest hotel in the world of its time. It was the largest wooden structure ever built anywhere. In it was epitomized a unique way of American life that will most surely never be seen again.

THE FLAME TREE

IN A SECOND-STORY CHAMBER of a coquina rock rooming-house facing the Plaza de la Constitucion in St. Augustine, Jenny Totten lay resting on the massive mahogany bed. A small proud smile spread over her lips, vanished, and then returned again. "I'm a married woman," she confided to herself. "This is the afternoon of January twelfth in the year eighteen hundred and ninety-three, and I've been married a week."

Jenny's body wasn't heavy enough to make much of an impression on the stiff counterpane. She was medium-sized and neatly boned, but not frail. At seventeen she was nearly complete; her breasts were full, high and delicately tipped. Her hair was so black it had a sheen of deep blue in it. Her clear white complexion was marred only by a delicate sprinkling of freckles that reached across her straight little nose and then started timid voyages onto her cheeks.

To rest better, Jenny had slipped off her corset. She had put her mousseline dress back on, for she didn't care to appear in the afternoon in a wrapper. She had, however, discarded all except one petticoat. Unlike Ohio, from where she came, it was warm in Florida in the middle of winter. It was comfortably nice on the large bed. She wriggled in her own warmth, filled with the delicious shame of being married, while she fondly recalled how this had come about.

In the company of her Aunt Erminia, she had met Tip Totten two months ago at the post office back in Yancey. An acquaintance presented him. She saw a tall lean young man with shaggy hair and open, weathered features. His eyes, dark duplicates of her own, became luminous, lighting with pinpricks of fire, when they came upon her.

Tip's sudden discovery and instant admiration was so complete and unguarded that it disarmed Jenny. He made no acknowledgment of the introduction. The sight of her, he admitted later, left him speechless. He had merely been able to watch her as she went out the door with her aunt. He confessed that he had never even seen that she was with anyone else.

Aunt Erminia, when they reached the street, complained not about this, but about his manners toward Jenny. "The nerve of him to stare at you like that."

"I think he liked me."

"Well, I don't like anybody as rude as that."

"Maybe he's only shy."

"That's just as bad. Worse, in some ways." Her aunt was a lady of decided opinion, frankly expressed. Even then she sensed in Tip a danger to her plans for her niece. Bringing up Jenny since both her parents died of smallpox when she was ten, Aunt Erminia had aspirations for the girl that went beyond an uncouth youth from the backwoods.

She snorted and made her attitude all too plain when Tip came calling. Aunt Erminia was not impressed with the three mink skins Tip brought as a present. He suggested, "I thought you might find them good enough for a muff." They were the most beautiful skins Jenny had ever seen.

2

The muff her aunt made for her, scoffing at their donor, was the envy of the town.

Tip told Jenny of himself as though presenting his background for her possible consideration. He lived ten miles out of town in a log cabin with his parents and two brothers. They hunted and trapped for a living. That had largely been his education. For the rest his mother instructed him, and he had a few years at school when he became old enough to walk back and forth to town.

Tip tramped the ten miles each way to see Jenny. He did not hide what he wanted from her. He didn't actually expect anything, but only hoped. "I'm a poor catch," he told her. "Not in your class at all."

"Tip," she said, "there aren't classes of people——"

"Oh, yes, there are," he differed. That was the first time he surprised her. "And we'd better realize it. You're one thing, and I'm another. I don't say one is any better than the other. But they're different. Maybe we don't belong together."

Nothing had been said of belonging together. Jenny was accustomed to her suitors pleading their causes with fervent protestations of how much they were made for each other. Tip was unique.

The practical part of her woman's mind recognized that his love for her was not merely a blind groping; he wanted to establish it on a sound basis, rejecting her if she was not right for him. Startled, Jenny saw his own high standard. She wanted to be good enough to meet it.

She looked at him on a cold day they walked together. The bare hand by which he held her arm was blue with chill. Impulsively she took it and drew it into the silken

3

interior of the mink muff. Their fingers found each other. Hers warmed his, and as they did so Jenny felt a melting sensation come over her that left her weak.

They stopped, and faced each other, their hands still together in the muff. In a half-strangled voice he said, "I couldn't give you anything like you been brought up to have."

"That doesn't matter, Tip."

He blurted, "I only got about two hundred dollars saved from my share of the skins."

"That's an awful lot of money."

"It ain't, and you know it."

She placed his other hand in the muff. They held on tightly, secretly beneath the glistening fur. Looking down at it, she drew his eyes there, too, and said, "That's what matters, Tip."

Their fingers grasped even tighter, almost fiercely.

"You mean it?" he demanded.

The fact that he couldn't believe it yet touched her like delicious pain. She looked up, to find his burning stare on her, and she nodded.

He gave a great sigh, as though he had been pursuing something for a long time, and only now came within sight of it.

Without knowing in the least what they did, they kissed, right there in public on the open street.

On the way back to her aunt's house Tip first mentioned Florida to her. It was always summer there. Game was profuse in contrast with its disappearing fast in Ohio. Skins were good, life easy. Immediately that became a part of her because it was a part of him, and now of themselves. Aunt Erminia was shocked and appalled at their announcement.

4

She informed Tip baldly, "You aren't a fit husband for her."

"Ma'm," Tip replied agreeably, "that's what I been telling her."

"You won't—you couldn't—make a happy marriage."

"That," said Tip politely, "I expect is a thing we'd have to judge for ourselves."

"Where are you going to live?"

"We ain't talked that all the way out yet, but maybe Florida."

Aunt Erminia attacked cruelly, "You don't even use good grammar."

"I got to be taken like I am, ma'm. Or not taken. That's why I want Jenny to think some more about it before we go ahead."

In panic, Aunt Erminia demanded, "You aren't thinking of getting married right away?"

"I guess," said Tip, looking at Jenny, "we got a feeling for each other that calls for it as soon as Jenny is sure."

The aunt appealed to her niece. "Jenny!"

Jenny was sorry to disrupt the world her aunt had built for her, but she was driven by a stronger and different kind of love than she had for her relative. Without looking at Aunt Erminia, Jenny announced, "I'm sure now, Tip."

In desperation at the threat of losing her niece to so distant a place as Florida, Aunt Erminia offered to let them live in her house with her. When Jenny refused this with affectionate thanks, her aunt wanted to give them five hundred dollars as a wedding present, a sum she couldn't exactly afford, but which she felt Jenny needed more than she did. Tip put his foot down on this. "I don't want my wife bringing more than twice the money I got."

He allowed Aunt Erminia to give them a hundred dollars. At that point he at least won her respect. She still didn't accept him as a proper husband for Jenny and blamed him bitterly for taking her away.

Jenny had no time to reminisce further about her marriage. Through half-closed eyes, which she closed instantly all the way, she saw the door open softly and Tip appear.

He moved silently across the big square room and stood for a moment looking down at his young wife. He thought of her like that because he was four years older, all of twenty-one. This made her seem hardly more than a child who needed protection.

Gazing down at Jenny, Tip couldn't tell if she slept or played a game with him of pretending to be asleep. He didn't care, just so long as she was here. Sometimes Tip thought he would die for loving her. In the possession of her he was still enthralled that anyone could be as she had proved herself to him. He worshiped her without stint or reservation. She was almost holy to him. He could not keep his eyes off her or the thought of her out of his head. He regarded himself as the luckiest of men to have her. He anticipated her every desire and wish and moved, if he could, to meet it before she expressed it.

Tip took off his high-buttoned blue serge suit coat and hung it over one of the thick mahogany posts of the bed's sturdy footboard. He followed this garment with his waistcoat, being careful not to let his heavy gold watch chain rattle. He lifted one foot and then the other and took off his boots. Then he eased one foot on the bed beside Jenny, stretching out well beyond her.

Still her eyes did not open. Not until he turned his head,

his face within inches of hers and their noses almost touching, did her lashes come up. Their eyes met in sudden, close, welcome recognition, and lighted. His slow smile widened and the sight of this broadened the smile on Jenny's lips. With intimate delight they regarded each other.

Tip waited, though he could barely contain himself, until her hand reached for his cheek. He accepted the invitation quickly. As he held her close, one arm about her slim waist, they kissed, long, deeply and repeatedly.

"You ain't got any right," he whispered, "being this beautiful."

She denied his compliment with pleasure. "I'm not beautiful. That's for when you're older; it's for grand ladies all dressed up."

"All right, then, you ain't beautiful."

"*You* aren't supposed to say it."

He grinned, then, and told her, "Anyway, you're the prettiest thing that ever lived." Gazing into her black eyes close to his own which snapped with the same color, he said solemnly, "You're so pretty sometimes it makes me scared."

"Why should it make you scared, Tip?"

"I don't know. But it does."

Jenny didn't understand this feeling of his any more clearly than he seemed to know it himself. But she was glad both for him and for herself that she might be attractive. She had a husband who thought she was beautiful and she lay with him on a bed in St. Augustine, over a thousand miles from home, and told him, "You've been gone a long time. We got here this morning and you've been away half the time."

"Only three hours."

7

" 'Only?' " She expressed fond aggrievement. "It seemed like three days."

He stopped teasing her, and held her more closely. "Three weeks," he amended.

Pleased, she whispered, "I love you."

He buried his face in the warmth and softness of the side of her throat, and murmured, "I love you, too." He held her still more closely.

She gave a low choke of response that was like a cry. "Oh, Tip!"

WHEN AFTER A TIME they parted, Tip lay on his back, one arm under Jenny's neck, the other flung up above his head. She lay on her side, watching him.

Suddenly the loud blare of a band came in through the open window from the square. Tip looked toward the window, and Jenny raised her head to look also, and listen. She lifted herself to one elbow, and then got up. She left the bed and crossed the room to the window. She stared out for a moment before she called, without looking around, "Come and see."

Tip joined her at the window. The far end of the ancient square opened onto a wide bay over whose surface a few sailboats skimmed. The stone buildings on the other three sides were those of hotels, rooming-houses like their own, restaurants, tobacco shops, several barbers, a theater and a small Catholic cathedral. In the plaza itself grew large graceful palms. On an octagonal-shaped covered stand a band now played furiously. All about promenaded smartly dressed people, while some sat on benches, listening to the music and examining the strollers. It was the fashionable hour in St. Augustine.

Jenny was taken with the gay and bright scene. She stood looking at the entertaining spectacle. Her lips parted and her eyes were bright. "Let's walk about, too," she proposed to

9

Tip. "Though I'm a little scared of all those society million-aires."

"I'll bet," said Tip, "some of them ain't millionaires, a lot of them ain't society and a lot more not too long ago didn't have any more money than us." He took her hand, to lead her down to the plaza, but she held back.

"I've got to change my dress. And do up my hair."

"You look fine just like you are."

"Not in this dress." Jenny waved a hand at the people below. "Don't you see?"

Tip stared down. He shook his head, puzzled, seeing but not understanding.

He didn't change his dark blue serge suit, for that was his best, but he did wash at the bowl and pitcher in one corner of the room and combed his hair with a neat part in the middle. He took a long time at these activities, for he knew that Jenny in back of him was undressing and then dressing. She had opened one of their fiber trunks. He turned only when she requested, "Hook me up."

She had brought out her very best daytime gown. It was of wine-red damask. It fitted her snugly, showing off her young, full figure to every advantage. Its straight foundation skirt with its short train, had superimposed on it a shorter overskirt draped in back to take the place of a bustle now out of date. The upper bodice was of passementerie, rising to a high lace collar.

Twisting her head as Tip made connections with hooks and eyes, Jenny wanted to know, "Is it too wrinkled?"

"I can only see a couple of little wrinkles that don't amount to anything at all." Tip's hands still shook a little whenever he worked so intimately at her clothes.

Jenny made an exasperated sound that meant the dress was horribly wrinkled from hem to neck. Hastily she combed out her hair and then piled it into the highest pompadour she could manage. On top of this edifice of hair she carefully perched a little red straw hat; she hoped her costume was not too red, and was glad she had decided against feathers on the hat. After giving a last glance at herself in the tall mirror set in one of the doors of the large wardrobe, she was nervously ready.

When they reached the plaza and joined the promenading people, Jenny lost her nervousness, replacing it with an absorbed admiration for the silk and paillette-studded velvet styles to be observed on every hand. Never had she seen such grand, dignified people and up-to-the-minute fashions. Both, she was sure, were straight from Fifth Avenue. They walked to the lively strains of the band, and it was like being in a stirring parade.

Jenny saw that leg-o'-mutton sleeves were being revived, and made plans of her own. She liked the new princess gowns. She stared at one whose train was being coquettishly uplifted by its owner, to reveal quantities of rustling frilled petticoats and then, for an instant, a glimpse of black stocking.

Jenny gasped.

Tip said, "You got just as good-looking an ankle, and you show it sometimes, too."

"Her stocking was silk, real silk."

"Some day," he promised, "I'll have enough money to get you a pair."

"Will you, Tip? *Will* you?"

They sat on one of the benches and listened to the music

coming from the bandstand. Jenny watched the continual style parade and recognized some of the people. She had seen their pictures on the society pages. She recited their names to Tip, who was not greatly impressed. But in spite of himself he had to pay attention to one. Among the promenading people was a special couple. The wife was a tall, stately beauty, exquisitely gowned and the cynosure of many eyes. Her husband was a handsome young man in his early twenties. Light-haired, he sported a small mustache. He was dressed richly but carelessly, as if he didn't care much how he looked, although he still appeared to be excellently groomed. Through merry blue eyes he surveyed the world with light-hearted expectancy.

His eyes now lighted upon Jenny. The young man perceptibly hesitated in his stride. He appeared nearly to stumble, and his wife, not noticing Jenny, but glancing quickly at him, caught her arm tightly in his as though supporting him.

As they passed on, Tip said calmly, more surprised than anything else, "He ogled you, right out."

Jenny, gazing after the couple, said nothing about what the man had done, but asked Tip, "Do you know who he is?" There was a catch in her voice.

"I know he's got bad manners."

"That's Cleve Thornton. He inherited twenty million dollars and a mansion on Fifth Avenue. He's never done anything all his life except drink and—well, chase chorus girls. Now he's married and people wonder if it will last."

The Thorntons came back along the path, in the wake of other walkers. This time Cleve Thornton looked long at Jenny. To her enormous shock he winked at her and murmured with obvious admiration, "Well, well . . ."

His wife now noticed Jenny. She gave her a venomous look that twisted her pretty lips into a grimace. She admonished her husband in a low, decisive tone, "Cleve!" She jerked at his arm, pulling him along.

The incident only lasted a few seconds, but it was long enough to make people stare. One woman clicked her tongue. Jenny, her face flushed at being the object of such attention, gazed open-mouthed after the Thorntons. Tip observed, "I don't know whether to laugh or go after him."

Jenny placed a hand on his arm, as if to prevent a scene.

"He must be drunk," said Tip.

"He must be," Jenny breathed. At the full realization of Cleve Thornton's boldness, she flushed more deeply. "Wasn't he awful?" she demanded. "To do such a thing with his wife! To do it at all!"

"If you think," Tip suggested dryly, "you can take time from your society admirers, I'd like to tell you what I found out about where we thought to go."

"Yes, Tip." Jenny heard what he said in spite of still watching for another glimpse of the Thorntons.

"Florida south of here," Tip went on, "is mostly homestead country and below that raw scrub and near jungle. They called the West the last frontier, but this is really it—the last American frontier. That's what we're headed into, Jenny—if we go."

She turned to him, then, with her full attention. She asked, in questioning surprise, " 'If we go?' But that's what we planned."

"We'd better study on all sides of it," he suggested. "These Palm Beaches down on Lake Worth, the place we read about in the magazine, and the man I met told me about, are two hundred and fifty miles south of here down the coast. Practically nobody from here has even been there, and just about all of them say they don't want to go. Mostly because there're only small settlements on both sides of the lake."

Jenny knew that he spoke against it because he wanted so much to go there. He maligned it for her sake, not wishing to take her into territory more primitive than they had believed.

"How do you go from here to Lake Worth?" she asked.

"Not that we're going," Tip replied, "but there's two ways. They say that no matter which you choose you'll wish you hadn't taken any. The first is traveling by Flagler's railroad to the end of the line at a place called Cocoa. Then you get a steamer down the Indian River—that's the big long lagoon running along just inside the coast and ending up at the Jupiter lighthouse. From there you take a narrow-gauge to the head of Lake Worth, and after that another steamer the rest of the way."

"It sounds like a lot of changes."

"It is. The other way is by sharpie schooner down the coast. It's outside on the ocean, but it only takes a couple of days on a brisk wind. It's a sea voyage that maybe you wouldn't like."

"We've never seen the ocean, Tip. When does a boat leave?"

"Now wait a minute," Tip cautioned. "There's something else to be thought about before you put foot on any boat. Flagler ain't planning to stop with his railroad and plans for hotels where he has them now. He's talking of building them along down the coast, maybe some day clear to the end of the peninsula."

14

"Who is this Mr. Flagler?"

"You've heard of Henry M. Flagler. He's one of the ten richest men in the country and used to be the chief partner of John D. Rockefeller. He still owns a big part of Standard Oil. After he resigned from active work he came to St. Augustine and got interested in opening up Florida."

Mischievously, Jenny inquired, "Are you going to be a locomotive engineer on his railroad and shoot deer from the cab?"

"I could do that, too," he said. "And you touched on part of it. Flagler needs hunters for his construction gangs. He needs one right now. I talked with his agent, a man named Denbaugh, and he offered me a position."

Jenny stared at him. "You're thinking of hiring out to somebody as a hunter?"

He nodded.

"You don't want that," she said. "You can't work for somebody else. It isn't in you to be owned by another man. You must be your own man and you know it."

He acknowledged her understanding of him by looking away and muttering, "I could do it."

"You're only thinking of me," she accused.

"A thing I like to do," he said stubbornly.

"Perhaps," she said softly, "where we mean to go will grow up around us. I need you as you are and want to be, Tip, more than I need a town and comfortable things. I want to be with you in your way."

"My way could be this." Still without looking at her, he swept an arm to indicate St. Augustine.

It was a moment before she spoke again. Then she pleaded, "Tip, let's go where we started out for."

He stared long at her, and took her hands and pressed them in his. "There's a schooner leaving tomorrow for down the coast." Doubtfully he said, "If you think you could stand the trip."

"Of course I can."

He began to show enthusiasm. "This sharpie is called the *Margaret D* and it has a flat bottom that can take us right into the inlet at the Lake."

Jenny nodded, and turned to look at the styles again. This would be her last chance. She didn't tell her husband that they were connected with other reasons she chose not to stay here.

Though greatly admiring the very latest fashions, she knew she could never keep up with them as displayed in St. Augustine. And to live in the sight of them would be unbearable. Then, too, she had been curiously disturbed at the look in Cleve Thornton's eye when he winked at her. She didn't want such a thing to happen again. She wondered how anyone so handsome could act the way he did. She could not down a sense of being flattered at his behavior toward her. She tried to stifle it by speculating on what his wife was like, and what having him for a husband must entail.

LATE IN THE afternoon of the second day of sailing down the coast on a smoothly glittering sea the *Margaret D* came opposite a narrow inlet. Here Cap Jim Bethune, a giant of a man with a black spade beard, took the wheel and swung the trim sharpie boldly toward the land. Gerald, his one man crew, a dark-skinned little man who spoke with a cockney accent, scrambled forward to watch the bottom and call out depths. As the boat approached the mouth of the inlet both Tip and Jenny were startled to hear Gerald cry, "She's goin' to 'it!"

They braced themselves, and Tip, in anticipation of being wrecked, wondered if he could swim with Jenny in the swiftly flowing current of the inlet. The sharpie hit bottom with a dull thud, shuddering for an instant. There was a loud rasping sound. But that was all; the boat sped on smoothly, safely. Cap Jim grinned at them, spreading his beard. "That was the centerboard drawing up in its slot as it hit the bar. We're over."

They glided into a long lake perhaps a quarter of a mile wide. Lake Worth placidly led both north and south as far as the eye could see. Its shores were lined thickly with mangroves, sea plums, pines and coconut palms which drooped their long, graceful fronds over the water and occasionally dropped a nut, which splashed, bobbed and then floated.

Slowly, in the lessened breeze that reached this inland water, they sailed south for several miles. Not until then did they catch a glimpse of any habitation. On the east, reef side of the Lake, placed on a point of land extended farther by a wooden dock, was a low one-story gray building with a thatched roof.

"That's the store and post office of my brother and me," Cap Jim informed them.

A few other houses and a small boarding inn, all of frame and shingle construction, were in evidence. "That's Palm Beach," explained Cap Jim. "You can see about all of it. Across there," he said, pointing over the lake, "is West Palm." The shore line there was broken at intervals to offer the sight of a house. "Something over a hundred people there," said Cap Jim, "and not nearly that here."

Staring with great interest as the sharpie was worked up to the dock in front of the general store at Palm Beach, Jenny said with reverence, "It's beautiful here."

The sharpie nudged the dock, was made fast, and her sails were lowered. As they came down, a middle-aged man appeared on the dock. He had a drooping mustache turned slightly gray. He jumped aboard. Over steel-rimmed spectacles he peered at Tip and Jenny.

"This here is my brother, Doc," Cap Jim boomed. "He's called that because he's the only doctor around here—if you can use that name for handing out patent medicines."

"Welcome to the Lake," Doc Bethune told them. He stared at Tip's bundle of guns sewed in waterproofed canvas, and when he learned the newcomer's profession, said, "We can do with a hunter. We'll sell your meat if you're of a mind to let us. Handle your skins, too." He peered at Jenny.

In her paletot traveling coat of checked brown and tan, she made a fetching picture. Doc's eyes twinkled behind his spectacles as he took over their affairs. "They can stay at the Doolittles' over in West Palm until they get settled," he informed his brother. "You better get them across before dark."

Without waiting to consult the Tottens further, Cap Jim yelled to Gerald, "Get the passenger luggage in a rowboat!"

Cap Jim rowed them over, with their baggage piled high in the prow of a long rowboat. They arrived at one of the wooden docks that broke the thick mangrove shore and tied up. Cap Jim took the larger trunk on his shoulder and in his other hand transported Tip's gun bundle. Tip took the smaller trunk and the heavier of the two suitcases. Jenny, over Tip's protest that he could come back for them, took the small suitcase and her hatbox. They trudged into the town.

A few sand streets were laid out in fairly regular blocks, with others of like nature straggling away at odd and crooked angles. Facing the lake front a short distance back were a general store, a barber shop and a feed and grain establishment. The best frame houses were those they had seen on the lake front. Most of the others were not much more than shacks; several of these had turned silver under the rays of the fierce sun. A number of people lived in tents whose canvas was stained with dirt and weathering.

Jenny's face fell when she saw what the town amounted to. She had a sinking sensation. She wanted to keep this from Tip, but she didn't succeed when he, walking ahead of her and behind Cap Jim, turned and discovered her feelings in her face.

They stared at each other. "It ain't much better than a shack and tent town," he said.

"It isn't so bad," she told him. "And it can't get anything except better."

"It could do quite a bit of that," he told her.

"Look at that house," she said. "It's like the South Seas."

Through trees with strange-looking leaves and fruits on them they saw a thatched house; thick palm fans covered the roof and sides.

There were several of these houses in evidence as they made their way along, following Cap Jim. The sun was hot, and when they reached the shade of a tremendous banyan tree, whose roots dropped to the ground from large limbs to support them and then began to grow, they stopped to rest, putting down their burdens.

At one side of this tree, in its copious shade, a boatbuilder worked in the open. He was a small, wizened little old man who looked up from his labors as they appeared. From his mouth, astonishingly, there hung a long, slim, white, sharp rattlesnake fang. Evidently he used this as a toothpick, for now he put down his tools, stopped his work and manipulated the fang methodically to pick his teeth as he regarded them. He didn't leave his place by an uncompleted boat as Cap Jim introduced him to the Tottens, saying, "This here is Mr. Varney."

"Howdy," said Mr. Varney. He worked his toothpick while he took in the newcomers, his little eyes resting with frank, open and respectful admiration upon Jenny. "I'm from New Bedford. Which means I build a good boat." He said this as a simple statement of fact, not a boast. "You need a boat any time," he told Tip, "and can pay a fair price, we can do business."

"Being so far north a Yankee," warned Cap Jim, "look out

for your fingers if you ever shake hands with him on business. He'll keep a couple of your digits."

"More likely," said Tip, gauging the little boatbuilder, "he'd leave a couple of his in somebody else's."

Mr. Varney acknowledged his appreciation of Tip's sentiment by working his toothpick furiously. He told Jenny, "I see you looking at my pick, ma'm, not that I blame you. I guess I'm the only one ever to use a rattler fang for a toothpick. But I can tell you it makes the best there is. I've wore out half a dozen in my time," he explained. "You ever kill any real big snakes," he told Tip, "I'd surely be grateful if you remembered me."

Tip assured him he would.

Jenny tried to keep alarm from her voice when she asked, "Are there many snakes here?"

"Some sizable ones," Mr. Varney told her cheerfully. "Some deadly poisonous, some not."

Jenny looked about at the ground, as though large snakes would appear at any instant.

They made their way on down the sand street. Cap Jim said it was called Banyan Street on account of the tree. A few houses and shacks stood on it. A block past the tree was located the largest structure, a two-story frame building with an open, pillared porch running completely around it. Unpainted, as were most of the buildings, its lumber had only begun to show the signs of weathering. On its front was a sign which said, "Doolittle Cottage."

As they mounted the steps with the luggage and put it down on the porch, from out of the front door came a couple to greet them. The woman, who looked to be in her middle twenties and who wiped her hands on her apron, was fair and regulation in size and shape. The man was extraordinary. Probably thirty, he was shaped a good deal like a gourd, with a long neck and a bulging stomach. His face was red and fat and jolly-looking.

"I brought the Tottens to the Doolittles," Cap Jim roared. He punched a big fist into Doolittle's great stomach. "You look like you needed some trade. They're from Ohio, same as you, and they just been married. Now I ain't got time to hang around any longer." Abruptly, he departed, taking the steps two at a time and not listening to the thanks Tip and Jenny called after him.

They turned back to the Doolittles. The pot-bellied man exclaimed heartily, "From Ohio! Put your fist in mine." He held out his hand to Tip, and they shook. "We're from Cincinnati. How about you?"

Tip shook his slim head. "We're from Yancey, at least my wife is. I come from the country about there."

"Quite a way from Cincinnati," said Doolittle. "But being Ohio people is good enough for us." Enthusiastically he asked his wife, "Isn't that right, Grace?"

Grace Doolittle had not been as quick and easy in her welcome to Jenny as her husband was with Tip. She hung back for an instant, looking at Jenny eagerly. "A bride," she murmured. "Come to this wild place." Then, without further reservation, she went to her and said, "I know what you need, having come all the way you have." She took Jenny in her arms, kissed her and gave her a hug.

Jenny's eyes filled. She hadn't known that this was exactly what she needed. The trip, the excitement of marriage, final arrival at their destination and the sensation still of riding the schooner, all left her a little bewildered and slightly homesick. And now to have this warm reception, almost from home folks, was too much. Her tears spilled over, and she wept while she clung to the other woman.

Concerned, Tip went to Jenny, but Grace told him, "This is a woman thing. You can't do anything about it. Let her cry for a minute. It will do her good."

Tip stared, troubled at what he thought was unhappiness in Jenny, as she wept.

"Well, well!" cried Doolittle. "Guess she's glad to be here. And she'll find she is, as you'll find it, too, Totten. This is the greatest country with the greatest future that——"

"You can tell them at supper," his wife interrupted.

"Of course, of course!" Doolittle exclaimed agreeably.

A little later, at the meal, there was no ceremony about seating, and little about serving, each helping himself from the nearest dish and passing it on to his neighbor.

"Right at this particular minute we haven't got any other boarders," Grace explained. "We had some last week, and we got some coming next, but you're the only ones right now."

"What she means to say," Doolittle explained, "is that I guess that won't make you mad as newlyweds." He slapped his thigh a resounding crack. "Gives you a little more privacy."

"It wasn't what I meant to say at all," Grace protested. "You're embarrassing our guests."

Doolittle glanced at their guests with genuine concern. "Wouldn't want to do that. You're not embarrassed, are you?"

Jenny laughed. "Not very much."

"Your husband is," said Grace.

They looked at Tip. "No," he said, "I'm not." But it was

evident that Doolittle's remark, and their gaze now, made him self-conscious.

"Only want to help you," said Doolittle apologetically. "Don't want to hurt anybody, not for a minute." He shoveled food into his mouth, but it didn't stop him from speaking. He always spoke as if in a hurry, often leaving off the first words of sentences. "Like to tell you about this Lake country."

Tip broached the subject in which he was mainly interested. "The hunting must be good."

"Hunting?" asked Doolittle. "Guess it's good, all right. People used to do lots of it at one time, I've been told. If you want some sport, you'll find it easy enough."

"Tip doesn't do it for sport," Jenny announced. "It's his business."

"Business?" asked Doolittle. "You hunt as a trade, it's the work you do?"

"And trap," said Tip. "Sometimes, back in Ohio, I acted as a guide, too."

"Planning to guide here?"

"If it can be done."

"Not right now, but in time there will be people, if you want to follow that." Clearly, Doolittle didn't think much of a hunter's life as a profession. "I meant to speak of other things to do. Pineapple raising is the big rage right now. There's a fortune in it."

"Have any fortunes been made yet?"

"Well, not exactly, but good money has been made. Why don't you try that?"

"I don't know a thing about it," said Tip.

"Then try citrus. They say people up north are getting

to like oranges and this new grapefruit more all the time. Or, if you don't like citrus, there's always winter truck vegetables. Fetch big prices."

"When did they ever do that?" Grace demanded.

"Will just as soon as the railroad is built down and they can be shipped in a hurry," declared Doolittle.

Grace addressed the Tottens. "All this is to get you to buy some farming land from him."

"You see," Doolittle went on, unabashed, "my wife is in the boarding-house business and I'm in the real estate business. Of course, it's only in a small way now, but when things open up—and they will any minute now—it will be big. Maybe," he asked Tip, "you'd like to try real estate?"

Tip shook his head. "Thanks, but I know even less about that."

"He's a hunter," Jenny explained as though the pot-bellied man couldn't understand.

Doolittle looked at her as potatoes went into his mouth. "You hunt, too?" he asked.

"Tip has tried to teach me how to fire a rifle," she said, "but I can't hit the side of a barn."

Doolittle stopped trying to locate Tip in a profitable business, and began to discourse about the section generally. "What you see here now," he said, "isn't far from virgin jungle. Why, up until a year or so ago the mail was still carried to Miami along the beach, the only road. Carrier walked barefoot, easiest way on the sand. Used to leave from the Bethune store. Now the mail is taken down the lake by boat and then on a trail by mule stages." He added, "Not that Miami is any worth-while place to take it, being no bigger than us."

25

The fat man forked in food busily, and went on to prophesy that change was going to come quickly to the Lake area. "This is next for Flagler. I know," he squashed his wife who showed signs of wanting to interject, "that's only been talked about for a long time, but now he's close to it. Got to be here," he explained to the newcomers, "because there's no place else for him to go. He can't go west into the swamps and he can't go east into the ocean. May be sooner than even I think," Doolittle claimed. "When it comes," he advised Tip, "you ought to be in on what will happen to land and houses."

"All we want," Tip told him, "is about an acre near the town, or in it, to build a small house on."

"Got any idea," Doolittle inquired, "what milled lumber costs down this way?"

Both the Tottens shook their heads.

When Doolittle told him, Tip's eyes went to Jenny in consternation. They could afford nothing like that.

Jenny turned to Doolittle. "What are those thatched houses we saw?"

Doolittle waved a fork perilously loaded with food; nothing fell off. "Cabbage houses," he dismissed them.

Jenny appealed to Grace.

"That's what folks built when the place was first settled," Grace explained. "And still do, when they don't put up tents. They're called cabbage houses, or palm fan houses, because the thatch is cut from the cabbage palmetto—that's a palm that has a bud you can eat that is a lot like cabbage in taste. The lumber is driftwood found on the ocean beach and rafted across the lake." At the yearning look on the faces of the Tottens she said, "They hardly cost anything at all."

Tip and Jenny conferred with glances that agreed a cabbage house would suit them and Tip asked Doolittle, "Is there anything to stop us from building one of them?"

Doolittle shifted his stomach as though to make room for more food. "Nothing at all," he said. "But you ought to take the long view and have vision. Cabbage houses won't be worth anything when the railroad comes. The kind of people who will arrive here then won't want to live in a house like that."

Alarmed, Tip inquired, "Is anything the matter with them?"

"Well, they're hardly modern. They rustle some in the wind. They—" He gave a start and stopped. His wife had kicked him under the table.

To the Tottens Grace said, "They're a perfectly good kind of a house and kind of romantic."

"We'll have a cabbage house," declared Jenny. "I think that's what we'll like."

Tip thanked her with his eyes and bent to his food.

Doolittle took up the subject of their land next. "I can recommend a thirty-acre tract to the north of the town, suitable for a pineapple plantation. Later it can be cut into lots that will sell for high prices." He recollected, "But you only want about an acre, as close in town as you can get."

Both the Doolittles thought.

"What about the royal poinciana site?" Grace asked her husband.

Doolittle looked up. "The very thing!" he cried, and then amended, "If you can pay as much as fifty dollars?"

"We can," Tip stated proudly.

"Won't say it's a bargain," Doolittle told them, "because

you don't want a bargain, you want good land. You could get an acre for thirty-five farther out, but this one has a special kind of thing on it."

"It's a tree," Grace explained. "We built here because John thinks this is where the business section will grow first. I wanted the acre we're telling you about. On account of the royal poinciana tree that grows on it. That's a tree that blooms all over, not now, but in summer, the reddest thing ever. It's so red sometimes it's called the flame tree."

"I saw a picture of one once," Jenny recalled. "It was colored up, and it was gorgeous. I've always remembered it, but I never thought I'd ever see the real thing."

"There's only the one tree on this side of the lake," Doolittle pointed out. "Others over in Palm Beach, but just this one here. It——"

"Now don't you give them any sales talk about it," scolded Grace. "They'll either like it, or they won't. We won't tell them anything more about it until the morning. Not until they see for themselves."

Grace would let her husband say nothing further about it, no matter how curious Tip and Jenny expressed themselves to be. They were left with a sense of curiosity and expectation about the land picked out for them, and the thing that grew on it. They thanked the Doolittles for taking such an interest in them, only to have Doolittle say, "Glad to be of service to somebody from home."

"Home?" asked Jenny. "Isn't this your home?"

Doolittle looked startled. He became sober. Then he brightened. "Guess it is, at that. Should be by now; we've been here two years. Only, to this time we've been thinking of Ohio as home. But I expect from now on it's right here."

He looked at his wife, and she nodded. "And we don't intend to keep on running a boarding-house in our new home," he went on. "Some day I'm going into real estate in a regular way, with a regular office instead of just having one in my hat. Then we'll really settle down and have a family, too." He turned to the Tottens. "You figuring on having children?"

Jenny moved her head eagerly in the affirmative. Tip nodded and slightly colored.

THE NEXT MORNING the Doolittles took them about four blocks south from their boarding-house. The way led mostly through a trail in the scrub, though it crossed several sand roads that the erstwhile real estate man referred to as streets. They passed a number of shacks, a few good houses and several tents. At some of these the Doolittles stopped to introduce the newcomers, who were welcomed with warm curiosity.

They reached the acre they had come to see. It was marked in a very rough way by trees located near its corners, in two cases Australian pines, in one each a coconut and a cabbage palm. In approximately the middle of it, separated for some distance from any other growth, the poinciana tree lifted itself ten feet from the white sand.

Its smooth gray spotted trunk was spindly, its branches darted out in surprising directions to take eccentric turns. Only a few fernlike leaves hung from it, and a number of long brown seed pods dropped in a dispirited manner from the limbs. These seed pods seemed too large for the tree, being nearly two feet long, several inches wide, and a quarter of an inch thick. They rattled lightly in the breeze, as if to say that the tree was so poor a thing it had to call attention to itself in some manner.

In appearance, at least at this time of the year, the royal

poinciana hardly lived up to the first part of its name. Outside of its being the only thing of its kind to be seen, the flame tree looked like nothing very special.

Tip's disappointment was plain, but Jenny looked receptively at the little tree, as though seeing in it hidden qualities.

Grace offered all she knew about it. "You should have seen it last June. The whole tree blooms just like a plant, the most beautiful thing you ever saw; you can hardly believe it; and it will get big, maybe forty feet high; imagine it then."

The royal poinciana, she explained, was a native of Madagascar that immigrated to Florida. It didn't follow the local custom of blooming in winter, or even the temperate one of flowering in spring. Perversely, as if to show its exceptional quality, it waited until the beginning of summer, usually the last of May or the first part of June. Then nothing could hold it back. It burst forth like a dam giving way, and kept up a riotous cascade of fiery blossom through most of the summer.

Jenny stood gazing at the small tree. It was dwarfed by tall, magnificent pines that reached proudly toward the sky, by sturdy cabbage palms with their latticework of broken fronds, and by towering coconuts. Jenny had no eyes for the more successful growth, but only for the little royal poinciana. From the picture she had once seen, and from Grace's enthusiasm, she could visualize what it would be like.

She glanced at Tip. Her look contained what he rarely saw in her, a naked, selfish wish. She softened it by saying, "Maybe you'd like somewhere else."

"I like it here all right," he said, telling her he chose it also because she did. "Unless you want to see the whole place before we decide."

31

"Grace said this is the only poinciana on this side of the lake," she reminded.

He gave a last warning. "It's off by itself out here, out of the way, with no other house in sight. You'd be pretty lonesome with me gone hunting overnight."

She considered that, swallowed, looked at the poinciana again and decided, "I still like it here."

"It's done, then."

Jenny's eyes went gratefully first to Tip and then once more to the little tree. It being hers, for the first time she walked over to it, and took up some of its sparse leaves, spreading them on the palm of her hand.

Tip had never seen her so taken with anything as she was with the thought of the young royal poinciana blossoming for them. A surge of gladness came to him because she was so pleased with the land to which he had brought her. Part of his fear about bringing her here left him. His glance went to her and remained. Sensing it, she looked up to ask, as if in apology for making the request. "Do you think you can build the house so the tree will be near the bedroom window?"

"I don't see why not," he told her promptly.

"My," Grace said, "that's what I would have liked."

Her husband slapped his great belly. "You've got something else to look at."

Wistfully she said, "But not as pretty."

Doolittle guffawed.

Now that where they would settle and live was decided, Jenny, gazing about, thought that it was a long way from Ohio. Even St. Augustine, and the world of Cleve Thornton, seemed far away. But she was content and filled with anticipation.

Tip hired Mr. Varney to help him build the palmetto fan house. The little boatbuilder lived in a cabbage house himself located south on the lake shore. He furnished a boat in which they rowed over to Palm Beach where, on the outer beach, they found and gathered driftwood for the structure. Jenny went with them on the first few of these forages. "Lots to find on the beach besides the bones of ships," cackled Mr. Varney.

Jenny was delighted with the treasure house of the ocean beach. She ran about like a child, picking up bright shells, exquisite pieces of white coral, sea beans, dried starfish, seahorses and bits of sponge for which she was sure she would find good use. She exclaimed at lengths of giant bamboo and other exotic growth that had washed in from the Bahamas which lay just over the horizon of the sea.

Besides filling her uplifted skirt with valuables that lay on the beach, Jenny helped the men in finding driftwood. The beach was littered with planks, timbers and boards, all from wrecked ships. There had been a hurricane the previous fall, several ships had foundered along the coast, breaking up, and their debris spread the length of the beach. It took time and some searching to locate the right kind of planks and timbers. The men worked north while Jenny, going south, saw a great deal of lumber she knew they would like. Using Tip's pocketknife, she cut long-stemmed sea oats and stuck them in the sand to mark the spots. The feathery brown plumes soon waved down the beach for several miles, and the men, going to the marks, found what they wanted.

Tip looked at Jenny with appraising gratitude in his love, which showed in his eyes narrowed by the new strength of the sun found in their adopted land. The same sun, together with the nearly incessant breeze on the ocean front, burned Jenny's face a painful red and caused Mr. Varney to advise, "You best stay out of the open for a spell until you get more used to it."

Jenny, looking at herself in the mirror of the dresser in their room at Doolittle Cottage, agreed with him. In addition to her face assuming the hue of a bright beet, her freckles had spread over her cheeks and even onto her forehead.

Tip told her, "You stay here and order our furniture from the catalogue."

Grace, with many cluckings and much figuring of selections to fit the lean Totten pocketbook, helped Jenny in filling out the order blank. It was arranged that Cap Jim would bring the furniture from Jacksonville. He would accept no immediate payment for this service. "I'll take it out of your skins!" he roared at them. "You keep your cash money for getting settled and built in." Barter was the way most business was done at the lake, for there was no bank, and actual money was scarce.

Mr. Varney entered into the spirit of getting the house built as soon as possible so the Tottens wouldn't have the expense of staying at the boarding-house too long. He and Tip carried the lengths of driftwood across the quarter-mile width of Palm Beach and made several rafts of them in the lake. One by one they pulled these over to the other shore by attaching them to the boat and laboriously towing them across. Then they carried the boards and planks to the building site.

When they started to work here, Jenny, her face back to normal again but with a flush of tan, attended the proceedings once more. Sitting on a pile of driftwood lumber in the shade, she received many visitors who came out of neighborliness or curiosity—usually a combination of both—to inspect the building. They watched, and sometimes helped, while the foundation was put in place. This consisted of foot-high piles of flat stones erected at the corners and at a few places between. The heaviest of their timbers were laid on these and spiked together. Then they began the framework, using lighter planks. Over this, when it was in place, were nailed narrow strips, leaving six-inch spaces between. The flooring, next laid, was of ship's decking, hard-sought and carefully selected. Bleached nearly white from much holystoning, it would require only scrubbing to keep it resplendent.

Once the skeleton of the house was erected, the sheathing was a pleasant task, and in this Jenny was again of help. Wearing a wide-brimmed straw hat to shade her face from the sun, Jenny cut many of the fans. From cabbage palms low enough for her to reach she took the partially bunched variety which made a thick thatch. She learned to avoid saw palmettos, with their cruel, sharp stems, by the hard experience of mistakenly grasping them.

She watched for snakes in the scrub where she worked. Often she thought she saw one and drew back, tense and terrified, her heart beating fast, only to have the suspected object turn out to be a twisted stick or a length of stout vine. At her fear both Tip and Mr. Varney told her that most snakes were more afraid of her than she of them; the rattler was the only one which would hold its ground, but if not startled or stepped on, it would not strike. To this Jenny nodded a belief she could not actually accept; her skin crawled at the mere thought of a snake. The fact that she saw none did not lessen her fear of them.

The men thatched the house with the broad palm fans.

They nailed them near the stem, upside down, generously and many times overlapping. The cabbage house, consisting of a tiny parlor, a kitchen, and two bedchambers, was shaped in the form of a right angle. This shape more than carried out Jenny's wish, for both a bedroom and a parlor window were almost within touching distance of limbs of the poinciana. The flame tree could be seen through the mosquito netting that served as windowpanes. Already Jenny regretted the times rainy or chilly weather would require the closing of the wooden shutters. Even before its promised blooming, she loved the little tree.

In the middle of February, right after the house was finished, Cap Jim brought their simple solid wood furniture. They had not been able to afford stylish mahogany veneer. But the plain dark-stained bedsteads, chairs and tables, including one for the kitchen where they would have their meals, seemed to fit the palm house. Anything fancy would have been out of place. When it was all moved in, and they had carried their things from the boarding-house to their new home, Tip looked around and said, "It ain't so bad."

"It's fine," said Jenny. "Listen to it talking to us."

They listened. In the breeze the cabbage house rustled slightly; the fans stirred and whispered.

"Still," said Tip, "it ain't good enough for you."

Jenny spoke to him sharply for the first time in their lives. "Don't you talk like that, Tip Totten! Don't you say anything against it. This house is good enough for anybody."

He gazed at her, noting the blaze in her black eyes as she defended their home. Choking fondness was in his voice as he murmured, "That's the last I'll run it down."

TIP'S FIRST HUNTING was done only a few miles out of town. Not wanting to leave Jenny alone overnight yet, he was away merely for a long day at a time. On three sides of the town it took only a short time to get to the game. He passed a few small citrus groves and a pineapple plantation or two, with the prickly fruit growing low on the ground, some of it under the partial shade of slat houses, and then he was in hunting territory.

He found that the Florida deer was smaller than the northern kind; bucks averaged only a little over a hundred pounds. He always remembered the first one he got. He sighted to hit it just below the forearm so that the bullet would not spoil the upper skin where it tore out jaggedly on the other side. He fired. The bullet did not at once stop the buck. He ran valiantly and kept running even as he died. His small antlers ploughed the sand with the force of his rushing fall, breaking his neck.

From him the Doolittles had their first haunch of venison. The Bethunes across the lake and others on this side got free venison before Tip began to sell his meat. He received a good price for wild turkeys. They were hard to get, not because they weren't plentiful, but because it required exacting technique. Back in Ohio Tip had been an expert at this. The call of those here was no different from those he knew formerly, so that his imitation, to attract or throw them off guard, was equally effective. He could give it so realistically that the actual thing and the false could hardly be told apart.

First there came from his throat, faintly but clearly, a flutter of delight, a low chuckle, and then the same sound rose in a rich, staccato guttural, hurrying in volume until it was almost hysterical before shutting abruptly off, only to begin again. He made a sporting thing of getting the erect, slender birds, refusing to shoot them on their high roosts in a pine or cypress. He waited until they flew off and then shot them in the air. If he missed, there were always others. When he didn't miss, the turkey cocks, with their glossy bronze breasts and scarlet blue wattles, flashed to the ground in their bright colors.

He set a trap line that could be attended in a single day. At first he couldn't believe the quality of the otter he caught; they were larger, fatter and their pelts thicker and richer than any he had ever seen before. It was much the same with raccoon. He didn't care about the quality of a skunk when he found one in a trap.

Deer were so profuse that he could almost pick the size he wanted. Quail whistled in the palmetto scrub and prolific families of them trotted out, heads held ridiculously high, to march stiff-legged in a single line to another shelter, or to whirr into the air and be brought down by Tip's quick shotgun.

"It's a lazy man's country," Tip told Jenny. "Anywhere else you got to go out and find the game. Here it practically climbs into bed with you."

Each day Tip looked more longingly toward the Everglades. They lay back there, not far, yet not so near that

38

exploring them could be done unless he camped out overnight. Winging to them with measured beat in the sky he saw ibis, egret and heron. Once he saw a panther heading fast toward the Everglades, as if knowing that there lay sure and broad sanctuary.

Always Tip had heard of the mysterious region, and now he yearned to see it. No one in the community could tell him much about it; some of the other men warned him away from the place, saying he would get lost and never return. This made Tip want to go the more, even if alone. He did not suggest to Jenny that he go. He meant nothing more when he told her of the life he saw headed toward the Everglades, describing what he thought must lie inland, and telling of the old Seminole Indian trail that led southwest. But more must have been in his tone, for one evening she said, "Why don't you go to the Glades?"

In a long look at her he took in everything she had sensed about his desire. The deep sympathy of their union permitted them silently to discuss everything about the subject up to the point where he asked, "Will you be all right?"

With cheerful assurance, intended to encourage him to get about his business and not worry about her, she said, "Why shouldn't I be?"

When Jenny awakened the next morning he was gone. She marveled that he could have risen from their bed and departed without disturbing her. It seemed uncanny to her and was a source of wonder and admiration. She busied herself about the palm house so she wouldn't think too much of the possibility that she had been too quick in saying she would be all right if left alone. Now she didn't look forward to the night. She had never in her life stayed by herself in a house, particularly a frail structure like this set off by itself in what she thought of as the tropical wilderness.

She did her housework, sweeping the dust out the doors, front and back. She tidied up. It didn't take long. Actually, there was little to do in such a household. No work at all was required in the second bedchamber. Here, as they planned it, their first child would wail. At present it served another purpose. Tip skinned and butchered his animals at the spot where he brought them down. In this way he had only to carry the furs and lean meat, often heavy enough. But he brought the skins home to stretch and cure. They covered the four walls of the extra bedroom, hiding most of the slats and the thatch where it showed through. At first Jenny thought she would be bothered by the faint, sickly odor that came from the skins, but soon she became accustomed to it.

She sat on the bed in this room, looking around at the pelts of deer and other animals. Mrs. Cleve Thornton would never occupy a room like this. All her rooms would be plastered and wallpapered. Again Jenny found herself thinking of Cleve Thornton, and she could not fathom why. Her interest in him made her feel guilty. Yet she could not refrain from smiling at the recollection of his wink.

Jenny wondered what her aunt would think if she could see where she had been left alone. With the thought that Tip would not be here tonight, the house felt empty already. She listened to the talk of the house as the breeze rustled the thatch. Seldom still, it was comforting and friendly, like having company. Sometimes it whispered softly. When the wind came up it sighed slightly, raising its voice, and in a brisk breeze it chattered like a gossipy woman. As the fans began to dry out, turning from green to brown, and became crisp, the house spoke still more. Sometimes Jenny pretended to be tired of its incessant talk, and replied to it, saying, "Oh, be quiet," or, "Stop that!" Today she did not advise it to be still, but welcomed its chatter.

She heard the conch shell being blown over at the business establishments on the lake front. Someone had brought in a catch of fish. She wished she needed some, for it would be an excuse to go and see and be with people. She resolved not to give way to this, but to remain on her own.

She left the house and went outside, walking among the bright periwinkles that she encouraged to grow in the sand. The pink and white little flowers, whose plants lifted them courageously sometimes a foot high, bowed to her in the breeze. She nodded back but saved her greater greeting for another thing.

The royal poinciana was much the same as it had been slightly over a month ago. Daily she waited for it to change, but it was not ready, its time not yet come. In the watching and by the attention she gave it, Jenny established a close association with the tree and its promise. It was her friend who would do many things for her, and who was always there to be relied upon. She had need of it now.

Going to the tree, she touched it, at first lightly with the tips of her fingers, then fully with her whole hand. She leaned against its trunk and put her arm about it. She might have been embracing a person as she stood there giving and drawing companionship from the flame tree. The poinciana, in turn, reached out with a branch that grew in the shape of a crooked elbow. The breeze carried the sparse leaves on the end of the branch to touch Jenny's shoulder like a caressing hand. She was solaced in her loneliness.

She was surprised that she experienced no mounting fear of the approach of nightfall. She took precautions against its possibility, drawing sufficient water from the well to last her until morning and closing all the wooden shutters of the house, which had to be done from outside. This would make it too warm inside all night, but it was better than having only mosquito netting between her and the wild things.

She restrained herself from lighting two lamps instead of only the one she needed, and ate a lonely supper. She dawdled over doing her dishes so as to be busy part of the evening. Afterward, she sat in the stifling air of the parlor and tried not to listen. The house now was silent; the breeze had dropped as it usually did at sunset. An owl hooted softly, sounding as if roosted in the poinciana. Jenny hoped the bird would stay, but after a time its call sounded no more.

A loud crackling sound came from the scrub. She decided that she was not afraid at all, or only a little, not more than the amount anyone would feel. She took pleasure in the discovery of learning that her anticipation was far worse than the reality. Previously she had thought she would not get completely undressed for the night, in case something got in to attack her; but when it came time to go to bed, she took off all her clothes and got into a nightdress. Climbing into bed, it was only after an instant's hesitation that she blew out the light.

She lay there in utter darkness, listening again. There was almost no sound; what noises came were familiar and for that reason, welcome. She smiled to herself as she fell asleep long before she ever thought she would.

She was awakened by a maniacal screech right outside the window. She jerked to a tense sitting position in the bed,

42

shaking like jelly. Something clawed at the thatch. The shriek came again, and Jenny recoiled. It seemed to come from inside the very room, as if the thing had gained entrance. The noise resounded off the walls, filling the chamber with terror.

The insane cry was identified as that of a wildcat only when Jenny came out of her shock after its third terrible call. She recognized it, then, for she had heard it before, from afar. The wildcat had chosen this unlucky night to pay a visit to the house; Tip had warned her it might some day come.

In spite of knowing what it was, Jenny was completely unnerved. It wouldn't have been so bad if the animal didn't, at intervals, claw at the house. Tip had assured her nothing like it could get in, but he wasn't here now to make this convincing.

With trembling fingers, Jenny scratched a match and lighted her bedside lamp. She got up and knocked on the slats of the house with the heel of a shoe, to try to scare the animal away. It snarled at her so close by that she drew back and did not try that again lest she enrage it further.

She went to the other two lamps in the house and lighted them. She lighted the lantern and placed it in the kitchen. All rooms were now illuminated. Jenny didn't know what good this would do, but it might do some, and it made her feel a little better, though not much. She got back into her clothes for additional protection and sat in the kitchen, as far as she could from the presence of the beast outside.

The wildcat remained about the house all the rest of that night. There was no telling what attracted it. It wandered around, shrieking at intervals. It meowed, loudly, and Jenny told herself she was foolish, that this was no more than a big cat. She took this back when it screeched again. She could hear it clawing at something, and once there came the sound of its big pads landing on the ground with a series of thumps; it had climbed up in the poinciana and jumped down. Jenny prayed it wouldn't get on the roof.

Shortly before dawn it went away, leaving Jenny limp, half-dozing in a fret of fear, spirit strained and mind fatigued.

She didn't venture out until the morning was well advanced, and then only after peeking through openings she made with her fingers in the thatch at all sides, closing them up again. She knew the wildcat had long departed, but she could not help herself.

Its footprints were all about in the yard. The trunk of the poinciana was scratched from its claws. Jenny glanced up into the tree as if to discover the beast there.

The visit of the wildcat was the least of her experiences. That afternoon she stepped out of the front door of the cabbage house and nearly walked into a rattlesnake as thick as her calf and over six feet long.

Fortunately it wasn't coiled and in position to strike. This enabled her to jump a few feet back, her muscles acting that far automatically before conscious fear paralyzed them. The giant rattler continued to occupy the place he had taken as unquestionably his, head raised inquisitively and slightly higher than the many erect rattles on its tail. Large white diamond markings gleamed on the black and gray scales that moved one over the other.

Jenny opened her mouth to call out. No sound came. Her throat was so dry that no cry could pass out of it. She closed her mouth and swallowed. She tried again. This time she

44

was able to utter an agonized shriek. Encouraged, she developed it into a scream that well equaled that of the wildcat. She stood there repeating it.

Her presence and her cries appeared to annoy the immense snake. Its rattles now began to vibrate. A sound came like the buzzing of angry bees. Slowly, methodically, as though knowing its business of killing thoroughly and confidently, the thick, supple body of the big snake writhed into position to strike. Thick coil piled upon coil to give the lethal thrust greater power and range. The tiny dark eyes were angry near the sensitive pits that marked the reptile for a viper. Coldly it gauged the distance to its victim.

If Jenny saw, she could do nothing to help herself. She was hypnotized with fear and frozen with awful fascination. She shrieked louder when the long, black forked tongue of the snake shot out like lightning, licking the air, as though sending this small emissary to reconnoiter before getting ready to use its deadly hypodermic fangs.

It was fully prepared. The head went still higher and slightly back, to gain momentum for its fatal thrust. The buzz of its rattle sounded insistently, and struck a shriller note. This was the final and full warning.

The whole body of the long rattlesnake quivered an instant before its strike, and still Jenny could do no more than stand before it, ready to receive it.

THE MORNING TIP had left for the Everglades the sun sifted at a sharp slant through a blue mist among the trees. He took his shotgun, though he meant to do little hunting on his first trip to the Glades. He intended simply to see them. Carrying a full knapsack of food, he followed the Indian trail, faint and often completely overgrown, but still there for those who could read it.

The mist rose as the sun came farther into the sky. Both pines and palmettos began to thin out as he walked on steadily. Now there was no trail or path, merely the sand which gradually began to turn from the startling white of the coast to gray, and then into a black that became fine silt, a mucky peat laid down thousands of years ago.

Finally, Tip reached a region that could be most nearly described as a prairie. Yet it wasn't exactly that. The tawny land was flat but watery, being as much swamp as dry surface. The grass that stretched to the rondure of the earth heaved in waves and ripples in the breeze. It was shoulder tall and on its edges were sharp saws that could tear a jagged scratch in the skin. The flatness of the land was broken here and there by clumps of high-lifting palms. These hammocks were like inviting islands in the ocean of grass.

Other live islands of birds were white against the brown sawgrass. Some filled the air at his approach; others paid no attention whatever, but went on with their fishing, sticking their long bills into the brown water and coming up with small catches. Frequent ponds, as though reserved for them alone, were black with thick carpets of ducks.

Tip stopped to stare and listen. The breeze in the sawgrass, now sighing, now swishing, was the theme of a symphony. Water splashed as life in it moved violently. There was rustling of wings and sharp calls. A bull alligator roared from afar, and once a panther screamed.

Tip saw that the Everglades was little like the storybook versions of it, which told of tangled jungle. Most people would be disappointed in the sight. But to him this strange land, and what he could read in its signs and sounds made his black eyes sparkle. It was like a time in the beginning of the world when it was empty of men except for himself. He doubted if the great expanse had ever been much hunted —or fished, he thought, as a tremendous large-mouthed black bass came out of the water almost at his feet, and then slapped back in again.

As he made his way on, now having to pick his footing carefully between water and land to find a route, Tip visioned a hunting camp here where he could stay for weeks at a time. In his enthusiasm he even picked out a place for this, at a bend in a stream winding from the west and entering a small lake. He pictured bringing Jenny here. At the thought of showing her the Glades and sharing it with her, he quickened his step to go on and investigate it so that he could return the sooner and describe it to her.

He was deterred a little at the number of thick, repulsive cottonmouth moccasins to be seen and heard. The repellent, deadly snakes seemed to be everywhere. One reared its snout in a narrow stream he meant to jump, and hissed at him.

Although he knew it was foolish and a waste of a shell, Tip leveled his gun, saw the white open mouth in his sights and pulled the trigger.

He leaped over the body of the dead snake as it began to float away. He turned at a rushing sound of water to see long black jaws snapping up the snake. He had furnished a tidbit for an alligator.

Tip's skin tingled. He looked forward to catching his first gator. Gray crocodiles were here, too, with narrower snouts filled with an even more wicked set of teeth than the alligators, and of a greater ferocity.

He spent that night in a far palm hammock, one so large that he could explore only a small part of it. He risked drinking the Glades water and suffered no ill effects. Long before the abrupt Florida night descended the mosquitoes were so profuse that he had to take to the pillowcase he had brought with him for this purpose. Making his camp and lying down, he drew the case over his head and tucked it securely inside the collar of his shirt. He buried his hands beneath his clothes to keep them from the ravenous insects. After a long time, he slept.

He was awakened in utter darkness by the movement of something touching him. He was startled, but there was little time to be afraid. An animal the size of a large cat had come up and was partially hunched against his shoulder. Tip didn't move and breathed only slightly. He didn't know what it was that failed to be disturbed by his scent. Perhaps it was making a friendly gesture. With a prickling sensation, he enjoyed the association of the wild thing until, after a moment, it moved off. It was like being accepted by this primitive land and the creatures in it.

In the morning he looked for tracks and came to the conclusion that it had been a young panther. Long ago Tip had stopped trying to understand the queer things animals sometimes did apart from their usual strict rules and habits.

He ate his breakfast while watching birds lift from their night grounds to start the day's feeding in other places. A limpkin wailed, greeting the day mournfully. When dense flights of ducks came over, flying confidently low, he brought down two with his first shot and three with his second.

It was from the beak of another bird that Tip found something to take back to Jenny. The big blue crane was standing in water almost up to its ridiculously knobby knees. Its long neck was raised to the sky in position to .swallow a baby alligator whose head it had already engulfed. The alligator, perhaps eight inches long, frantically waved its tiny legs and tail.

Tip gave a yell. At the same time he bent and picked up the end of a broken palm frond which he threw at the crane. It didn't hit the bird, but whistled close by its head. Its beak jerked, sending the little alligator flying through the air, to land almost at Tip's feet. The crane took off, protesting at this rude invasion of its private affairs.

Tip looked down at the stunned young reptile. It lay on its back feebly waving its half-webbed feet in the air. He picked it up. The small creature came more to life and looked at him from beady dark eyes. It gave no thanks, but now struggled to get away from this new giant, opening its mouth, absurdly threatening.

Tip thought it would make a good pet for Jenny. He took

a length of cord he carried, tied the snout of his catch, and then fastened it on one of the straps of his knapsack. With his ducks slung over his shoulder, and stirred by what he had seen, Tip started home.

He hurried to get back to Jenny the faster. He couldn't know that he raced the striking speed of a rattler.

Two blocks from the cabbage house he heard Jenny's scream. Tip didn't stop to listen further. He ran, furiously, his long legs carrying him forward with great leaps.

He arrived on the scene to one side of Jenny, just as the rattlesnake was about to strike. Tip's shotgun was ready. He brought it up instantly and fired.

The blast of the shell brought Jenny's scream to a stop. Instead of striking, the head of the rattler twisted sharply. It started to raise itself and then fell to the ground, its head nearly severed from the body. The body itself convulsed and writhed as though trying still to strike. In the process of death its rattles sounded ominously.

White-faced, Jenny whirled and saw Tip standing a few feet from her. He lowered his shotgun.

She threw herself at him. He held her, stilling her hiccoughs of low cries nearly as soon as they began, and soothing her, said, "I shouldn't have gone and left you."

"Oh, Tip! I was—there was a wildcat last night—and then this . . ."

His words were gentle and right, his tone serious. "From out in the Glades I heard somebody calling me. I expect I got here right about just in time."

"I know I shouldn't be scared——"

"I'm scared myself," he told her, "when I see the size of him."

50

They looked down at the still writhing body of the huge rattler. Jenny clung to her husband. He kept speaking to her in a low voice. She quieted. He kissed her, and one of her arms slid around his neck. Her hand then came into contact with something slick and alive. She jerked back, parting from him, and cried, "What's that?"

He unslung his game and knapsack and took up the baby alligator. He hoped to divert her attention from the snake. "Something I brought you," he said, holding up the alligator and untying its snout. "He's a cute little fellow."

He held it out to Jenny. She didn't take it at once, and when she did it was gingerly and reluctantly. She didn't like the feel of it. The monster in miniature promptly opened its jaws, revealing a gaping white mouth full of rows of teeth, and hissed at her.

Jenny dropped it with a cry.

Tip stooped and picked it up. He straightened with a surprised look in his face before understanding came.

Jenny's voice was agonized. "I'm sorry I don't like what you brought me, but coming right after last night, and the snake——" She stopped, her hands reaching out as she pled, "I'll try again."

He shook his head. "No. It ain't a proper thing to bring you, not anything that spits at you and that will grow twelve feet long or more, and chew you up. I'm the one sorry for bringing it." He looked around. "Now it appears this all has been a bad experience for you, one thing right after another. I don't blame you for a minute, because I blame myself. I don't think it'll come like this ever again. You've sort of had bad beginner's luck. But I'll get these things away from out of your sight." He kicked the now still rattler's body, turning it over to expose its white belly. "I don't suppose you'd want to make anything out of his skin. It's a beauty."

Jenny shuddered.

Tip didn't skin the snake even to sell, lest it be a reminder to Jenny. He saved only the head so that Mr. Varney could have two fresh toothpicks. He took the small alligator to the lake and there released it. As it swam away swiftly Tip knew that he couldn't take Jenny to the Everglades. He wouldn't return there himself until she had become more accustomed to conditions here. He wouldn't even hunt in this district for a few days, but stay around home until she got her confidence back.

As he returned to the palm house Tip could not down a slight, unreasonable sense of disappointment that his wife had no feeling or understanding, and therefore only fear, for wild things.

IN APRIL the Lake communities were electrified to hear the rumor that Henry Flagler was at last actually going to extend his hotel and railroad interests to the Palm Beaches. It was whispered that the great man had already been here secretly, in the dead of night, leaving in the same way, and that he had made negotiations for large tracts of land on both sides of the lake.

If he had really been here and conducted such business, he had done it well, for none of those from whom he had supposedly bought options for land spoke a word to corroborate the stories. It was said that silence was a part of the goods purchased from them. Flagler needed this so that few would be the wiser and prices could not be jumped on him while his agents signed up homesteaders on the way north for a railroad right of way.

Gossip flew thick and fast that all this was the gospel truth, that it was not true, that nothing would be done, that many things would be done at once. The whole population on both sides of the lake was agog with a fever of speculation. The latest shred of information, real or supposed, was passed on with passionate fervor. Usually it was elaborated. Sometimes it was scorned. People were hopeful and skeptical in the same breath.

For some days no one could run down the truth, if any,

connected with the rumors. Then, late one evening, Tip and Jenny heard a knock on their door. They admitted an excited John and Grace Doolittle.

Grace began, "We've come to tell you——"

"Close the door," Doolittle stopped her. He spoke and acted like a conspirator. He put down the kerosene lantern he carried to light the way, looked behind him into the Stygian darkness along the path they had come, and carefully shut the door, after which they all trooped into the parlor of the cabbage house.

"You act like you'd just committed murder," Tip advised as they sat down.

"What is it?" Jenny asked, alarmed at the manner of their friends.

Grace started again, "Flagler——"

"It's true," Doolittle announced in solemn tones. "He was here the way the talk goes. I talked with him, did business with him. He came in a boat at night and left before dawn."

"We've come to let you know so you can get in on it," Grace explained.

At first the Tottens didn't understand their possible connection with Flagler's plans. Only when Doolittle delineated it further did they comprehend.

"You're the only ones we're telling," the pot-bellied man went on, "because we know you can keep quiet and because we'd like to see you benefit. Now here's what's been done: Flagler's bought out the Bethune land."

Tip asked, "What are Doc and Cap Jim going to do?"

"Move their store over here. Post office, too. Flagler's bought a larger tract to the north of them also," Doolittle went on. "Both are where he'll put up his hotel, and I'll tell you about that in a minute. He hasn't stopped there, but acquired more land in Palm Beach, and a lot more over here. He's going to build a bridge across the lake, a railroad bridge, but you can walk across it, too, on a special footpath. He's going to start everything right away, and the official news will be given out any minute. You've only got a little while more to act," he told Tip. "That's why we're letting you know tonight."

"You mean you want me to buy land for speculation?" Tip asked.

"You can make a fortune at it," said Doolittle. "Anyway, a lot of money. I've already made more than enough to carry out all our plans, and I'll make a good deal more——"

"Have you got the money?" Tip inquired.

"Well, no; it's on paper so far, but it's as good as gold. Happens this way in every place Flagler gets to. Will happen bigger here than any other place." Doolittle took a piece of paper out of his pocket. "Now I got a list of lots here I can tell you about."

Tip shook his head. "I thank you all the way for thinking of me like this, and taking the trouble to come here and place your confidence in us, which will be respected, but like I said before, I don't know anything about real estate."

Doolittle turned that off with a wave of his hand, not taking it seriously. "Guess you don't know what's going to happen here."

"I think I do," said Tip. "And I'll be glad if you can turn it to good profit for yourself. But not knowing the ways of such things, I'd better stay out of them."

Grace saw Tip's stand before her husband. "Why!" she exclaimed.

"For illustration, to show you," Doolittle went on, "right now, even if you hadn't put a house on it, I'd give you three hundred dollars for your acre. And that's a dealer's price."

Jenny drew in her breath, but said nothing.

"I believe in every man keeping to his last," Tip said, "and hunting is mine. I wouldn't have much of anything to put into land, anyway."

Doolittle stared at him. "Mean you don't want to do it?"

"I thank you again, John, but that's right."

"You're crazy!" The fat man waved his piece of paper wildly, as if to fan some sense into Tip. "You'll never get another chance like this as long as you live."

"I expect, then, I'll just have to live and regret it."

Doolittle threw up his hands and appealed to Jenny. "You talk to him," he advised.

Jenny had been looking at Tip, who now asked her, "You want me to do this?" His tone promised that he would follow her wishes.

She had her reply ready and gave it softly. "I wouldn't ask you do anything you don't want to."

Tip gave her a long look before he turned back to Doolittle, saying, "You see? Neither of us has got any sense."

Grace informed Jenny fondly, "That's the first true thing your man has said."

"I can't believe it," Doolittle grumbled. "Never knew you were stubborn."

"Like a mule," Tip agreed cheerfully. "You see, I figure that I'd worry so much about the price of my land investments going up and down that I couldn't hold a rifle steady on a deer. My hands would shake so much I'd miss him clean when I fired."

Doolittle didn't appreciate the joke. Sounding slightly aggrieved, he asked, "You don't like real estate?"

"I don't think it's for me when I've got no feeling for it. The same as you have no feeling for hunting."

Doolittle could understand that. He nodded, reluctantly accepting Tip's decision.

"Tell us about the hotel," Jenny requested. "Is it going to be as grand as the one in St. Augustine we saw?"

Doolittle brightened. "Grander and bigger. It's——"

This time his wife took the story away from him. "It's going to be different. All frame. Two blocks long and six stories high. The plans are all made up. It will be painted yellow, with a white trim, the same colors as the railroad buildings. It's going to be the very latest thing, the most modern hotel in the world, with central steam heat, real gas light and elevators. Think of that, right here!" Grace was as impressed as her husband. "Isn't it wonderful?"

"I suppose it is," said Tip. He spoke without much enthusiasm.

"Why," said Grace, "you sound as if you don't like it."

Tip glanced at Jenny. "I do. Except I didn't think it would come so soon, and I sort of hate to see the wilderness go."

"Tip means he likes it for me, but not himself," Jenny explained.

"There's the name of the hotel," announced Grace. She looked at Jenny. "You'll be interested in that."

Jenny stared at her, sensing something personal in what her friend now had to say.

"From the trees that grow on the site," Grace revealed, "the hotel is going to be called the 'Royal Poinciana.'"

Jenny's gaze flew out the window. Through the mosquito netting, in the faint light cast by the oil lamp, she could see, as a fuzzy shape, her own royal poinciana. It seemed to give her a quick and certain connection with the great hotel to be built across the lake.

She was glad Mr. Flagler was bringing his enterprises here. She thought of them as comprising civilization. After the episodes of the wildcat, the giant rattlesnake and the baby alligator, she hadn't been sure she could stand it here. In having this secret thought she felt treasonable to Tip. Now she need accuse herself no longer.

With a start, she also realized that the styles she had so short a time ago evaded remaining with in St. Augustine, would be brought to her here. The world of Cleve Thornton, probably he himself, would be coming to the Lake. It seemed dreamy and incredible.

Jenny had the odd sensation that something was chasing her.

JENNY EXPECTED SO MUCH from her tree that, shortly after the middle of May, when it began to show signs of blooming, she was afraid she might be disappointed. She felt she had placed her love and faith in an unknown thing that was now about to fail her. To stave it off she almost wished the poinciana would not flower.

She need not have worried. At the first breaking of its hundreds of buds, Jenny was filled with an inordinate admiration.

She couldn't believe anything had such color. All day long, and with Tip when he returned late in the day from his hunting, she watched it unfold. It burst dramatically. The yard-long, foot-wide clusters of blossoms covered the entire tree with a brilliant red. It was like a blazing umbrella, aflame against the blue sky, making the colors of each more vivid by the contrast. Soon there was so much blossom that it seemed as though the tree had no foliage, the delicate leaves being lost in the startling, five-clawed, orchidlike flower.

The carmine petals, like glowing embers, spilled profusely and wantonly upon the ground to provide the earth with a vermilion carpet. Jenny picked up individual blossoms to look at them close. She studied the star shape the burst green pod assumed. This formed a background for the larger spoon-shaped petals flushed with scarlet. Among some of these, as

59

if for variation or contrast, was a white petal flecked with red carried out to its fluted edge. From the center ten blood-red stamins reached out boldly, topped by orange and black pollen which shook off as a fine dust when lustily ready to impregnate the female blossoms.

Jenny liked nothing better than to lie in bed mornings—with Tip long gone to his hunting, not allowing her to get up and prepare his breakfast before dawn—and look at the poinciana with the early sunlight pouring through it. Often she was awakened by a redbird which came to the tree and called in at her shrilly, "What cheer! What cheer!" The bird was so nearly the same color as the extravagant blossoms that it was impossible to see it until it moved. Jenny played a game of finding it, while the redbird tried to move without giving itself away, often succeeding.

Jenny was so grateful to the tree for being beautiful beyond all her expectations that she stood under it, with her face lifted, so that the falling petals alighted on her cheeks, sometimes covering one of her eyes like a delicate benediction. The faint, slightly sickening fragrance of the bloom reached her, and she breathed it in as though she could not get enough of it. The flames of the poinciana seemed to burn a deeply satisfying and soul-stirring warmth into her, branding her for its own. "Thank you, oh, thank you, tree," she murmured.

At the same time another royal poinciana was blooming. Ground had been broken for the hotel on the first of May. Jenny went over to see it. She rowed across the lake in the light boat Tip had had Mr. Varney make for them.

Barges had arrived, pulled by tugs. They made trips to the head of the lake and the terminus of the eight-mile-long narrow-gauge bridging the land gap from the Indian River;

this was called the Celestial Railroad because its stations were Jupiter, Mars, Venus and Juno. There the barges took aboard the laborers who arrived by the hundreds, pouring down from the north. Jenny saw them loaded to their edges with men, and the tugs pulling them also filled to the gunwales with swarthy, or blond, thick-muscled foreigners.

She saw the women with them, square-jawed, wide-hipped, some of them painted. She wondered what their lives were like, but did not shudder for them, for they seemed gloriously happy, smiling, gesticulating and jabbering with animation. The men called out to Jenny in her little boat, usually with foreign words she did not understand but whose import she could guess. Once she was addressed in English. "You want mans? Me!" She pretended not to hear. The other men laughed. The women laughed, too, thinking it a great joke. Jenny didn't tell Tip for fear he might ask her not to go on the lake.

The Flagler interests established a community for the Hunkies and their women a little south of where the hotel was to go up. There sprang into existence a white city of tents. It grew until a thousand men and nearly a hundred women lived there. Another section, to the northeast of the hotel, was populated by Negroes and their women, and was known as the Styx. Both were unsavory, reeking of sweat, whisky and lust.

A hundred yards back from the lake shore the ground was cleared for a long distance north and south. From her boat Jenny saw the foundation built on top of the ground; there was no basement. Concrete was mixed and poured, bricks laid, and scaffolds erected. Hills and mountains of building materials began to arrive. Steamers carried them to Jupiter.

Here a small army of men loaded them on the Celestial Railroad, which groaned under the weight of its freight. At Juno another army transferred them to the barges. At Palm Beach they were finally unloaded for the third time.

All that summer the noise of a hundred hammers in operation was carried by the southeast breeze across the lake. The long structure rose steadily. First it was a framework of smooth clean lumber through which the sun could be seen rising every morning. Soon the framework was sheathed. The six-story building, with also a ground floor, two blocks long, altered the horizon line to the east. It joined man's creations here and not only became a part of them, but dominated everything by its sheer size.

While the hotel was rushed toward completion, the building of the railroad was pushed south. The hotel would need trains to bring the wealthy society guests. The immense hostelry, so boldly built in a virtual wilderness, could not live or exist without such service. The race to see which would be first finished, the hotel or the railroad, was run furiously. The Flagler interests spurred their workers on both projects, driving them mercilessly and imbuing them with a senseless rivalry. Men were killed because of the haste, but the work did not stop to mourn them. In the fall the hotel was half completed and the rails had reached Ft. Pierce, fifty-seven miles away.

At the same time West Palm Beach acted as if it were in the race, too. People poured in. Land values jumped overnight, jumped again the next night. A small hotel, as though inspired by its greater across the lake, and several more rooming-houses, were the first to go up. These were followed quickly by a livery stable, grocery and hardware stores, a pharmacy, a bakery and that epitome of sound civilization, a bank. The post office was moved across the lake into its own tiny building when the Bethune brothers gave up their general store. In West Palm Beach the Bethunes started the first department store and called it the Mercantile Bazaar. Cap Jim hauled its goods by his sharpie because Flagler had corralled all the other means of transportation.

These establishments were located on the few streets that had so far been laid out, mostly along the lake front and two avenues that led from it. These were shelled by the process of having wagonloads of oyster shells dumped on them which were then crushed and flattened by a steamroller. The result was a dazzling white roadway from which only occasionally a sharp edge thrust itself to cut a shoe or a bare foot.

The mangrove shore of the lake was broken at frequent intervals, baring the water. Sections cut up into lots by Doolittle, Flagler and others sold like hotcakes. Still more people came; the town now had a population of nearly a thousand. Strangely, in this southern place, south of the real south, the people were mostly Yankees. The soft southern drawl was rarely heard; it might be a northern community.

The excitement over all this activity reached its peak when the Royal Poinciana beat out the railroad in the battle to be completed first. It was not far ahead, but sufficiently so that it was clearly the victor. One day in February the hotel was there, finished and ready, shining lemon-yellow on the palm-studded landscape. It seemed as if it had sprung up overnight. It was the very newest wonder of the hotel world and on Sunday next open house would be held at it so that the community could see what had been built.

ALONG WITH EVERYBODY else, Jenny burned to know what the big hotel was like. Because it might interfere with the rush work, no local people had been allowed inside. Seeing it only from the outside had long been unsatisfactory. Jenny was curious to see it all. And from the first, because of its name, she felt she had a special interest in it. This was almost a right, recognized by other people. Knowing of her royal poinciana from coming to see it in bloom most of last summer, they spoke of the other, identifying her in this way with the hotel.

The entire community turned out for the open house. The lake that afternoon looked as if a regatta was being held on it. Every craft available was used to take people across. Mr. Varney started a ferry service that made repeated trips. His ferry was no more than a small motor launch, open except for a low cabin forward which it was necessary to stoop to enter. A wooden seat ran around the cockpit, surrounding the motor on three sides. The Doolittles traveled grandly on this instead of rowing across. Doolittle, as chairman of the town commissioners, was known unofficially as the Mayor, and he wished to preserve his new swallowtail coat, a badge of office hastily ordered from Jacksonville for the occasion.

Grace, with Jenny's help, lived up to her husband's position. Jenny, who loved nice clothes, had had little opportunity to get dressed up. This was a main chance. She had stayed up nights working on gowns for both Grace and herself. Grace, who did not admire clothes the way Jenny did and thought them something of a waste of time, could not help herself from looking very attractive in an afternoon ensemble of gray silk which had a bell skirt and an overhanging bodice of pink satin.

Jenny herself looked slim in a princess gown of creamy linen, with a snug-fitting bodice and leg-o'-mutton sleeves. Her skirt was given fullness with a froufrou silk petticoat. She felt so good walking beside Tip, who had climbed uncomfortably into his high-buttoned blue serge suit for the first time since they arrived over a year ago, that she even admired the outfit of the town marshal's wife.

Emma Duncan was broader in body than she was solid, with large blobs of flesh high before and low behind. Today she was important and proud in green taffeta. She carried a silk parasol of a light shade of green and wore a dark green sailor hat. She was somewhat monotonously of one color, which was reflected rather gruesomely on her plump face. Staring at Jenny, she said, "You look the very latest fashion." But her expression belied her compliment, for she seemed to resent Jenny's smart appearance.

Tip rowed Jenny across the lake. She sat in the stern and waved to people they knew in other boats making their way to the same rendezvous. The boats landed at the wide dock built out in front of the Royal Poinciana. Here Marshal Duncan stood, with his pistol strapped to one of his skinny hips, his shined-up handcuffs dangling from the other and his celluloid collar glittering in the sun. Officiously he directed the tying up of the boats, assisting the ladies to land. He sent the arrivals on their way up the broad promenade leading to the entrance of the hotel.

Off this walk, along the way, led serpentine paths. Pools in which goldfish flashed and small fountains were here. Flaming hibiscus hedges were interspersed with blood-red Turk's-cap, both bordered by all kinds of smaller blue and yellow flowers. Circles and half-moons of blooms were on every hand, and between them rose dozens of varieties of palms, including coconut, date, royal, fishtail and screw with its large prickly seeds. Crotons and lantanas, in deep or pastel hues, hedged other flowering plants. Fruit trees had been transplanted fully grown. In open places were velvety green lawns of Santa Lucia grass and here, as if to show them off especially, grew half a dozen royal poinciana trees just like Jenny's.

Finally, there was the hotel itself.

People stood craning their necks to look at the high cupola which lifted itself above the noble main portico. Their eyes followed down from this over the sheer yellow wall of the structure. The white trim set off the green shutters with splendid effect. Broad steps led up to the main piazza. Here immense white pillars reached two stories high. About them and along the spacious veranda leading in both directions across the front of the building, were placed dozens of green wooden rocking chairs.

Before the main entrance stood Denbaugh, Flagler's expansive head agent, with the unctuous quick-eyed manager of the hotel, Mr. Bemerill, to greet the people. They introduced themselves, shaking hands, and the manager told Jenny, "Mr. Flagler regrets that he can't be here to greet each of you in person. He would have particularly liked to do this, but business affairs prevented."

Jenny had a sense of disappointment that Flagler was not here. She wanted to see the great man. She turned, startled, when she heard Denbaugh say, "Tip, I still don't see why you won't hunt for us. I don't mean work for us on salary as I proposed to you in St. Augustine, but get meat for us as I asked you to do last summer."

Tip pointed to Jenny. "Here's my reason. To get you any of the amount you need for your construction gangs and the hotel now, too, I suppose, I'd have to go into the Everglades. That's where your other hunters are ranging now, with the game starting to get skinned out along the coast. And to go there means leaving my wife alone all night, which I don't want to do."

Jenny said to Denbaugh, "He didn't tell me he wasn't doing business with you on my account." She turned to Tip. For an instant she thanked him privately with her look. "The land has been cleared all around us now, with new houses going up and neighbors near. You can go again. I should have seen how much you want to."

Tip searched her with his own gaze. Still looking at her, he said to Flagler's agent, "It looks like you're going to have your meat."

"Good for you, Mrs. Totten," Denbaugh told her.

Bemerill said to Tip, "I wouldn't be surprised, later on, if some of our guests might want you to guide them on hunting trips, if you'd care to do that."

"I been thinking along the same lines myself," Tip said.

"Let us know if we can do anything to help," Denbaugh offered.

Tip and Jenny passed into the hotel, where an orchestra played softly in some far place.

They stood in the beautiful rotunda. This room, the main lobby, was nearly a hundred feet square, and reached two stories high to a skylight. Completely covering its floor was a sage-green carpet, so soft that it was like a thick lawn beneath their feet as they crossed it. The rotunda was furnished with the very latest style of wicker furniture, the broad chairs having comfortably rounded arms. In the center of the room, growing from a large pot hidden beneath ferns, was a tremendous fan palm.

Leading from the rotunda were the parlors, reading and writing rooms and card rooms, all visited by peeking into them and exclaiming at their lavish furnishings. Here, too, were the Fifth Avenue shops, not open today, but their windows already displaying their wares. Jenny lingered before the glittering jewelry of Greenleaf and Crosby, and the gown, rug, hat, flower and candy shops. They stared at the posters of far lands exhibited in the "Ask Mr. Foster" travel agency.

The Tottens walked down one of the wide corridors stretching a block long to the entrance at either end of the hotel. Here a suite of rooms was open for inspection. It consisted of a sitting-room furnished with the same kind of wicker as the public rooms, and two bedrooms which had fresh green mats on the floor to match the figured green wallpaper. The bedrooms contained gorgeous mahogany furnishings, and between them was a bathroom. Even though the bathroom had all the appurtenances that are usually contained in such a room, a chamber pot could be seen peeping from beneath one of the beds. It was no ordinary pot; it had been specially made for the Royal Poinciana, with gold-encrusted

68

borders and green palms painted on its cover and sides. In the parlor, even though it was only a low story to the ground, a rope fire escape was coiled over a hook near the window; in case of fire you threw it out and climbed down.

In this part of the hotel the Tottens saw one of the gold strap-metal elevators operated by pulling up or down on a rope that passed through the cage. Here also they peered into the vast dining-room that could seat a thousand people. Jenny exclaimed, "Think of it—a thousand chairs!"

Everybody speculated on how the Flagler interests would ever fill the hotel. Some said they wouldn't, that the place, even before it opened, was a white elephant. Those who agreed with this didn't believe there were enough rich people in the country who could be brought to this remote place to make it pay.

Tip had a bemused expression on his face. His comment was one of wry awe. "It's a lot different from us across the lake. There's going to be another kind of life here, all right."

He led Jenny back to the rotunda. They had not seen all yet. They mounted the wainscoted oak stairway. On the landing blue, green and yellow light came through the leaded stained glass windows. They entered through a richly ornamented arch into the spacious octagonal ballroom. For the moment it was empty. Jenny, who could not contain herself at all she was seeing and had to express her feelings in some way, danced out on the floor, skating across it gayly. "Watch to see if anybody comes," she put Tip on guard. Instead, Tip watched her, admiring her grace, so that people came in and stared, to make Jenny stop, abashed.

Returning to the first floor, they passed under the stairway and through a corridor. On the left was the stock brokers' office. Of this only the men were allowed to enter the bar. Word was passed about to those known to be interested that it was in operation, with drinks on the house. Tip went in there, while Jenny passed into the palm room opposite, used for afternoon tea and (it was whispered) cocktails, the wicked mixed drink coming into vogue.

It was here that the orchestra played, hidden behind potted palms. And here was the largest crowd, for fruit punch, tea and cakes were being served. A buzz of comment filled the room, trying to compete with the music of the orchestra.

Jenny found Grace and compared notes with her. "John is in there drinking, probably too much for him," Grace confided. As they drank tea their husbands joined them. Tip had a smile on his face and a twinkle in his eye. Mayor Doolittle was expansive. "This is the greatest thing that ever happened," he declared, "not only to our section, but to the whole of Florida!"

It was not difficult for Jenny to catch some of his fire. She exclaimed, as Grace had once asked, "Isn't it wonderful?"

"Why," said Grace, "you're just as excited as John. You look just the way you did when we took you to the flame tree."

Jenny, glancing away as though to deny this, tried to keep the flush in her cheeks from becoming deeper.

Tip stared at her as though seeing something fully for the first time.

FOR A FEW WEEKS, until the railroad could be completed from the head of the lake, where it had now reached, guests for the Royal Poinciana were brought by ferry barge. Even with this awkward method of transportation, many came. It was soon evident that there would be no trouble in filling the hotel. It was the dead of winter in the cold nation. Word about the luxurious hotel and its location in a bland, nearly tropical place went swiftly back north. Reservations began to pour in. Finally, there was a waiting list. And nothing could indicate its success more than the affectionate nickname the big hotel began to be called almost immediately. It was referred to as the "Ponce."

During this period West Palm Beach was rocked by two events. The first was the necessity to remove the now soiled tent city of the workers directly south of the hotel. The only ones satisfied with this were the several hundred men given employment on hurrying the construction of the railroad, the bridge and later the building of a depot and train yards. These men, with their women, moved over to West Palm, while the others, faced with no employment, accepted free transportation north.

To the horror of all decent citizens the tents were moved across the lake and erected on railroad land between the forks of the terminal Y of the tracks being laid. The Hunkies and their women were seen on the streets. Two saloons in tents opened up overnight on Banyan Street, and it was said that one building had been turned into a disreputable rooming-place. Another became a dance hall where a mechanical piano, that simply sprang from nowhere, tinkled day and night.

Little protest was voiced by the responsible people. Many were now employed by the Flagler interests or dependent on them in one way or another. People merely crossed the street when meeting the Hunkies. Children were kept away from the railroad section in the west of the town. Many people did not dare to venture out at night. On Saturday nights Marshal Duncan had his hands full on Banyan Street.

The second event that stirred the town at this time was the arrival of the first train. Coming so soon after the open house at the hotel, and following so closely on the heels of the Hunkies being permitted to settle in the community, it was almost too much to bear. Normal life was completely upset and in some cases even suspended.

It was said that Mr. Flagler himself would ride the first train and make a speech from the back platform of the rear car. For some time Jenny had wanted to see the great man. With their royal poinciana trees she felt she and Mr. Flagler had something in common. They were the only ones to be so associated.

On First Train Day, as it was termed, the regular affairs of the town shut down entirely. Jenny prevailed upon Tip to stay home from his hunting and attend. The most difficult part of her persuasion was to obtain his agreement to get dressed up again. "If I keep on this way," he objected, "I'll be wearing out that suit."

"But, Tip, the first train will come only once."

"I'll agree with you on that."

"Then you'll do it?"

"I wouldn't want that first train to have to come again," he told her with concern.

He was laughing at her. But she didn't mind.

Jenny knew that all of the other women in town would wear the same gowns they had for the open house, or their second best. She alone had in reserve something better than she had previously displayed. This was her red damask she had worn in St. Augustine, altered slightly to meet the current mode. She had not shown it here because there had never been an occasion. She hoped she would not be resented and thought to be showing off. She could not resist risking this, for she enjoyed dressing up and looking her best more than anything else.

Early in the afternoon everybody headed toward the northwest part of town, convening there three blocks back from the lake. Here the railroad tracks ended. In place of a depot, which did not yet exist, there stood the soiled tents of the unwanted Hunkies, who gathered in a boisterous group of their own at the very end of the tracks. They sang and played rough games and from time to time a bottle was tipped toward the sky, its neck plunged into a wide, gluttonous mouth.

The good people of the town contented themselves with carrying small American flags on sticks. Others had whistles and horns. A few brought cowbells with them. From the Ponce came the orchestra. It played to entertain the crowd waiting for the first train ever to pull into the community or to reach this far south in the United States.

As Jenny, holding the skirt of her dark red dress, arrived

on the scene with Tip, her eyes shone with anticipation. She didn't think to pay attention to any envy of her as they pushed their way politely through the crowd to join the Doolittles at the trackside.

The mayor doffed his hat to her ostentatiously as he looked her over and said pompously, "Our fair city shines in the light of its fair ladies."

"What he means," Grace interpreted, "is you're certainly one for pretty clothes, Jenny. Other women are hating you."

Tip looked around and observed, "Seems like you're being looked at, all right."

Jenny glanced about. It was true. She had made the mistake of looking far too fashionable. Her skin was too white and glowing against the dramatic contrast of the damask. Other women stared with open hostility at her or stole looks and then peered away, speaking among themselves.

Jenny knew what they were saying as well as if she could hear them or read their moving lips. "Putting on airs," they assured each other. "Humph! A clotheshorse! All she thinks about is fixing herself up." She wondered if any of them were saying, behind the sickly smiles some of those she knew awarded her, "Thinks she must belong over at the Ponce."

Covered with confusion, Jenny shrank back, instinctively trying to conceal herself behind Tip and the Doolittles.

"Never you mind," advised Grace.

Tip assured her, "Nobody ever got hung for being pretty."

"Look at me," said the mayor. "I'm the only one with a swallowtail. And I'm not hiding." He slapped his stomach. "Couldn't if I wanted to."

Jenny took courage, standing up for her appearance. She

had nothing to be ashamed of. She couldn't fathom why she had felt the way she did. Her chin lifted.

Doolittle, as the leading town official, was scheduled to make a speech commemorating the event. He awaited the arrival of the train more anxiously than any other. Everybody craned his neck, staring up the tracks, to be the first to see the train. They tried to listen for it through the noise. There were several false alarms, one of which the band joined, playing furiously until its leader realized it was all for nothing.

Finally, above the buzz the crowd made, there came from the north an unmistakable, long low whistle.

A shout went up. The train was coming at last.

It kept whistling steadily while far up the tracks and still out of sight. Soon black smoke shot forcibly above the pines and then curled high into the sky. The ground vibrated, sending a thunder into people's chests and shaking their souls.

With resounding shrieks from its whistle, and its bell clanging madly, the locomotive, making the sand earth pound, came into sight. Its front, from cowcatcher to smokestack, was decorated with long palm fronds.

The crowd went wild, calling, yelling, waving flags and blowing its own whistles and ringing its own bells, while the orchestra now played its loudest. Men shook hands, congratulating each other, or pounded friends and even strangers on the back, and women embraced.

The powerful pulsating locomotive passed and after coming to a stop, the engine settled down, steaming slightly, with a grinning, sooty-faced engineer and black fireman looking out of its cab. The crowd milled about the cars, which were filled with people who had wanted to ride the first train. Some were guests going to the hotel.

Jenny scanned the faces of those leaving the cars. She found herself, strangely, looking for Cleve Thornton among them. She was startled. She had heard nothing of his being on the train. He wasn't here. Yet why did she repeatedly think of him? What was there about him that attracted her thought? Why did she pore over the society columns in the newspaper to see mention of him, searching for actual news about the rumor that his wife was divorcing him?

Standing near the steps of one of the cars, Mayor Doolittle waited impatiently to board it as soon as everybody had descended. What looked to be the last person got off, and the mayor started up the steps. He had no more than reached the platform when a tall, sturdy man of perhaps thirty, with a brown mustache, emerged from the door of the carriage. He and the mayor met forcibly. The man was knocked back into the car by Doolittle's stomach, while the mayor himself was sent off balance and fell backward down the steps.

He was caught by Tip and another man who saw what was happening, and set upon his feet on the ground. Doolittle gasped as the man into whom he had crashed made a second appearance and jumped down the steps to exclaim solicitously:

"My dear sir! I hope you're not hurt—I should not have come out of that door so fast—if you've been injured I'll be glad to do what I can, for I am a doctor."

Doolittle puffed, catching his breath, "Always knew my belly would hit something before I did. Not your fault," he assured the man. "It's my stomach's. Nobody hurt, unless you are, and you don't look it. A doctor, did you say?"

"Dr. Douglas Howard, of Titusville," he introduced himself

"A regular medical physician?" Doolittle inquired with interest.

Dr. Howard corroborated this by smiling and repeating Doolittle's term.

"We need one here," the mayor told him, and then in clipped tones said, "Got to get aboard the train and speechify, but after it's over, come and have a glass of wine with us." Hastily, he introduced Grace, Jenny and Tip, and then climbed aboard the train.

Dr. Howard looked about calmly. His eyes went to the town, taking in its raw appearance, its tents, sand wastes and its relatively few good buildings. His expression showed nothing. "I came down on the first train," he said, "because I've always heard about the Lake district, and I wanted to see if the town might be big enough to move here and practice. But it seems much too small."

"My husband will tell you all about how big it's going to be," said Grace.

"If you've got ears to listen," said Tip.

"Listening to other people," offered the physician, "is the most of doctoring. Especially when they haven't got anything the matter with them."

"They're going to have the speeches," said Jenny.

The crowd was flowing toward the rear of the train. Accompanied by Dr. Howard, Grace, Jenny and Tip followed.

People stood pressed thickly all about on the tracks at the observation platform of the end car. Many spoke of Flagler, eager as Jenny to catch a glimpse of him. Jenny stood on tiptoes and stretched her neck to see.

The crowd stopped its noise-making, and the orchestra dribbled off in the middle of a rendition when a group of dignitaries, including Mayor Doolittle, appeared on the platform from inside the car. A man in the crowd called excitedly, "Flagler's there! That's him!" Others differed, saying it wasn't Flagler.

Jenny examined the men quickly. None of them, she thought, was Mr. Flagler. Besides not recognizing him from his picture, there was not enough dignity to them. To be certain, she glanced at Dr. Howard. He sensed her gaze and turned to her, shaking his head and saying, "Flagler wasn't on the train. He isn't here."

Jenny felt disappointed, a little cheated.

Denbaugh, who led the officials on the car platform, held up his hand for absolute silence. He made an announcement, speaking publicly in the staccato manner of the orator:

"Mr. Flagler has asked me. To tell you. How sorry he is. That other pressing affairs. In the interests of the great state of Florida. Have unfortunately kept him. From being with us today."

A groan went through the crowd. Denbaugh proceeded to make appropriate remarks and introduced several other men who made much the same remarks. Then he presented Mayor Doolittle.

Doolittle, patently enjoying himself and glancing down occasionally in recognition of his wife and friends, made a speech, extolling the Flagler interests. He related and listed all the excellent things they had done and would do for Florida and the Palm Beaches. "Henry Morrison Flagler," he declared, "is a benefactor to mankind and to the state, a pure benefactor."

The crowd listened attentively, drinking in every word when the mayor concluded, "What less than a year before was an almost inaccessible pioneer settlement here is now introduced to the world as the queen of winter resorts of the world! I give you," he cried, "the Queen!"

The celebrating noises started all over again, louder than ever, and were joined by the deafening whistle and bell of the locomotive, which now sounded hysterically. Buzzards floating in the sky had never heard anything like this; they veered and flew higher. Dogs, which had slunk to safety at the approach of the train and who had come out again timorously to investigate, scuttled away once more. The Hunkies, gathered in their own group, tipped their bottles straight up at the sky and then howled coarsely, like animals.

THE CELEBRATION CONTINUED for the rest of the day. It was a time of confused excitement, of many unplanned comings and goings, of laughter over almost anything. The stimulus of a community experiencing a complete revolution in its affairs made itself felt in every corner. Even Marshal Duncan overlooked certain things which, watching tight-lipped, he resolved would never happen on a normal day.

Doolittle and Tip took Dr. Howard on a tour, to show him everything. The physician expressed his admiration of the ocean beach. He knew how the Gulf Stream, close to the shore here, warmed it and changed the aspect of the land from here south. "That's what you've got here that we haven't up the line," he said. "It's one of the things that attracted me to look you over." He was interested in the Everglades, and listened to Tip's description of the region and his offer, "I'll take you out any time you want to go."

"If I were to move here," Dr. Howard said, "I'd take you up on that." He looked at the town again and shook his large head. "I'm afraid there isn't enough population to support a doctor."

"It's going to grow," protested Doolittle. "What you see now is nothing." Doolittle appealed to his sense of humanity. "Need you pretty bad here—Doc Bethune has been killing us, or at least letting us die—for too long with only his patent medicines."

The doctor shook his head. "I'm sorry, but I'm afraid you'll have to swallow them a little longer. The bills a doctor can collect of what's owed him wouldn't take care of my own bills here. Even though I'm a bachelor. At least it would be thinner going for a time than I would want to take on."

Tip had been silent for some while. Now, as he sometimes surprised Jenny, he startled Doolittle. The mayor had opened his mouth to argue further with the physician. Instead, he found himself looking at Tip, who shook his head. Doolittle subsided.

"I guess we can't expect you to do it, then," Tip told the doctor. "And that's all there is to it." He looked at the physician's face, which glistened with perspiration from the exertion of their tour. "Now I know you'd be more comfortable in the shade at Doolittle Cottage. The ladies will keep you company while John and me attend to some business we got, and then we'll join you, too."

Doolittle, catching on quickly that he and Tip had some heretofore unknown business together, backed him up. "Of course," he said. "A cooling glass of wine is just the medicine for you," he joked. "And you're to stay the night with us as our guest until the train returns in the morning. Longer, if you want."

If the doctor, expressing his thanks for this hospitality, suspected anything in connection with it, he gave no indication of doing so. He found it pleasant to sit for an hour with Jenny and Grace on the open porch of the boarding-house while they pretended not to see, or at least not to acknowledge, the evidences of sinful life on Banyan Street. These were rather hard to ignore.

Across from the boarding house a tent saloon stood. From the porch of Doolittle Cottage, through the wide open canvas flaps, the rough board bar could be seen and patrons standing at it. Women hung about its entrance and accosted men as they emerged, sometimes being thrust roughly aside, sometimes going off with them. From up and down the street came loud voices, the sound of music, of dancing, of quarrels and even fights. Once a woman screamed and men yelled imprecations in a foreign language.

Jenny confessed to herself that she was more curious about them than shocked by the institutions on the white-shelled street. She liked to visit Grace in order to observe them. She had only heard or read about such things in frontier towns. Now here they were before her very eyes. She was still astounded that the women, at least outwardly, did not appear unhappy.

When Doolittle and Tip returned, their faces flushed and looking pleased with themselves, Grace said at once, "You both look as if you've been up to something."

"Only something you'll like," her husband informed her.

With a glance across the street, Grace said, "I'm not sure I like anything around here any more."

"That's what I mean," Doolittle informed her. "You won't have to live in this red-light district much longer."

"What a thing to say!" Grace gasped. "What do you mean?"

"I've sold Doolittle Cottage. You're retired from the boarding-house business."

"Who did you sell to?"

"It doesn't matter. Now the doctor here would like his glass filled——"

"Who did you sell to?"

When Doolittle didn't answer, but concentrated on replenishing the wine in Dr. Howard's glass, Grace appealed to Tip, who told her, "Nobody would buy except those who want to be a part of the street."

Grace let out a wail. "Our place is going to be turned into a—a——" She couldn't say it.

"It's going to be called the Plaisance," Doolittle said. "We've got two months to get our other house built. I'm ordering the lumber tomorrow." He explained to the Tottens and Dr. Howard, "We're building on the lake front, south."

That was the choicest section of town. "We'll almost be neighbors," Jenny pointed out.

Grace looked about, at Doolittle Cottage, at Banyan Street, and said to Jenny, "At least I'll have that."

An old man came slowly up the sand walk. In his hand he carried a truss, holding it so that its kidney-shaped pad was high. He stopped and looked up at the people on the porch and quavered, "I heard there was a doctor in town. I ordered this here contraption by mail, but I can't get it to do me any good for my rupture, can't get the blamed thing to fit right. Which is the doctor?"

Both Tip and Doolittle pointed to Dr. Howard.

"I'd pay you if you can show me how it works," the old man told him.

The physician looked about, suggesting to Grace, "If you'd let me use a room . . ."

Grace rose and led the way inside, with the old man climbing the steps and following them. While he was being attended, Grace returned. Jenny, examining her husband and Doolittle, questioned, "Did you——?"

"We just passed the word around," Tip whispered.

When the doctor and the old man came out, the truss had disappeared. The old man, who walked now in more sprightly fashion, was pressing a silver dollar piece on a protesting Dr. Howard. "You got to take it," he said, before he hobbled down the steps and then away.

Reflectively, Dr. Howard took his chair again and lifted his replenished wine glass to his lips. Suspiciously, he glanced at his host.

"We happened to mention that you were here," Doolittle said.

"Hope you don't mind," said Tip.

The doctor took another swallow of his wine and looked at the silver coin in the palm of his hand. He tossed it a short way in the air several times and caught it so that it slapped onto his hand again. He put it in his pocket and observed dryly, "You seem to have mentioned me to the right kind of people. Is this," he asked, "another?"

Up the walk came a chunky, swarthy, dark-haired man. He was one of the Hunkies. His left arm dangled uselessly at his side.

In a genuinely startled tone Doolittle claimed, "We don't know anything about this one."

"No?" asked Dr. Howard skeptically.

"This one's on his own," asserted Tip.

In broken English the Hunkie spoke to the physician, singling him out instinctively. "I hear you doctor. I got broke arm. You fix?" He grinned, showing perfect even white teeth.

Dr. Howard had the man up on the porch, felt of the arm through his shirt and asked Grace for a pair of scissors. With this, while the Hunkie grinned even wider, he cut off the shirt sleeve. A reddish lump showed where the break was in the forearm. The physician studied it while he called for some short boards and strips of cloth. These were found and brought. Jenny cut up a piece of old sheet according to the physician's instructions. Then Doolittle held the Hunkie by the shoulders while Tip was asked to pull out the arm gently but steadily, and the doctor held it at the break.

The Hunkie's grin vanished as the pain came. There was a clicking sound of the two ends of bone snapping into place. The Hunkie echoed it with his gritting teeth. Grace held the splints in place while Jenny handed the doctor the broad linen strips with which to fasten them tightly to the arm, holding it rigid. One was placed about the man's neck to form a sling for the trussed member. The music from the mechanical piano up the street came as if in accompaniment throughout the process.

Doolittle wanted to know of the man how he broke his arm.

"Me and two my friends," the Hunkie explained, "celebrate train. My friends hold me." With his good hand he indicated his elbow and wrist. "They break." He grinned again. "Some day I break their arm. Give you more business," he promised Howard. "How much I pay you?"

The doctor waved a hand. "I'm not really practising."

"One dollar?"

"You don't have to pay me anything."

"Two dollar." The Hunkie reached into his pants pocket and brought out two silver dollars. He forced them on Dr.

Howard, said, "Now I need drink," and stalked across the street into the tent saloon.

All the time this had been going on, more people arrived. They stood about, watching, gathering into a tight little crowd in front of Doolittle Cottage. Now they began to call out.

"Can you fix me up, Doc?"

"You settling here?" a man wanted to know.

Howard waved a hand, making a meaningless gesture.

A woman called, "We've got lots of sickness piled up for you."

"We'll make it worth your while," a man promised.

The people began to crowd in, coming right up to the steps of the place, still calling out, and demanding that the physician let them know his answer.

"Too bad you won't be here," Tip observed.

"Maybe you'll change your mind," advised Doolittle. "Besides all these people and more, I can promise you something of a small steady income as health officer."

An obviously pregnant woman pushed her way carefully through the crowd and said, "I'll need a doctor for my baby; my first died being born because I didn't have a doctor."

"Come on, Doc," a man with a loud voice called out persuasively from the swelling throng. "The railroad and hotel are going to bring lots of people. We'll grow up fast."

Another demanded, "Ain't today told you we'll be a big town quick?"

From the crowd a thin man detached himself and came halfway up the steps. "Doc," he pleaded, "I got a cough I'm scared of and I need attention bad."

Dr. Howard stood up. He stared at the thin man and at

the pregnant woman, then at the Doolittles and the Tottens. His gaze lingered on Jenny before he turned his attention back to the crowd. He brushed his mustache reflectively with one finger while he addressed the people.

"How can I resist you?" he demanded. "You knock me down the minute I arrive. You break your arms and promise to break more. You bring me cash paying patients. You say you'll be a big town overnight. You pour wine down my gullet to take away my good sense. And finally you bring a whole crowd of customers. I'll be here to take care of you!" he announced, and then warned, "But you'd better not let me starve!"

"Hear! Hear!" cried Doolittle. The mayor heaved himself to his feet, held his wine glass high and proposed a toast to the doctor. They drank it while the crowd cheered.

FOR SOME YEARS Jenny had wanted Tip to take her to the Everglades. He had built a rough hunting cabin out there where he had already taken Douglas Howard, Doc Bethune, Cap Jim and other local men. During the winter season when the Royal Poinciana was open, a few guests who wanted to hunt and fresh-water fish tramped out. This business was growing, for still more people came to the hotel with the addition of another hundred rooms built on the north end. But Jenny felt excluded from this part of Tip's life and slightly jealous of not sharing it with him.

"It ain't because I don't want you out there," Tip refused her. "I have from the first. And I know the fear you're putting aside by asking; that's why I'm saying no. There still is only a trail most of the way, and the snakes and other things are thick the way they always been. I don't want you scared of the Glades so you'll never go. I work on a better trail every chance I get. When a horse and wagon can get out there, you'll come first thing."

"Tip, what are the Ponce men like that you take out hunting?"

"Just like anybody else."

"They must be different."

"Different?" he asked. "Why?"

"Oh, I don't know."

"They're only different because they can afford to stay there."

"Have you ever met any of the women?"

"No—and I've never met your admirer, Thornton."

Jenny had often wondered if he recalled the incident with Cleve Thornton. They had never spoken of it. Now she learned that he, as well as she, had thought of it from time to time. She was caught with interest as Tip went on:

"There's something I never told you I felt that time in St. Augustine. You remember how I said once you being so pretty sometimes made me scared. Well, Thornton making up to you like that is what I meant."

"Tip, you sound jealous." Jenny felt a curious delight.

"Not exactly," he denied. "It's just that I heard he comes here during the season."

"I guess he does."

Meaning came into Tip's voice. "You go over to the hotel quite a lot."

"I like to see it and the styles and people."

"Our place is here, on this side of the lake, Jenny. Across the Great Divide." That's what the lake was called now.

"Of course, Tip."

Jenny was touched at his warning that she might be stepping out of where she belonged. It stirred the memory of the handsome young millionaire who once looked at her so brashly. She knew she should have no feeling of being flattered, but the fact remained that she had it from the beginning. She had gone out of her way to read about Cleve Thornton's divorce, which finally had come about. She had searched for a glimpse of him at the Ponce.

After what he had done in St. Augustine, Jenny thought,

this was only a natural thing for a woman to do. She was sure it amounted to no more than this. There was nothing the matter with her keeping alive the recollection of her brief but startling association with him.

Her tree grew in the same way the hotel did. Jenny's attachment to it increased, for there was more of it to admire. It stood nearly sixteen feet high, reaching to the top of the cabbage house. Its deep tangerine bloom as seen against the dried and brown thatch might have represented a scene from its native island far away across the other side of the world.

The long seed pods of the flame tree always fascinated Jenny. In winter, hanging from the nearly bare limbs, they rattled in the breeze. In a strong wind they whistled as the air hurried past them. This gave another name to the poinciana, which was sometimes called the whistling tree. Jenny collected the flat, hard, dark brown pods and gave them as souvenirs to those interested who came to see the tree.

Tip told her that Seminole Indians he knew out in the Glades had them for baby silencers. "You'd better give one to Grace," he had suggested after the first Doolittle child, a girl named Medora, was born.

Delighted that a product of her tree could be put to such good use, Jenny presented a pod to Grace. Medora took to it immediately. It made an excellent combined rattle and teething ring. The seeds sounded sharply when the pod was shaken even slightly. It was nearly indestructible. Medora bit at it with her toothless gums to break her teeth through. And broken through, she chewed on it with her sharp baby teeth, making distinct marks.

Jenny sat with Grace on the top of the boathouse built out over the lake in front of the new Doolittle shingle house.

They occupied rustic chairs placed there. Jenny held Medora while the baby alternately shook and bit at the poinciana pod. Her lap made a cradle which she rocked back and forth by moving her legs at the knees, her feet stationary, her hips swinging. Her legs stopped moving for an instant when Grace announced:

"I'm off again doing what you've been trying to do. This time we hope it's a boy."

"Grace, that's fine."

"I suppose it is." Grace said this unenthusiastically because she wanted to deprecate its value to Jenny.

Jenny looked up, shocked.

"Of course it is," amended Grace. "Except it's been your turn for some time now, and I wish it could be you."

"I wish so, too."

"Has Douglas anything more to say?"

Jenny shook her head. "Nothing new."

"You're still young."

"I'm twenty-one now." Jenny spoke as if she were an old woman.

Grace laughed. "You still have plenty of time."

That was one of the things Douglas had said.

"Now listen to me, you two," the doctor lectured Jenny and Tip. "You've got a problem most people don't have, but still a good many do have. Some meet it right, others don't. I can't say it's easy, especially in your case, when you both want children so much. But you're becoming alarmed too soon. I've known many cases when it took a number of years, up to five or even as much as ten or more."

"We've been trying for quite a few," Tip pointed out.

"Then you've got some to go."

"Are those long cases you mention," Tip inquired, "the usual thing?"

"Not usual," admitted Douglas. "But pretty regular."

"Isn't it true," Jenny persisted, "that our chances are cut down?"

"Cut down," Douglas agreed, "but not eliminated. Now who's the doctor around here, me or you?" He glared at them both.

Jenny felt her lack acutely in connection with her Aunt Erminia. In her early letters, after Jenny described her life in Florida and invited her aunt to come for a visit, Aunt Erminia wrote back that it sounded so primitive that she would only come at a time of emergency, such as the birth of Jenny's first child. Jenny wrote that she would hold her to this, and would let her know the date.

Since then Aunt Ermina rarely wrote without making an inquiry about the date. Lately her reminders had been caustic. "What's the matter with that husband of yours?" she demanded. "If he hasn't given you a child by this time he can't be much good, just as I thought."

Douglas, appealed to again after this, advised them, "You may be trying too hard. There's something funny in nature about this. The more you want a thing sometimes the less you get it; nature seems to rebel and withhold it, almost enjoying the denial of it to you. I don't know why this is, except I've seen it happen that way many times. So take it easier. Get your minds on other things."

"Or," suggested Tip, "face the fact that we won't ever have children and make the best of it."

"I wish I could help you more than by just telling you to

have faith," the doctor said. "Some day we'll know more about this. But that's no consolation to you now."

Tip could follow his own advice no better than Jenny acted on it. From that time on a subtle change crept into their relationship. A tenuous wall was gradually erected between them through the years. They never referred to it, but it was always there, beginning to thrust them apart, insidiously and progressively interfering with the sweetness of their love.

One of the greatest of human urges and needs was denied to them. Jenny was desolate at having nothing to mother. The primal reason for her existence was removed. One of her main hopes and most poignant dreams was destroyed.

For a time she forgot that she still had Tip. Unreasonable doubts assailed her. She felt it must be his fault. She wondered if they were well-mated in any respect. She was a town girl with more schooling than he had. Perhaps her aunt was right and their marriage had been a mistake. Certainly it was precipitous and unfair to Aunt Ermina. Jenny missed her and found this Tip's doing.

Or possibly Florida had something to do with it and they never should have come here after all. She even speculated that in some manner things might be different if Tip had gone into the real estate business and lived more in town instead of being off in the Everglades so much. When in the vagaries of her roiled emotions she didn't blame him for that she held him accountable for other deprivations. Among them, dairy products were missing locally. No one kept a cow because forage was too sparse. The only milk obtainable was evaporated in cans. Few kept chickens, so that eggs were at a premium. Vegetables were scarce except when a farmer was lucky enough with the weather to mature a quick winter crop. In summer there were none at all. Jenny missed mostly a big glass of cool, creamy fresh milk. Often her system craved this. Somehow, all the delicious wild game Tip brought couldn't make up for that.

Their problem hurt Tip's pride. He was convinced that he would never have a son whom he could teach how to fire a rifle. He felt he would die without leaving any progeny behind. And perhaps children constituted the only immortality, everything meant by a life hereafter. None would live for him, so that all of him would pass away and disappear. He would have existed for no purpose.

He couldn't conceive that he was at fault, and therefore it must be Jenny. He didn't blame her as much as he felt sorry for them both.

Because their basic love was so great they felt a larger disappointment that its most poignant expression, so hopefully repeated, found no fruition. Their desire for each other lessened and began to take on an emptiness, producing nothing except the pleasure of the moment. The real significance of life passed them by.

The Doolittle children, because they saw so much of them, were the greatest reminders of their grievous lack. Medora, now six, and little Jack, four, were always present when they visited their house. Jenny thanked Grace for making no further deprecation of maternal pleasures. Instead, Grace understood when Jenny no longer went to see her as often as she once did. One day Jenny, while playing with the children, broke down, so that Grace sent Medora and Jack away while Jenny wept, "I wish we were the kind who don't care if they have children or not; there are some, I guess. But we counted on it from the first, both of us."

"I've hesitated to suggest it," said Grace, "but have you thought of adoption?"

"Maybe that's all right for some, but we've never even mentioned it because it wouldn't do for us."

Grace glanced with compassion upon her friend, and agreed helplessly, "Not with the way you want your own."

It was Medora and Jack who later upset Tip as much as they had disturbed Jenny that day.

For some time the cabbage house had been looking shabby and run down. Through the years Tip had renewed parts of the thatch that wore out and fell off. Nothing could alter the contrast of the primitive structure with the many new houses all about it. It was one of the few palm houses left in town. When they planned their family they had decided on what a new house of their own would be like. Tip's hunting, both for himself and for the Flagler interests, and his guiding for Ponce guests, had enabled him to pile up respectable savings. The house would have three bedrooms on the second floor, just like Doolittle's, so as to have plenty of room for their children.

Now, when Tip decided to replace the cabbage house, they did not change the plan. Even to speak of this would be painful to them. Building less rooms would be a formal recognition that they had given up all hope. They wished to cling to at least the illusion of being granted a miracle.

As Tip worked, nailing in joists and then putting up studs, the Doolittle children got in the habit of visiting the scene of construction and became interested spectators. Aside from the pang of regret that the sight of most children gave him,

Tip was fond of Medora and Jack. They liked him because he treated them with gravity, as equals.

Jenny, sitting on the front porch of the palm house one September afternoon, watched and listened to the children with Tip as he worked on the new house close by. The juvenile questions became very personal.

"My mama," Medora announced, "said I shouldn't ask you something, Mr. Totten."

Jenny became aware, recognizing this as a child's way of convincing herself that it was all right to do something forbidden.

Tip sensed the same thing about it. "Then maybe you'd better do as your mama says," he told Medora.

The little girl shifted her plump form and thought that over for a moment. She held onto her young brother's hand, keeping him safely out of the way of the building. "I'd like to know this," Medora persisted.

Tip gave her no encouragement. Jenny knew she should interfere right then and there. But she was held with an awful fascination.

Medora asked her question. "Why haven't you got any children, Mr. Totten?"

Tip didn't answer at once. He nailed a spike through a two-by-four. "Well," he said, "maybe I just never got around to buying any at the store."

Medora giggled, sounding just like Grace. "You don't buy us at the store. You have us." She considered that, not supplied with clear details. "Why don't you have any?"

Jenny wanted to call out, to stop it before it went any further. Tip hadn't seen her come to the porch, and she knew she ought to make her presence known. But words stuck in her throat, especially when she saw the strain come to Tip's face.

Yet he answered good-naturedly. "I guess it just happened that way."

"Don't you like children?" Medora inquired.

Tip hammered in another nail with loud bangs. "Well, I like those who don't ask too many questions."

Medora was not finished. "I shouldn't think you would build such a large house if you aren't going to put any children in it."

Tip's face worked as he tried to control himself. But the goad had sunk in too deeply and been twisted in the wound. He dropped his hammer, almost flinging it down. Without a further glance at the children, he left the new house and strode over to the old.

He discovered Jenny on the porch and gave a start. They stared at each other, stricken. He made a helpless, futile gesture and went quickly into the cabbage house.

Jenny walked out to the children, hushing their further questions at Tip's action. She sent them away and watched them go down the street, puzzled and vaguely offended. She knew, when she returned to the porch, that she couldn't go in to Tip. There was nothing to say to him, nothing to do. She could not reach or touch him, but merely listen to him moving about.

She wasn't surprised when he came out dressed in his hunting clothes, with knapsack and rifle. A set expression was on his face. He didn't stop or look at her as he muttered, "I'll be gone a few days."

There was no need to tell her that he had to be by himself in the Glades for a time. She could understand that, knowing

97

it was impossible to tell him that he took what the children said too seriously. That was the very effect they had on her as well. She let him go past her without saying anything. It was the first time he had ever left without a kiss. That hurt most of all.

Jenny stood there regretting that she had not interfered in time. She asked herself: What was happening to them? Where was their love? It should have sustained them in a crisis like this, but it seemed consumed by bitter regret and cruel disappointment.

TIP RETURNED THREE days later, carrying few skins. He had spent little time at hunting. They didn't mention his departure. Jenny wanted to bring it up no more than he. He glanced at the unfinished skeleton of the new house, but he didn't approach it. He seemed unable to take up work on it again. They did not refer to that, either, and Jenny wondered, after a week, what was to become of it.

At the end of that week another kind of storm than the one that had blown up between them announced itself by squally weather. The air became exceptionally humid, there were abrupt, quick downpours of rain and the wind began to rise steadily. No one spoke the word hurricane until the barometer began to fall in earnest, and then people took a serious view of the impending blow.

The vegetation whipped about as though vainly trying to punish the air. The rain now came in cloudbursts. The sandy earth drank the water greedily until it became saturated, then small spreading pools began to form. The clouds closed in on the earth. Jenny, looking at them, thought she could almost reach up and touch them as they scudded by overhead. They came across the ocean from the east, hastily dumped their wet cargo and passed over, disappearing into the west as though hurrying to a desperate duty, chased by some unknown terror that pushed them on.

The thatch of the cabbage house could no longer keep out the driving rain. Water dripped in a dozen places in the house. Tip and Jenny were kept busy setting pans about to catch it. With the wooden shutters closed to keep out some of the rain, the house was almost as dark as at night. Soon there was no further use in trying to catch or control the water now pouring through the roof and seeping from the walls. The floors were soaking wet. Occasionally actual spray found its way through the wall. The cabbage house shivered under the force of the elements attacking it.

"Get your things together," Tip said. "What you want to save. The way it's hollering now leaves no doubt about it coming here. We'll go to the town hall."

As though it would destroy them before they could leave, the cabbage house began to shake and slightly sway, emitting loud creaks. The thatch began to leave it. Rain came into the rooms as though the roof was a fine seive.

That sent them scrambling to collect their valuables.

Tip took almost none of his clothes. He gathered up his guns and traps and slung a bundle of skins across his back.

Jenny rolled her most precious dresses into a ball. She unrolled it and put several pairs of shoes in the middle. She grabbed useless things to take until she saw them in her hands and put them down again. As she worked in the bedroom the house shuddered under the pound of the storm. Jenny looked about the damp and dripping chamber. For an instant she knew fear. It was stark and gripping. She trembled. She felt that the whole force of the angry earth and all its elements were intent on destroying her. Having singled her out in particular, they seemed to be gathering to descend upon her.

She tried to ignore this feeling, gazing about in awesome realization. This was her first home with Tip. Things here were familiar and dear. Outside the window was her royal poinciana.

She stepped to the window. The mosquito netting had been half torn away and hung in wet shreds. She put her face to a chink in the shutter. Outside, close by, the poinciana writhed and whipped in the wind. A few of its minor branches had already broken off. The main limbs reached toward her as though now asking for the consolation the tree usually gave her. Her fear for the poinciana was real and lasting.

Tip called out, saying they must go. He had to yell to make himself heard above the roar of the wind.

Jenny joined him at the back door, which now rattled. The wind had shifted slightly as the core of the great hurricane worked north. When the door was opened the rain shot in with a blast. The drops of water were like hard pellets, stinging their faces. Tip took Jenny's hand with the one he had left free and pulled her out after him.

Even with his support she staggered. They sloshed toward the central part of town. Jenny had expected it to be worse outside than in the house, but not as bad as this. The driven water, in sheets, wrapped itself about them. Small articles were now flying through the air. These struck them, and they protected their faces by holding up their bundles before them.

The wind had become eccentric, as if out of control of the thing that unleashed it. Maddened, it blew according to its own vicious whim, first one way and then another, with undisciplined gusts. One instant they fought it, the next they were blown with it, their feet touching the ground just enough to keep their balance.

Jenny tripped and started to fall. Tip grabbed her arm roughly and held her. His fingers were like steel, hurting and steadying her. During the stress of that moment Jenny wished that Tip would often clutch her that way; it was like a fierce caress. She wanted the hurricane to blow them back together again.

During a short, comparative lull in the wind, she looked across the lake to see the Ponce. But the hotel was blotted out. Nothing could be seen even of the lake. In that direction the air was water-filled and seemed to become thicker by the instant, lashing all the living things of the earth as though to annihilate them.

At last they reached the tiny town hall which contained a chamber on each of its two floors, with an outside stairway to reach the second story. In front of the building, clad in a slick black oilskin coat and hat tied securely under his chin, stood Marshal Duncan. He was directing those who came here for refuge. To the Tottens he yelled above the noise of the wind, "Upstairs all filled! You go in the jail! Downstairs!"

Tip grinned and pulled Jenny toward the first floor front door of the town hall. The door was opened. They passed in, carrying with them small streams of water.

A short corridor led across the small building between a row of three steel-bar cells on each side. The cells had their doors thrown back. They were occupied by some of the most respectable people of West Palm Beach, who sat or lay on the bunks, or sat on mattresses on the floor. Mr. Varney leaned against the wall at the end of the corridor. A baby wailed. The air was hot and still, rancid with the smell of carbolic acid, used to keep the jail disinfected.

The Tottens found a place in the corridor between the cells. They opened up and spread out their belongings as well as they could in the limited space. Somehow they managed privacy in which to change their soaked clothes and hang them on the bars to dry. With dismay Jenny saw that all her dresses were ruined except for a few on the very inside of her bundle. A nearby woman sympathized; others simply stared; one made it plain by her attitude that she was glad Jenny Totten, who thought only of clothes, had some of her best things spoiled.

At a loudly voiced complaint of being in jail, Emma Duncan, who occupied a cot in the middle of one cell, announced, "You're better off here than upstairs; all Banyan Street is up there."

More people came, until the little jail was stuffed with humanity. Outside, through the door, when it was opened, the marshal could be heard yelling to others to go to the schoolhouse. The people inside were grateful for that. Already there was an oppressive atmosphere in the jail. The sound of the people upstairs moving around and sometimes calling out increased the sensation of being packed in for those below.

The small high windows of the jail admitted little light. Now, in the thickening atmosphere of the approaching blow outside, it became steadily darker. A few people murmured and called for light. Emma lit a single lantern and hung it from the top of her cell. The beam of this, more than anything else, made it seem like late evening instead of about four o'clock in the afternoon.

The marshal opened the outside door for the last time and came in to fasten it securely behind him. He joined his wife in their cell. He had gauged coming inside exactly, for then the hurricane struck. The flame in the lantern flickered and wavered as the senseless wind reached in to grasp it with eager fingers. The noise of the screaming air mounted to such a high pitch that it was difficult to hear anything else.

The closely packed people listened tensely. They glanced about as though the building would be blown down at any second. A few spoke, but it was with effort. They had to raise their voices to be heard. Inertia overcame most and they sat or lay silently, filled with anxiety, their senses dulled after long nervous strain.

Jenny sat on the floor huddled against Tip, who was the most relaxed person in the jail. From his attitude Jenny took her own, or tried to.

As she snuggled closer to him, he, sensing her affectionate movement, turned to look at her. Their gaze caught and lighted. It was the way it had been at first. For a moment nothing stood between them. The primitive, interfering desire for young was lost in a quick, selfish rediscovery of each other. They wished that they were alone so that they could express more closely the gladness of a flash of their original feeling for each other and perhaps develop it into full blossom again. As it was, they could only be grateful for the storm which tried to unite them.

They jerked to sitting positions, tautly separated, along with everybody else, as a splintering crash came against the side of the building.

THE LITTLE TOWN HALL shook and swayed. For an instant it appeared that it might be carried off its foundations. A woman screamed, another moaned in fear of approaching doom, several men cried out.

Tip was on his feet, alert. He was the first to breathe more easily when nothing else happened. People looked to him for an explanation.

"It was a tree," he said, "blown through the air, hitting the side of the building. I expect the storm is picking up some big ones." Reassuringly, Tip went on, "If the building stood that, it can stand anything." He sat down again.

Jenny saw that he didn't altogether believe what he said, but wanted to comfort the people. He, in turn, read her understanding in her glance.

Upstairs, even above the still growing roar of the storm, the Banyan Street crowd could be heard singing. Their songs were bawdy. Feet stamped and heels kicked on the ceiling to mark time. Mr. Varney spoke enviously. "They're drinking, having a hurricane frolic."

Those who had the will clucked their tongues. This was no time for carousing, but for prayer.

The marshal announced loudly, "We won't have any drinking here."

Tip whispered, as though speaking to Jenny, "He's wrong.

It gives people courage. It might save somebody who could have heart failure. And it's past time we had a nip or two." He looked at the marshal and kept his gaze on the law officer.

Steadily the sounds of the storm rose in pitch. The banshee rush of the wind about the building seemed almost unbelievable. It was incredible that the building could stand under the forces tearing at it. The wind reached a sustained screech that momentarily mounted in intensity with renewed gusts. From the beginning of the existence of this land it had known such onslaughts and had learned to succumb to them as a kind of retribution for the benefits bestowed upon it.

The faces of the townspeople showed the strain of listening to the storm even when they lapsed into an exhausted stupor. The marshal slept upright on the cell cot, leaning against the wall and supporting his wife who half lay with her head thrown back, her open glazed eyes seeing nothing.

Tip reached into his bundle of skins and his hand came out with a flat bottle. He uncorked it silently and handed it to Jenny, advising, "Have a swallow."

She had never tasted raw whisky. But she didn't question his suggestion. She took the bottle as though wishing to yield to him. A woman registered disapproval as Jenny raised it to her lips. The liquid burned her throat but she did not cough, even though tears came to her eyes; then her stomach tingled pleasantly.

Tip took a long pull at the bottle and handed it to his neighbor. It reached Mr. Varney and then continued to travel, noiselessly. Those awake watched; some men were nudged awake to get in on it. Glances went to the marshal and his wife to see if they would awaken and discover what was going on.

The woman who had criticized Jenny taking a drink cried, "Scandalous!"

The marshal came awake, demanding, "What? What is it?"

The bottle disappeared.

"They're drinking," the woman announced angrily.

"Who?" the marshal asked. "Upstairs?"

"Right here!" the woman cried. "While God stands in judgment on us, sending His punishment, they take to the bottle. It's——"

Mr. Varney began to sing a hymn. Others joined him, including the marshal and Emma, who was awakened by the controversy. To Jenny's delight, Tip joined in the hymn, singing lustily. As he sang, his eyes went to where his bottle still traveled surreptitiously. He seemed to enjoy the song. His eyes danced as he saw a man, hidden behind another, lift the bottle.

Jenny joined in the singing, adding her voice to Tip's. Their hymns competed with the ribald songs that continued upstairs. The marshal looked about suspiciously. Several times he sniffed, but he couldn't very well stop the hymn singing to ferret out the source of liquor fumes. He glanced overhead, half-convinced they were coming from there.

Jenny felt a hand on her arm. The bottle had come back. Furtively, she nudged Tip with it. He took it, investigating its condition.

"Tip!" Mr. Varney called. "How about it?"

Jenny was convulsed and filled with still more astonishment when Tip answered the man by making an interpolation in the hymn they were singing. "It's a dead soldier," Tip sang lustily, "who has gone to Jericho. A poor dead soldier, who has done his duty, has gone to Jericho!"

The singing both downstairs and up was stopped, momentarily, when there came another loud splintering sound of wood giving way. Heads flew up and white faces were turned to the walls as though excepting them to blow out at any second. The sound came and went almost instantly. Something substantial had been carried away. But the building still held.

Through the night the hurricane blew. The people in the jail breathed easier when it became evident that the wind would not rise above any state it had already reached, and that the building would hold. Slowly the storm slackened. Soon there were only healthy gusts. The worst was over, the time of danger passed. By dawn the wind had died to a mere strong breeze. Jenny, who had slept in Tip's arms, awakened to look about.

Even Tip now slept. Most people lay as though dead. There was no noise from upstairs.

Jenny felt tired, as though from long exertion. She lay against Tip, content to be close to him, and had no ambition to move.

The marshal was the first to stir. He got up, stretched and looked about. An expression of official satisfaction came to his face as he saw that all was well and the storm over. He started toward the door.

Jenny got up, disturbing Tip gently. He rose with her. They and others, now awakened and intensely curious to see what the scene outside was like, followed the marshal.

Sand was piled up several feet high outside the door. They had to step over it to get out. They also had to climb over the trunk and through the fronds of a coconut that partially blocked the way. It was this that had been blown against the building. They saw that it had hit at the branched end, fortunately softening the blow.

They stood in the open and for a moment enjoyed a feeling of freedom and release. Only after this did they glance about.

Not all the town was still there.

There were bare gaps where buildings had stood the day before. Trees stood at a slant. The vegetation was thinned out. Leaves were stripped from nearly every growing thing. The scene looked strange, like a different place.

The gaze of the Tottens flew to their own home.

The cabbage structure was not there.

In its place was complete emptiness.

Beyond, the framework of the unfinished house stood intact. The wind had whistled harmlessly through it.

Jenny and Tip did not have to look at each other or speak for them to know that now Tip would complete the new house.

More people were coming out of the jail to see what had happened. They exclaimed, or wailed, at the sights that greeted them. Some called out happily that their houses still stood. Others wept at the disappearance of theirs. Some had roofs torn off, or one side missing. A few remained intact except for having been twisted off their foundations.

All the docks at the lake had had their planks lifted off and carried away; only bare pilings remained. The Doolittle boathouse had been swept off by the furious water, though their house stood whole. Most of the shacks that Banyan Street people had erected in the north part of town were gone entirely. The marshal, looking there, remarked, "It's a good thing I made those people come here."

As if to answer him there came a shout from the top of the town hall. "Hey!" a man called. "We can't get down!"

Turning, they learned what had caused the loud splintering noise during the storm. The outside stairway to the second floor of the town hall at the end of the building had blown away. The Banyan Street people stood in the open doorway of the second floor council chamber, looking out into thin air.

Mr. Varney called up to them, "Looks like we got you where we want you now."

A man yelled back, "Looks to me like you spent the night in the right place for you!"

Several men went in search of a ladder to bring them down.

The town was awakening. People who had stayed in their houses came out to survey the damage. Others kept running back and forth, calling out information. The marshal had gone off to make a quick survey of the immediate town. He strode back to report that no one had been killed. One man, a newcomer, had died of fright. Another had his arm broken and Douglas was already setting it. From Palm Beach came a report that only a few shingles and shutters had been blown off the Ponce.

Jenny and Tip went to where the cabbage house had stood. They stepped onto its very site, now marked only by a few half-buried stones and planks. Otherwise, there was merely driven wet sand piled in eccentric drifts. The only other thing to show that it was the same place was the royal poinciana tree.

Jenny's eyes had turned to this almost as soon as she saw the house was no more. She examined it anxiously. The whole tree leaned over at a sickening slant. Like most of the rest of the vegetation all about, it was now leafless, and its pods had all been blown away. Many minor branches were gone, and several major ones were broken and hanging from the tree, whose raw wounds showed like white flesh. It was naked and hurt. Jenny wondered if it would live and looked at Tip, to ask, "Do you think——"

"It will come back," he assured her. "And grow straight again by itself. We'll trim it to help it along."

They began to take in more fully the entire significance of the destruction of the palm house. It marked an end of a period in their lives. They had built the house with certain expectations that had not been realized. And now, in a second house, they would take up another life.

What this would be neither knew. Jenny had realized during the night of the hurricane that the storm would not bring her back to the old basis with Tip. The moments it had seemed it might were only temporary and fleeting. The basic hurt each inflicted on the other remained in their mutual lack. It was the known fault of neither, yet that of both. The very sympathy they had for each other in their predicament, because this continually called attention to it, interfered with complete return to their original communion.

JENNY WAS PROUD of their new house and kept it spic and span. She gave visiting ladies no opportunity to find dust or other evidences of sloppy housekeeping with their quick glances. But the work failed to take up all of her time, even when she was particularly careful about the cleaning of the two extra bedrooms. She found that she forced herself to enter these, as though to prove their emptiness did not disturb her. She and Tip rarely referred to the rooms.

From the window of the northeast bedroom which they occupied, Jenny could see both her poinciana tree and the Ponce across the lake. The flame tree had struggled to an upright position, and sent out new branches to take the place of the broken and trimmed limbs. As for the hotel, there was still more of it to see. During the summer of 1901 a second and even larger addition had been made. This was in the form of an immense T built onto the end of the first addition. It contained four hundred and sixty-six more rooms. With many sitting-rooms and baths in this section it was a good deal larger than the entire original part of the Ponce.

Now the hotel had well over a thousand rooms. It could easily and comfortably accommodate thirteen hundred guests. It was the largest hotel in the world. It was the largest wooden structure ever built. There never had been anything even remotely like it anywhere, not even in Saratoga, which boasted of large hotels.

The larger the Ponce became, the more Jenny was absorbed by it. She was proud that electricity had replaced gaslight. She marveled at the hotel's mere statistics. A suite near the rotunda on the first floor cost one hundred dollars per day. Sometimes a party arrived by private train and took a whole floor in one wing at five hundred dollars per day. In the enlarged dining-room, which now could seat two thousand people, one man in charge of the water bottles did no other work than to keep them filled. Europeans of title were announced as staying at the Ponce, and Jenny wouldn't have been surprised if actual royalty came to it, for it was a royal place.

Jenny dressed carefully for her visits to the hotel. She did not consciously try to look as well groomed as some of the guests, for the quality of her clothes could never equal theirs in any respect. But in effect she achieved a distinction of which she was well aware. Now going on twenty-six, Jenny was striking in appearance. She had matured in poise and slightly in figure. Daringly, she passed a paper of rice powder over her face and used a touch of pomade on her lips. The first enhanced, the second defined, the lovely regularity of her features.

When Tip first saw the cosmetics on her face he stared and asked, "You got to use them?"

"Oh, Tip," she cajoled, "just a little. This is the Twentieth Century. Many women are doing it. It makes a woman feel—well, more like a woman."

"You don't need any help on that," he pointed out. He

examined her from head to toe. Admiration pricked his eyes. "You can't say you ain't beautiful now."

In gratitude for the compliment, she kissed him, leaving color on his lips, at which he protested. "Maybe you can wear it, but don't try to get it on me." Fondly she wiped his lips with her handkerchief, one arm encircling his neck. "Then you don't mind?" she asked.

"And if I did?" he countered.

Seriously and soberly she answered, "Then I wouldn't use them."

He gazed at the hurt appeal in her eyes. "A woman can get around a man," he sighed, "without any trouble at all. There ain't anything to it."

Grace relayed to Jenny what was said about her in town. "Emma says she won't deny you're a beauty," Grace told her. Surveying her, Grace went on, "And you are, Jenny. You always have been, except it's come out more."

"What else do they say?"

"No reputable woman—only those of Banyan Street—paints her lips. That's why I've taken it up."

"Thank you, Grace."

"You traipsing over to the Ponce is trying to push yourself where you don't belong. No good will come of it. It all amounts to thinking you're better than people here."

"Grace, do you think I ought to stop it?"

"Why should you? Not because of these old biddies. Make yourself as pretty as you can," advised Grace, "and go over as often as you want, if you like to do it, and I guess it gives you a lot of pleasure. I'll go with you myself."

Grace went with her several times to see all the Flagler wonders of Palm Beach, but most often Jenny went alone.

On an afternoon shortly after the first of the year in 1902, Jenny boarded Mr. Varney's ferry. She was the only passenger and Mr. Varney, toothless now so that he had no further need of a rattlesnake fang toothpick, cackled, "Goin' across to see your hotel?"

Jenny smiled. "I'm going across, Mr. Varney."

The little old man's chin nearly touched his nose when he spoke. "Never saw anybody who liked a building as much as you do the Ponce." He shook his head, trying to comprehend it. He peered at her as though he might see something to help explain it. He seemed to notice her with what male qualities remained in his wizened form. "With you around, Jenny," he cackled, "I don't see why Tip don't stay home more."

He looked hopefully up the dock for more customers. There were none. He cast off. He made no further conversation as they crossed the lake. He paid strict attention to the rather tricky maneuvering of his craft. Jenny was glad the course first lay straight across, to avoid shoals. This allowed the sights to be seen better. They passed among beautiful white yachts and broad-beamed luxurious houseboats moored in the lake; these came from the north every season.

The ferry turned and went north close along the shore. This afforded an almost unimpeded panoramic view of the yellow hotel, going right along in front of it for its whole length. It took some time, for the Ponce was now four city blocks long, not counting the top of the T, another block in itself. In addition there were several more blocks of two-story colonnades.

Jenny's eyes danced at the sight of it. Each time she saw it was like discovering it for the first time. She never tired of it. She resented the coconut palms growing on the shore that threatened to cut off some of her view.

The ferry, having no reverse, made a flying landing at the dock located near the end of the bridge. Two men among the group of people waiting for the return trip caught the lines Mr. Varney threw out and made the boat fast. Jenny took Mr. Varney's extended, spotted hand and was helped to the dock. She made her way up the path leading from it.

The path led, only a short distance away, to the tiny railroad depot of the hotel. Across the tracks was the Beach Club, or Bradley's, a casual white wooden building that looked more like a staid New England meeting-house than the most exclusive private gambling club in the world.

FROM THE DEPOT to the hotel there led a colonnade, single-storied for a short distance and then rising to two stories. The lower level ran into the ground floor of the Ponce; broad steps climbed to the second level which went to the main floor. Through either it was a quarter-mile walk to the registration desk in the lounge off the rotunda. If an arriving guest had his suite behind the great lifting wall of the T that formed the north end of the hotel, however, he need not travel all the way to the rotunda and back again; another registration desk was provided in the north parlor here at the end of the second floor of the colonnade.

Jenny entered, by a concrete path, the tropical gardens of the Ponce. They were even more beautiful than when the hotel had opened, with additional varieties of plants and flowers brought from the ends of the earth. She checked on the royal poincianas. She always did this, as though these belonged to her personally, and she had the say about them. To her satisfaction, they were in good condition; the Ponce gardeners seemed to understand how to treat them. They had just the right amount of sparse winter foliage. An excellent crop of the straplike pods clung to the spidery limbs, maturing properly to furnish a good supply of seeds. Jenny felt sorry for the winter people who never saw the trees in bloom.

She passed along the front of the hotel. It presented a towering yellow cliff relieved by the dazzling white trim and the thousands of green shutters thrown back. From four places on the high gables of the sprawling building flew immense American flags, while at the cupola the wind held out and waved the long buff Ponce pennant with its name appearing clearly in giant blue-green letters.

Along the winding paths people rolled in wheel chairs. These consisted of two bicycle wheels, with a smaller wheel in front below the footrest, supporting a padded wicker chair. In back was attached the rear half of a bicycle. This, pedaled by a Negro, gave the chair its name of Afrimobile. Seasonal hotel guests usually hired a particular man and chair to be at their disposal during their entire stay.

Jenny passed the main entrance of the hotel. At the top of the broad steps, between the high white pillars and down either side on the verandas, green striped awnings shaded people rocking in green chairs. Most of them were very special people, with names seen often in the society and financial columns. There were Astors and Whitneys and Wanamakers and Wideners and Stewarts and Vanderbilts and Harrimans. These and many others arrived in their private cars.

Jenny walked under the colonnade which led to the dock and boat basin at the lake shore. On its second story the orchestra played for dancing on the wooden platform set among the palms in the Coconut Grove directly south. Tables and chairs were placed among the trees. People took tea and danced. It was the fashionable place to be at this hour. A few, like those rocking on the verandas, or secluded in their suites, or gambling at Bradley's, were important enough to ignore this. But you had to be very important, or otherwise you were thought to be nobody unless you were present in the Coconut Grove at this hour.

She watched the dancing for a time and then walked on. She came out at the south end of the hotel. Here the little yellow horsecar ran from the Ponce to the ocean beach half a mile away. At the beach Mr. Flagler had built a second hotel, the Breakers; anywhere else the four-hundred-room Breakers would be a large hotel, but here it was dwarfed by its Gargantuan sister.

Together with bicycles and the Afrimobiles, the horsecar was the only wheeled vehicle Mr. Flagler would allow in Palm Beach. It was ridden mostly by children, and was like a perambulating nursery. Charlie, the burly old driver, sometimes let the children drive it back and forth. He kept them amused while their parents danced, played roulette or drank.

The car was pulling in at the end of its track as Jenny arrived on the scene. The open front platform was crowded with children, clustered about the driver. Inside it was packed with clamoring, yelling, sometimes fighting children, a small bedlam no one seemed to mind. Old Charlie, seeing Jenny, waved to her and called out above the noise, "You want to see something you been looking for a long time, you go peek through the fence of Whitehall."

Jenny forgot to thank him in her haste to cover the short distance, diagonally across the walk, to the square, three-storied, shining white marble mansion that stood here on the point of land where the Bethune brothers once had their store. Jenny knew that Whitehall was as wonderful as any palace in Europe. She also knew for whom it had been built, and what a romantic story it was. Mr. Flagler had had bad luck with his wives. The first one died. The second went insane. But his third wife!

When he was seventy, Flagler lunched with friends in Newport. A relative of this family was visiting them at the time. Her name was Mary Lily Kenan. She was in her early thirties, shy and pretty. She occupied a small top-floor room in the Newport mansion, and did the family mending. Mr. Flagler met her when she came to the dining-table, but had little chance to talk with her. He was taken by her appearance and modest manner. Furtively, the multi-million-aire pulled a button from his coat and asked if it might be sewed back on. Mary Lily got busy with her needle and thread, and while she sewed on the button for him, they spoke, apart. Flagler came to see her the next day, and they talked again, seriously and at length. The Newport family learned what they discussed when they announced that they were to be married. They were, after Flagler instructed the Florida state legislature to pass a temporary law for his con-venience, permitting a man to divorce a mad wife.

The couple, not much more than newlyweds, were here now in the two-and-one-half-million-dollar marble palace that replaced the Newport attic room. Jenny rushed to the mas-sive, wrought-iron gates and peered through the pickets. Immediately she knew the two people sitting in the wheel chair and being pedaled leisurely about the grounds inside.

At last she saw Mr. Flagler.

She could see that he was a tall man even though he was sitting down. He looked spare and old. He was clad in a white linen suit that hung loosely on his bony frame. He had great shaggy eyebrows, and a gray scraggly mustache over-hung his straight, severe-looking mouth. He showed no animation as he rolled past in the wheel-chair, not twenty feet from where Jenny stared. He looked straight ahead.

Jenny's glance had gone first to him. Now it went to the figure beside him.

Mary Lily was also clad in white, with overlaid creamy lace. She held a white lace parasol above her head to shade both herself and her elderly husband. She was slimly beautiful, with a round, pink, kindly young face. Jenny thought she had never seen anyone so grand, not even among the famous society ladies she frequently glimpsed at the Ponce.

As she passed, Mary Lily turned her head and saw Jenny. She seemed amused, in a friendly way, at the sight of the other woman peering in at her through the towering black gates. Even though Jenny, abashed, drew back a little, Mary Lily turned her head to keep Jenny in sight as the chair was pedaled on. Mary Lily smiled at Jenny and Jenny smiled back gladly. She was so touched at this gracious attention that she didn't realize what she was doing when she raised a hand and waved it. Laughing, Mary Lily waved back.

Returning to the Ponce, Jenny strolled around to its rear. There was a particular sight here which in some ways she admired above all other things. Several spur railroad tracks extended the length of the hotel. On them were parked private railroad cars, placed end to end. She counted them today, and there were twenty-eight. The tracks could hold nearly fifty and were filled to capacity each year at the time of the Washington Birthday ball.

Jenny's eyes sparkled at the sight of the palace cars. Nothing else so strikingly illustrated the wealth of the nation. It was a proud thing just to look at these private railroad cars.

Jenny continued on her course north to the end of the

hotel. She walked past the tennis courts and came to the depot. When she reached its platform she had circled the hotel, walking nearly a mile to do it.

She arrived in plenty of time. The orchestra had left the west colonnade and was seating itself, with its instruments, on the second story of the north colonnade. It would serenade the guests arriving on the train, due in a few minutes. As the orchestra got ready, from out of the Ponce, on the ground floor, marched Henry, the head bellman. The fringes of his gold epaulets jiggled as the proud Negro led his small army of bellmen. At Henry's direction they distributed themselves along the platform to be ready to grab the bags of arrivals. White baggagemen wheeled their trucks forward to get the trunks. These would be whisked into the proper rooms before their occupants reached them.

There was quite a stir on the platform today. A number of guests had also come down to the depot to greet friends arriving. Mr. Bemerill, the hotel manager himself, was on hand, which meant that somebody important would be on the train. The manager saw Jenny and greeted her stiffly, as though he had to keep up the dignity of his position. Henry greeted her more warmly; he had dignity, too, but seemed to find less necessity to preserve it. Jenny whispered to him, indicating the manager, "Who's coming?"

"Missus Astor," Henry informed her grandly.

The smoke from the engine could now be seen across the bridge in West Palm. Soon the rear of the train appeared, backing over the lake so that it would be in position to move out again after the private cars were detached.

The orchestra began to play a stirring march. Expectancy

on the Ponce depot platform heightened as the train rolled into the station.

Two private cars passed, followed by a diner, five Pullmans, and then the baggage car and engine with its tender, coming to a hot, pulsating stop.

Bellmen ran to be on hand at the vestibules. Porters shot out of these to place their footstands as the well-shined shoes of the passengers appeared. There were greetings and cries between newcomers and those who had come to meet them. Henry welcomed virtually everyone who had been here before, knowing them by name. Orders were shouted. The band played furiously.

Ladies held their skirts delicately as they appeared in the very latest New York fashions, details devoured by Jenny, who watched with hungry, worshiping eyes. Gentlemen lifted hats high after inserting their sticks under their left armpits, and bowed. People breathed deeply the soft warm afternoon air and spoke of having left ice and sleet hardly forty hours ago. In joy, some of them danced in time to the music being played in their honor.

Suitcases were grabbed efficiently by the bellmen, who could handle their size in luggage and carry it all the way to the rotunda. With it they even executed a few fancy steps in time to music.

Jenny watched carefully, trying to take in everything at once. She moved up and down the platform in order to see all she could. She stopped to watch Mrs. Astor descend from her car at the end of the train. Awaited by Mr. Bemerill below, she appeared majestically on the step, surveying the scene to see if it warranted her proceeding further. Evidently she decided that it would do, for she permitted Mr. Bemerill to take her hand and assist her to the platform. The grand lady was wafted off in a cloud of hotel manager, bellmen, companion, maid and two lady society reporters who had put in a last-minute appearance.

Jenny turned her attention to the second private car. No one had yet emerged from there. Now appeared a man who staggered rather than stepped, though once he gained the platform he was steady enough on his feet.

Jenny's heart missed a beat. It made her feel guilty, for there was no reason her heart should jump at the sight of Cleve Thornton.

He was older, with slight lines of dissipation in his face. But he was still handsome; he had style and was engaging. His blond mustache was sporty, his blue eyes merry, as he surveyed the scene expectantly.

Almost the first thing he saw was Jenny, for she stood quite nearby.

She was totally unprepared for a repetition of the scene that had taken place nine years before at St. Augustine, and a bold elaboration of it. He caught her entirely off guard when he came up to her, took her in his arms, placed one of her hands on his shoulder, took the other in his cool fingers and then began to dance with her right there on the depot platform.

Jenny was so startled that she had no time to resist. The orchestra was playing a waltz, and when the musicians saw what was going on below, they livened the pace of the music. People laughed.

Still Jenny hadn't altogether taken in what was happening to her. She had the disarming impression that Cleve Thornton remembered her. Then she knew that this was only in her own mind. She had thought of him from time to time over the years, but it was extremely doubtful if any recollection of her remained to him. She was sure of this as the strong fumes of liquor on his breath reached her.

She became conscious of their dancing together, smoothly, gracefully. At the same time she realized, like being struck a blow, what she was allowing him to do and the public spectacle she was making of herself.

She stopped stock still and tried to draw away from him. In a low, protesting voice she said, "No."

"Yes," he told her, hanging onto her hand. He looked at her closely. "You're exquisite. Who are you?"

At that she jerked away from him and ran.

She heard people laughing as she rounded the corner of the depot. Her face burned with the surprise and shame of what had happened. She hated Cleve Thornton for doing it.

Finding that she was alone, she stopped, her heart beating rapidly. Slowly her sense of curiosity overcame her shock. She stepped to the corner of the depot and peered around it.

Cleve Thornton had caught sight of a few wheel-chair men who had come to meet the train, singling out one of them. Choo Choo was a huge black man. He sat on his wheel, making sounds that exactly reproduced those of the real engine standing on the track. He chugged. He rang the bell that hung from his handlebars, making a dingdong sound. He blew a whistle. He hissed with imaginary steam. Most people believed he imitated a train merely as an act to entertain people or to draw interest in himself and get customers. Jenny knew that he was quite crazy and sincerely believed he was a train.

"Choo Choo!" Cleve Thornton cried.

Choo Choo let out a great whooshing jet of steam. He

rang his bell furiously and pedaled his chair back and forth.

These two, it was plain, knew and appreciated each other.

With supreme effort, gargling out the words as though his boiler was overheated and about to explode, Choo Choo awarded his friend the supreme compliment of actual words.

"You ride dis train," he pleaded. "Don' go walkin' in lak enny ol' common millionaire."

After he said this Choo Choo went off into a tremendous series of train noises, offering his entire repertoire. He worked himself up into knots being a train. Watching him, Jenny thought he might wreck himself at any instant.

"Wonderful!" Cleve said. "You're a better train this year than you were last, Choo Choo. You must be my special private train again, and I can do nothing less than ride on you now."

He got into the chair. Jenny watched Choo Choo pedal him off around the walk in front of the Ponce. Cleve declaimed to all who passed. "Palm Beach is well named," he said. "There are palms on every hand, especially human palms. They are always held out, continually waving and creating a gentle draught on the pocketbook. And their battle cry is, 'No quarter—nothing less than a dollar.'"

JENNY HAD the suspicion that Cleve Thornton thought she was a Ponce guest. She pictured him trying to find her among the hundreds of ladies staying at the Ponce. Or perhaps she flattered herself in her effect on him, and he had already forgotten her again. If he did search, the thought of his futile quest gave her delight. On the other hand, she felt deceptive and could not comprehend why she did. She was sure that if he found out she was not a guest he would never look at her again.

At this thought she caught herself up sharply. Why did it occur to her that he might make advances a third time? She wanted no such thing. Her cheeks burned at the recollection of his brazen rudeness and the scene he had made with her at the hotel depot. The story was all over town. Some people spoke to her about it, while others contented themselves with glancing at her curiously.

She was afraid Tip might hear of it before he came in from the Glades, as he did each Saturday and Sunday. When he arrived she looked quickly at his face. He had first stopped by at the Mercantile Bazaar where his weekly message arranging for hunters from the Ponce was left with the Bethunes. He held the unopened envelope in his hand. With relief Jenny saw that he had not been informed.

She told him at once, while he unslung his paraphernalia

and she helped him with it. She blurted out the story exactly as it had happened.

Tip laid aside his rifle and dropped a roll of skins on the floor before he replied, "He remembered you a long time."

"Oh, but he didn't. It's just his way of making up to any . . ."

"Good-looking woman?" Tip finished for her.

"He's despicable."

With her aid Tip took off more of what he carried. Jenny waited for anything further he had to say. She was sure he was thinking it over. A slight crease came to his forehead at the top of his nose. She watched it, knowing it for a sign of his working out a problem.

The crease disappeared. He said, "I thought you were going to keep away from the hotel."

"I haven't been over there since, Tip. I like to see it, but I'll certainly keep away while he's there."

His next words comprised a suggestion. "Wouldn't it be best to keep away all the time?"

Jenny had feared and was prepared for this. "Oh, Tip, don't ask me to do that. I haven't much to do, and that's one of my few pleasures. There isn't any harm in it except when things like that happen. And I'll keep out of the way of letting anything like that ever happen again."

Tip said no more. Though he disapproved of the strong attraction the hotel held for her, he did not insist that she stop going to it. As before, when he had first spoken of this and showed jealousy, it roused tender feelings in Jenny for him. She felt again the desire to be closer to him, to share the life that he led apart from her. In this lay her own jealousy.

"I want to go to the Glades with you now," she announced. "And see your camp. I should have gone a long time ago."

"I thought we understood each other on that, Jenny."

"I only understand I want to know what my husband does," she declared. "Maybe that's . . ." She didn't complete her statement, but she might as well have said that perhaps it was one of the troubles between them. "You said you'd take me out when a horse and wagon could get there. They can now; they've been taking Ponce hunters out."

"I'll keep my promise," Tip replied, "in the spring, as soon as the hotel closes and no more business for me comes from there."

"I want to go now," she importuned, "next week. I don't want to wait. I can go between your hunters."

Tip looked at her, and saw how determined she was. He didn't know what to answer right away. He took up the message he had received and opened it, reading. The crease returned to his brow, deeper than before. He kept looking at the piece of paper for a long time, pondering. Once he glanced up. His expression seemed both troubled and amused before he looked down again.

Piqued, Jenny asked, "Don't you want me out there?"

"You mean right now?"

"Next week."

Tip poked the sheet of paper with one strong finger. "Thornton has hired me and the camp for all of next week."

Jenny stared.

"Maybe," Tip went on, "it would be a good idea if you came out next week like you want."

Jenny still stared.

"If you keep going to the hotel," he said, "the way I see

you mean to, you'll be bound to run into him again even if you try not to. But if he sees you as my wife, that ought to be the end of it."

Jenny waited for him to continue.

"He wants to do some fishing and hunting," Tip went on. "And drinking, too, I expect. But mostly he wants to see me catch a crocodile alive the way I been doing for some with both crocs and alligators. He says he wants to help at this, and he can if he's of a mind to. You can come right along on that, Jenny, and watch."

"Are other hunters going to be there?"

"Thornton wants the place all to himself and is paying the biggest price I ever got." He elucidated further why he made his rather extraordinary suggestion. "Now I don't mean to make a fight of it because this man has looked twice at you. All I aim to do is to let him see he ought to look some place else in case he ever wants to look again."

"You think it will do that?"

"That's the way I'm figuring, and that's the way I think it will work."

"What if it does the opposite?"

"Then I'll tell him in plain words."

Jenny thought swiftly. Tip's idea startled her. She hardly looked forward to it. But she decided that he was right. When Cleve Thornton learned who she was, his guide's wife rather than a guest of the Ponce; and when he saw her attitude toward him he would have some respect for her, enough to prevent any further advances. She began to generate enthusiasm for the project.

She told Tip, "It will be a good thing to do."

"Then you'll come out for the day with Doc Bethune the

middle of the week. Doc wants a day in the open and he's bringing me some supplies and building materials for making the camp bigger. Also, I got an order from a northern zoo for a crocodile and Doc can bring it back that night." He made one more statement, a question. His manner of putting it sounded like a combination of consideration for his wife and a mild challenge. "There ain't any reason all this should be uncomfortable for you?"

"Not especially, Tip. Except—should we say anything about St. Augustine?"

"I don't see where that enters into it enough to mention."

It was left that way.

Jenny studied and planned and decided and changed her mind half a dozen times about what she should wear on her day in the Glades. She was hesitant in many ways about her appearance. She did not want to wear good clothes, but at the same time she didn't care to be unattractive. She feared looking too dressed up in case Tip might think this was for the sake of Cleve Thornton. Yet she rebelled at being frowsy in the presence of a handsome man worth twenty million dollars, no matter how much of a waster he might be or in what manner he may have insulted her.

In the end she decided on the sensible course of wearing exactly what she would if she were to be alone with Tip, a turkey-red checked calico cut like a Mother Hubbard. On her head was a crisp sunbonnet to match. Even so, her face was framed prettily, her body clad becomingly. With secret pleasure she noted that she looked well in almost anything. She was one of those lucky women who lend as much to clothes as clothes do for them.

Apart from this, Jenny looked forward to the trip and the

event with an eagerness she could barely control. It was like finally learning something unknown and long withheld about her husband. Added to all was the anticipation of seeing a large crocodile caught. She understood that a crocodile was more dangerous than an alligator, which was bad enough.

Doc called for her shortly after dawn, his eyes still sleepy behind his spectacles. He drove a brown mare hitched to one of the open Mercantile wagons loaded with lumber, kegs of nails and other materials. Jenny climbed up beside him on the board seat. It had only a little spring in it. She settled her skirts, Doc clucked to the horse and they started out.

The sand road led southwest from town for several miles, and then became a trail. In places it was barely discernible; in others a corduroy road had been laid down, sometimes with pine trunks, sometimes with tough spongy palm logs.

Doc yawned and Jenny, in spite of her excitement, followed suit. They laughed at each other. Jenny saw the beginning of the sawgrass. The wagon jounced, their bodies rolling with it. The mare stepped gingerly between clumps of grass and at the edge of streams. Once she shied and was about to bolt, until Doc brought her up sharply with the reins. He had to hurt her mouth to stop her and bring her to her senses. When she quieted and stood skittishly, a sharp, low hissing sound could be heard from nearby.

"Moccasin," said Doc.

Jenny looked fearfully at the grass hiding the water where the snake lay. She drew back against Doc on the seat.

Doc clucked the mare on; she pranced and glanced back nervously.

Sometimes the trail constituted the only bank of dry land running through water on either side. Jenny admired clumps of palms that dotted the Glades; this was what Tip had told her about. Often there were only a few in a group. At other places were hundreds, forming individual jungles.

Several times they disturbed flocks of ducks. Stretches of water were covered with so many thousands that it looked like dark, moving land. Frightened, they moved as one, seeming to walk on the water for a short distance, skittering over it and shirring it. Then, sending up sheets of spray as they gained momentum to fly, they took off, leaving the surface stirred as though from a sudden squall. The sky was darkened as they circled overhead and departed for another pond, or, after the wagon passed, cautiously returned to the one from which they had risen.

Jenny had an uneasiness at the prospect of the meeting ahead. The nearer they came to Tip's camp the more excited she became. She told Doc, "I've never seen it here, you know."

Doc spoke to her as he did to the mare. "Now settle down," he soothed.

She could not. She stood up when she thought she saw the camp ahead in a large thick patch of palms. The wagon lurched, and she nearly fell out. She was saved by Doc grabbing her skirt and pulling her down. "Don't do that again," he ordered.

She straightened her clothes which he had nearly pulled off. That would have been a fine way to arrive.

She looked up and saw that she had been right about the camp.

It was set on the curve of a barely defined waterway coursing through a flooded area. The stream entered a small lake, filling it with dark clear water before winding off again into the south. By the bank of the lake the side and roof of a small man-made structure could be seen. Beyond, under more palms, stood a larger building in the course of construction.

The utterly peaceful spot had its own wild brand of beauty. Jenny thought that it was like something in a painting. She didn't blame Tip for wanting to be out here but only for not letting her come long before.

They saw Tip ahead. He had been watching for them or had heard the sound of the wagon wheels. He waved, and they waved back. The mare, as though sensing this was a destination for which to be grateful, broke into a trot.

AS THE WAGON drove up and stopped, no other figure was in sight, though Jenny glanced about to catch a first glimpse of Cleve Thornton. Tip greeted them warmly. He seemed more at ease here than in town; he fitted this country, and it was his. "Good for you both," he said, "for getting out in such fine time. We'll have a big day." He helped Jenny down. They kissed, and he asked with concern, "See any snakes?"

"One made the horse shy."

"You'll see more," he warned, "so be prepared." He waved a hand. "How do you like my camp?"

Jenny looked about more closely. This, then, was where Tip spent so much time away from her. Here was his headquarters for his hunting, trapping, fishing and guiding. This was what he had kept from her for so long.

"I expected it to be rough," she said, "but not beautiful."

As though her remark had been made of him, Cleve Thornton stepped out of the small building.

He was clad fashionably in casual light canvas hunting clothes, worn with his usual air of expensive carelessness. He looked no less smart because they were stained in places with evidences of successful hunting and fishing. He stood straight and did not waver in his stride as he came forward.

Jenny felt a single flash of panic at not knowing what Tip

135

had told him about her coming. She learned only that Tip had identified her as his wife when Thornton asked, "Your wife has come?"

"This is Mrs. Totten," Tip told him.

Jenny stood waiting, saying nothing as Cleve Thornton addressed her. To her chagrin she found again she could not still a slight quickening of the beat of her heart. She blamed it on the possible awkwardness the moment might bring.

Thornton began, "I'm happy to meet you, Mrs. Totten. Tip explained you were coming out to—" He stopped, for then he looked full into her face. He failed to identify her instantly, but he knew something about her was decidedly familiar. Then it dawned upon him.

His blue eyes widened as he gave an involuntary exclamation. "You're—" He caught himself, flashing a glance at Tip and then back to her.

Jenny realized that his practiced sense of discretion cautioned him that Tip might not know of the Ponce depot incident. She tried to be politely hostile, but could not keep amusement from her voice when she said, "It's all right, Mr. Thornton."

He understood then and smiled broadly as he turned to Tip. "I see what you've meant to do, Tip. And I accept the lesson. I deserve the rebuke. I take the gentle hint."

Tip included Jenny in his reception of this. "My wife and me thought it was a good time for her to come out." He kept his gaze leveled on the other man.

"A good time, indeed," Thornton turned back to Jenny. He hadn't flushed with any shame. She saw, summoning a scorn for him, that he must have faced such embarrassing situations many times before. And except for that first moment he took this one in his stride. Still looking at her, but addressing his initial remarks to Tip, he said, "I don't blame you in the least for warning me off. If I had her I would do the same." Bowing to Jenny, he continued, "My apologies to you are in order, Mrs. Totten, and gladly and hopefully offered."

She struggled not to admire his charm and manners, but failed to keep herself from being won at least partially. She murmured, "There is no need."

Tip looked from one to the other of them. Of Thornton he asked, "We've got that straight?"

"Straight as a die, Tip," Thornton stated. He laughed and touched his blond mustache. "I wouldn't want to look at it any other way with the kind of shot I've seen you to be these last few days."

"You ain't so bad yourself," Tip conceded. Candidly, he added, "When you don't drink too much the night before."

"You see, Mrs. Totten," Thornton explained quite as if she didn't know all about it, "demon rum possesses me. It is my life work and career. I am exceedingly successful."

His joking eased the strain among the three of them. Jenny was curiously disturbed on the one hand, and relieved on the other. She determined to ignore Cleve Thornton as much as possible today. She had other things to do.

Doc had unhitched the mare and tied her in the shade of palms. He was unloading the wagon. Thornton, upon being introduced to him, surprisingly offered to lend a hand. Grunting at having a multi-millionaire help him, Doc accepted.

Tip didn't refer to the incidents of her arrival as he led Jenny about his camp. He showed her his dock on the pond and the two rowboats moored there; one of them was the boat they once kept back on Lake Worth, and seeing it was like greeting an old friend. "In them I take out the Ponce swells like Thornton," explained Tip.

He took her to the buildings. They reminded her of the palm house and the unfinished frame house before the hurricane. One which was completed, was a board and batten cabin. The second was to be a bunkhouse. "I only been able to put up a few hunters at a time before," he said. "But with this I can do a wholesale business." He outlined the layout of the four rooms it would contain; with two sets of bunks in each it would put up sixteen people.

Proudly Jenny assured him, "It's as good as any business back in town, Tip."

He scratched his head. "Except for keeping the accounts. I never like paper work. Sometimes I get mixed up."

The suggestion she made was an impulsive plea. "Couldn't I do it for you?"

"Well, it's kind of complicated. You got to be out here sometimes to know how to handle it. We'll see," he temporized.

She resented, for a sharp instant, his not allowing her in that part of his activity. She swallowed her feeling, telling herself he wanted to wait to see how she liked the day here.

Tip went on, as though avoiding the issue further, "It's a funny thing how rich men like to rough it. I got an idea it makes them feel good, knowing they don't have to do it unless they want to. And by comparison with what they're used to, it sets them up. I've watched it a good many times. There's even one or two, if you can believe it, who are more comfortable here than at the Ponce."

He showed her inside the cabin. There was room for a cot and two bunks, one above the other. A cookstove, a table and a few chairs comprised most of the furnishings. Jenny walked about in the cabin, to all corners. She visualized Tip here alone. She understood, as much as she could, how he had come here after being pricked so cruelly by the Doolittle children, instead of finding comfort by remaining with her.

It was strange not to be allowed to help with the early lunch prepared. Jenny knew Tip cooked the meals for his clients out here, but she watched in amazement while he fried bass caught that morning to a crisp brown on the outside and a steaming white deliciousness within. Chunks of hot potatoes, strong coffee, slabs of bread and baked beans were served by Tip who suddenly assumed a domestic air never seen at home. At home, Jenny thought. Looking about once more, the jealousy she had of his life here in the Glades struck more acutely than ever. She saw that he had two homes, and one of them was here.

They ate outdoors near the bank of the pond where a rustic table and benches were placed. Rather than being waited on, Thornton was enlisted to pass serving plates around the table. He looked questioningly at Tip, and suggested, "Shouldn't we celebrate Mrs. Totten's being here by a wee splash?"

"Not on your life," Tip informed him. "Or rather, not on my life. If you're going to help with catching this croc we're going after, you're going to have the full use of all your faculties. I don't want you making a mistake at the wrong minute. I'm thinking of myself more than you," he elucidated.

"He told me," Thornton complained to Jenny, "that if I took a drop this morning he would leave me behind and take Doc Bethune here on the crocodile hunt instead."

"Count me out of that," Doc protested. "I won't have a thing to do with the critters unless they're trussed up and ready for market. I'm not even going with you. An alligator's bad enough, but anybody is crazy to go fooling around with crocs."

"Maybe," Thornton said, "we could have a small toast to these bass. After all, I caught them, and they are worthy of admiration."

"Nothing doing," said Tip.

"Your husband," Thornton told Jenny, "is a hard man." He looked genuinely abused. "After all, I've got to have the stuff. I feel awful without it, not myself at all. And I feel that stage coming upon me now."

Jenny felt touched not at the appeal to her sympathy he made, but by the fact that he was sincere in his statement.

"You'll last," Tip predicted.

"I doubt it, I seriously doubt it, unless we get started soon." His handsome face looked strained.

"Then here we go," said Tip.

They left Doc to clear off the table and prepared for the crocodile hunt. Tip stowed all the equipment for this in the larger boat. He loaded in several coils of stout rope, together with some short pieces, a rifle and two stout pine poles three inches thick at the base and twelve feet long. These he placed so that their thin ends protruded beyond the bow of the boat. He directed that he and Thornton get in the boat containing these, and Jenny row the other craft.

They pushed off. Jenny enjoyed the familiar feel of the little boat she had known so well and had not seen for some time. The lunch had been excellent, the day was fine, the company of her husband and Thornton now exciting and the purpose ahead full of fearful stimulation.

Tip explained the use of the poles as both boats were rowed away from the dock and deeper into the Glades, entering the stream winding south. "One end of a big croc, or gator for that matter, is about as dangerous as the other," he said. "After you've got him and have his snout tied up, that takes care of the front end. He still has his tail to throw about. That's where the poles come in. You lash these down the length of him so he doesn't smash your wagon apart on the way in to ship him off."

Their route followed irregular waterways. In places herons were thick, rising with a shower of silent wings to whiten the sky, and then settle back again after the boats had passed. "They may tell our friend we're coming," Tip said. "If they do, we won't get him. He's sizable, running to around nine feet, as big as anybody wants to tackle a croc the way we're going to. I've had my eye on him for a long time now, knowing just where he suns himself."

Tip had his eye on other things. Jenny had never seen him so alert. His glance shifted quickly about. Some of this she had observed at the lunch table. Tip had watched Thornton and glanced at her. What he saw had satisfied him. Now he turned most of his attention to the water and the banks at the side.

From his boat he informed Jenny, "You've passed some moccasins already, but now they're going to get thick."

She kept her voice steady when she asked, "Will I see them any more than I did the others?"

"You'll probably hear them first. Keep your hands on your

oars. Don't put them in the water. If one climbs on your oar, don't get excited."

"Just wriggle him off," advised Thornton.

Jenny felt faint. Fearfully, she watched and listened.

Turtles slipped into the water at their approach. Once something unseen around a bend crashed through the brittle undergrowth on the bank into the grass. "What was that?" Jenny asked.

"I don't guess any more," Tip told her. "There's too much it could be, from a big wildcat to a panther or even a bear."

There was no doubt about the moccasins when they came to a place where they nested. Jenny saw her first one coiled on shore. The stubby, nearly black, ugly fat snake seemed to look straight at her from its awful little eyes. She felt sick.

The second one was in the water, close by the boat. It was fishing and paying no attention to her, but she shrank back, catching a crab with her oar and making it splash.

"Stop rowing a minute," Tip said, "and listen."

Both boats drifted. Jenny then saw the moccasins all about, on the banks and in the water. One slithered across her drifting oar, its body bloated from overfeeding. There came a distinct, threatening, dreadful hissing from many cottonwhite throats.

Jenny learned, then, Tip's wisdom in not letting her come out here. She tried to keep her face from blanching.

She could not conceal this from Tip, who asked, "You want to go on?"

"Yes," she forced herself to say.

"It ain't as dangerous as it looks and sounds," he assured her. "Don't mess with them and they won't touch you. But keep clear of them."

Jenny kept clear, shrinking when one came close to the boat. They thinned, and she relaxed a little.

"We're getting near the place," Tip called in a low voice, informing both her and Thornton. "Now listen: There's a current that will carry us near to where he's out on the bank. Don't row any more, but just steer with one oar at the stern to let the stream take us to him. The two of us have got to get out of our boat before he knows it. That can be done because they haven't been disturbed enough here yet to be too scary. But he'll try for the water. If he makes it—and he can travel faster than you think—we'll lose him."

"You haven't told me what to do," Thornton said.

"First thing I want you to know," Tip said, "is that no matter how ferocious a crocodile is, it's also a delicate creature in some ways and can be injured with too rough handling."

"So," said Thornton, "can I."

"I want to get this one intact," Tip instructed him. "You got to be special careful of his legs when we get to tying him up—if we get that far. There ain't any other rules. It's a wrestling match, no holds barred, with some lassoing and tying thrown in. You may lose some skin. All you do while you're losing it is let me handle the head. Don't you get anywhere near his jaws and watch the tail. If you're sorry you wanted to do this in the first place you can still back out and nobody will blame you."

"I wouldn't miss it for the world," said Thornton.

The two boats drifted. Tip led the way. He shook his head at a flock of snow-white egrets that rose before them. A moccasin struck at his steering oar. Tip paid no attention as its fangs sank into the wood and yellowish drips of poison could be seen on the oar. Jenny shuddered as it let go and swam away.

She caught Thornton looking at her. Tip's gaze now was elsewhere. Thornton seemed to be reading her feelings and thoughts. From his look, which was a flash of frank, renewed admiration, she understood that his finding out that she was not of his world made no difference to him.

She resented both the message and the fact that he could give it at this time of incipient danger, and in Tip's presence. He had calculated it cleverly. She wondered how he would acquit himself in the moment to come.

Tip motioned for her to steer closer to the right shore. They rounded a point and his hand made almost frantic movements, indicating that they should land.

Jenny could see nothing as they silently made the shore. Tip got out, crouching behind grass, and pulled the prow of each craft a few feet up on the bank. Making no sound, he unloaded the poles and then took up the long ropes. He indicated that Thornton should get out and follow him.

Jenny couldn't make out the crocodile until Tip led Thornton to it.

The huge gray reptile lay in the sun on a high flat bank. Only his head was visible. There was a lot of that, over two feet. His eyes were closed. He was snoozing, with the rest of his body overhanging the bank, out of sight.

Jenny forgot all about moccasins and watched the men. They crept forward, around young palmettos and other growth. Tip walked peculiarly, lifting each foot high and placing it carefully upon the ground, to make as little vibration as possible. Thornton, watching him, followed suit as best he could.

They stopped at their last possible place of concealment while Tip dropped one rope on the ground and arranged the other. He dangled a noose held by a slipknot. He motioned to Thornton, and they emerged into the open.

They were within twenty feet of the crocodile before it finally sensed them. It came suddenly alive, eyes open, raised quickly on its short stubby legs. At that Tip no longer crept. He dashed forward, holding out his rope. He was between the croc and the water.

The crocodile opened great jaws to exhibit jagged long rows of glistening white teeth. This was merely a preliminary warning. It gave a bellow that shook the earth. Then it snapped its snout shut and began to travel toward the water.

Tip dodged around its head, and went in at its side, kicking it sharply near the belly. It was like kicking a huge boulder that gave a little. The irritation must have been felt, for the crocodile stopped, twisted its head and opened its jaws again in warning. This time it hissed. Its jaws closed with a sound like a pistol shot. Two tusks that rose alongside the upper jaw gleamed wickedly. It started for the water again.

Tip didn't throw his rope. His hand darted, and he placed it over the head of the croc, drawing the loop all down the length of its head to its neck. Then he pulled it tight. At the same instant he yelled to Thornton, "Don't let him get to the water! Got to get the rope around him again!"

They both threw themselves at the crocodile, grabbing it about the middle, tackling it. Thornton hesitated no more than Tip. The beast stopped momentarily. Its powerful tail thrashed, sending dirt flying; if a man had been in the way he would have been carried off his feet, his legs broken.

Thornton's hunting jacket tore with a ripping sound as he fought the writhing brute.

The crocodile heaved, digging its clawed feet into the ground. It moved forward, carrying the two men with it, lifting to heave again. They dug their own feet into the ground and were dragged just the same, though more slowly. They were thrown about, Tip once going half under the body of the croc until it rolled off him. He was unhurt except for the place where the horny hide sandpapered his arm. He struggled with the rope in the flashing melee. He managed to get a second loop around the body of the reptile back of its front legs, so that the rope would not pull free.

The croc had almost made the water, dragging them with it, when Tip yelled to Thornton, "Get the rope around a tree!"

Thornton grabbed the end of the rope, jumped up, avoided the wildly switching tail by a hair's breadth and got to a stout small palm. He threw the rope around its bole, pulled it tight and turned. He was just in time to see Tip execute the most dangerous part of croc catching.

The beast had carried him to the edge of the water before the anchored rope stopped it. Infuriated now, the croc kept snapping its jaws. It moved wildly from side to side, rolling this way and that. Twice more it gave its soul-stirring bellow. An odor of musk filled the air, and from time to time there was a loud hiss.

Tip was watching his chance. He tried with one hand for the snout each time the long jaws closed. They opened again too quickly for him to reach it. Jenny, who was now on shore to see better, cried at him not to try it. He seemed not to hear as finally he made it.

The great snout had no more than snapped shut when Tip's fingers closed over its end. Surprisingly, the man held it closed. The leverage was far in his favor. At the same time the big croc quieted, as though acknowledging that it was at least temporarily beaten.

Tip, breathing hard, looked at Jenny. His eyes twinkled at her concern. "That's the way you catch yourself a croc," he panted.

Thornton, holding on to his rope, suggested coolly, "Why not let Mrs. Totten have the honor of tying his snout?"

"I don't think she'd want to," said Tip.

Tip, because of his exertions, did not catch the note in Thornton's voice that he was laughing at Jenny and challenging her. The millionaire sensed how full of fear she was of wild things. He had gathered how this had been a means of separation between her and her husband. Thornton was telling her she couldn't close the gap.

She took a short piece of rope from the other craft. She was glad neither of the men could see any evidence of the trembling of her legs as she made her way to the scene.

To Tip's great surprise she approached the crocodile. "If you're going to do it," he cried, "keep here at the head."

She could not prevent her hands from shaking as she put one of the short lengths of rope, at Tip's direction, around the crocodile's jaws near the end. She knew only that she would do it if it was the last thing she ever accomplished. Her desire was confused. It was connected with showing Tip that she could come to the Glades country and with showing Cleve Thornton that he was wrong about her not being able to be a part of it.

She kept her eyes on Tip's hand as she tied the knot, pull-

147

ing it as tight as she could. She tried not to think of what would happen if he let go or the crocodile twisted free. The odor of musk was almost overpowering.

Jenny completed the tying. Tip ordered her to step back and she was glad to go, standing off at a distance, quivering. She could not avoid Thornton's glance, trying to give him triumph in hers, only to be met with a sardonic expression in his. She hadn't convinced him. She realized that she hadn't convinced Tip, either. Her hands had shaken too much, showing that she could have no equanimity to cope with capturing wild crocodiles.

"What do I do now?" Thornton wanted to know.

Tip let go his grasp, replaced by the rope. "Tie your rope around the tree," he instructed Thornton. "Then we get the poles and the rest of the rope around him before he gets onto the fact that he could still tear away."

The poles were put lengthwise down each side of the croc. Amid wild thrashings, they lashed these fast and then caught up the struggling crocodile's legs. "Go easy on him," Tip admonished, and Thornton, nursing a bleeding arm, replied, "Tell him to go easy on me."

Finally, the crocodile was stretching out straight with the ability to move only the few inches that it could bend the poles. The men rested. Tip produced a bottle he had hidden in his boat and gave it to Thornton, who drank greedily.

"You're a true friend, after all," Thornton told him.

Jenny heard and saw little of that. Another tension had risen in her. It was greater than any Cleve Thornton roused. It was an anger, the fury a person has for one he loves who has foolishly risked his life. Now that it was over, she realized to what extent Tip had been in danger.

Her first expression of it was quiet. "I didn't know it was as bad as this," she said. "You're going to get chewed up some day if you keep on."

Tip merely replied, "You both did fine."

Enraged to bursting out with her full feelings, Jenny scolded sharply, "You've got to stop it!"

Tip glanced at her and admitted, "I've been thinking along those same lines myself."

"You've got to do more than think!" she cried. "Stop it! Don't ever catch another crocodile or alligator!"

Her sudden angry concern made both the men look at her.

"You don't have to do it," she lectured. "If you keep on, you're going to get an arm torn off or even be killed."

"It could happen," Tip mused.

"Don't do it again," Jenny pleaded. "Say you won't. Promise that you won't."

Tip regarded her. He was moved by the depth of her feeling. It appeared to persuade him. He gazed at the size of the crocodile. "Well," he said, "maybe you're right, Jenny."

"Is that the last one you'll touch?"

"That's the last one I'll touch," he promised.

Thornton, holding the whisky bottle in his hand, studied them both. "I can see that Mrs. Totten is right," he told Tip. "You've made a wise decision."

He kept his tone clear of any further meaning than the sincerity of his words. But in the flicker of his glance Jenny understood that his interest in her was not over. It would continue, perhaps now heightened by having her called further to his attention. Most men would have taken Tip's warning. Thornton did not. Jenny saw that he would press any opportunity that might arise.

She wanted to tell Tip. But she had nothing to go on except her sure woman's intuition. She would not be able to convince him. She could not even mention it to him. If and when the time came she would have to fend it off herself.

THE PRESENCE OF Cleve Thornton kept Jenny away from the Ponce for the rest of that season. She didn't care to risk opening herself up to seeing him again and any scene that might involve. She hated him for driving her away from the sights at the hotel. She loathed him for being what he was.

With his staying there every season she wondered what she would do in the future about visiting the Ponce. She resolved not to let him keep her away permanently, and sought for a way to prevent this. A thought that had long been in the back of her head now seemed a solution to her dilemma. Before even admitting this entirely to herself she had to establish contact with a new institution in the community.

A small telephone system had been installed with old second-hand equipment. The central office consisted of a high, straight switchboard located in an alcove at the rear of the pharmacy. Its stiff, long mouthpiece stuck out almost to the large nose of Miss Alice Potter whose pale gray eyes attended her work through pince-nez spectacles tethered by a cord to her shirtwaist.

Jenny had often seen her at work. She went now to stand by the switchboard with a special mission in mind. She watched for a moment while Miss Potter picked up a cord, plugged it into a hole just below one of the small metal flaps that dropped down with a tiny clatter when a subscriber made a call, and said, "Hello." It was from this that telephone centrals were called "Hello girls," though it was difficult to apply the term to Miss Potter because she was so far from being a girl.

After she completed the call Miss Potter nodded at Jenny, the movement shaking her brown pompadour, which was tousled from the headpiece of her telephone set.

"Being a central," Jenny began, "must be awfully exciting. I don't see how you work all those plugs and switches and things."

Miss Potter answered another call, making the connection as if illustrating what she now said, "It isn't as difficult as it looks."

"It isn't?" Jenny stepped closer to the switchboard. "It seems awfully complicated to me." She purposely made a foolish remark, hoping to provoke a detailed explanation. "When the little flap drops down you answer and——"

"No," said Miss Potter, "that isn't it at all."

"It isn't?"

Miss Potter said, "Watch."

Jenny watched something she already understood from observation, but she listened patiently while Miss Potter explained, "When the flap drops, the first thing you do is plug in that number, whose jack is right below the flap."

"You say," Jenny then prompted, " 'Hello'; and sometimes you ask for a number."

"That is correct. Having been given the number the subscriber wishes to call, you pick up the front cord, carry it to the jack of the party being called, and insert it." Miss Potter now illustrated, picking up cords and inserting them in the jacks, but not all the way, so that no actual connections were made.

"It's from there on," said Jenny, "that I don't understand." She was perfectly honest about this.

Miss Potter gazed at her with some suspicion. "Why do you want to understand?"

"Oh, just because I think being a telephone central is wonderful, and I'm interested."

Dubiously, Miss Potter regarded her again. "If you are sincere in your interest, I will continue with the other steps. You see these two buttons alongside the key?"

Jenny nodded.

Miss Potter went through the rest of the explanation in great detail, and when she was through Jenny repeated the entire procedure with only slight faltering.

Dryly, Miss Potter commented, "You have quite a memory, Jenny. Or quite an interest. I suppose next you'll be wanting to actually try it."

"Could I?" Jenny pleaded. "Oh, could I?"

Miss Potter considered the proposition she had broached herself. "It isn't very busy right now," she conceded, "at noon, when people are home for lunch." She slipped the headpiece from her hair and got out of her straight-backed chair.

Jenny shot into it as if it were a matter of life and death to have it manned without an instant lost. Miss Potter fitted the headpiece, lifting Jenny's wavy black hair, so that the instrument clasped over her ears, and instructed, "Hold your lips straight in front of the mouthpiece, not too close, but not too far." She adjusted Jenny's head so that it was in the right place. Just then a flap dropped with a click.

Jenny started to panic and grabbed first at a front ringing cord instead of a back answering cord. Even before Miss Potter's hand darted out to put her right she knew it was wrong and corrected herself. She took up the proper cord, plugged in, threw the key forward and cried, "Hello, hello!"

In her excitement she had to ask twice for the number and received it the second time from an irritated voice. But she plugged in the front cord correctly, pressed the right button, turned the crank for the right ring and then let the parties speak.

She felt exhausted.

Miss Potter nodded approval, excepting, "You don't have to shout. The current carries your voice. The more you keep it down the better and more distinctly you are heard."

The lesson went on until Miss Potter did not stand guard each time a flap dropped. Jenny learned quickly and took to the work with little further trouble. Miss Potter brought out her lunch from the box she carried with her every day, and ate it while Jenny practiced further on the switchboard. During a lull, Jenny made an inquiry that was more important to her than any other:

"Is this board the same as the one over in the Ponce?"

"So that's it!" Miss Potter exclaimed, nodding her head vigorously while she chewed on a sandwich. "I knew it was something more than you said."

"Is it the same?" Jenny persisted.

"You think," Miss Potter accused, "you can get a position over there."

Jenny lowered her voice so that the few people out in the front of the pharmacy couldn't hear. "Maybe I do," she admitted.

"You aren't satisfied any more just going over there. You want to *be* there."

Jenny kept on the main subject. "I wouldn't get a position there if the work isn't the same as here."

"It's near enough," Miss Potter acknowledged. "The only difference is that they have white signal lights. And you don't have to turn a crank while ringing. Actually, it's quite a bit easier over there than here."

"Would you show me," pleaded Jenny, "I mean, as if this was the Ponce board?"

With some reluctance, Miss Potter illustrated the different steps. Jenny went through them in pantomime, over and over again. She closed her eyes until she could do it without looking. Opening them, she asked, "If I did what I'm doing here, I could work the board over there?"

"If," Miss Potter said dryly, "you could get over there. All the girls are hired in the north and brought down every season."

"I know," Jenny sighed. "I'm not sure what to do about that, or even if I will try to do anything at all. Miss Potter, if you wouldn't say anything about this, I would be glad to come here and fill in for you every noon so you can go home and have a hot lunch. I know you'd like to do that and, of course, I wouldn't expect to be paid anything. I just want more practice. If you think you could trust me."

Miss Potter considered. The temptation to spread the news that Jenny Totten was now planning to work at the Ponce almost outweighed the prospect of having her lunch hour off. "Well," she decided, "I don't know if the company would mind."

From twelve to one o'clock after that Jenny trotted to the

155

telephone office in the pharmacy alcove and filled in. To Tip and others she explained, "Miss Potter is terribly overworked and I'm helping her out."

She felt her deception was not wicked enough to hurt anyone. She took Grace into her confidence. Previously she had apprised Grace about Cleve Thornton and now Jenny said, "He certainly won't have anything to do with anybody who works at the hotel, and anyway, it's against the rules for employees to associate with guests. Tip is planning to spend all his time next winter at his camp, not even coming in week ends, or only once in awhile. I've got to have something to do."

She wrote three letters asking for a position, all of them identical in explaining her experience, and addressed them, care of the Flagler Company in St. Augustine; one to Mr. Denbaugh, one to Mr. Bemerill, and one to Miss Morris, the head central at the Ponce. She didn't feel she knew the pouter-pigeon Miss Morris well enough to place all her faith in her, and so brought her acquaintanceship with the Flagler agent and the hotel manager to bear.

Mr. Denbaugh answered from St. Augustine that he was asking Mr. Bemerill to do everything he could to meet her request. Mr. Bemerill replied from New York that, in turn, he was requesting Miss Morris to make a place for her if this could be done. Miss Morris wrote from Saratoga where she operated the board at the Grand Union Hotel in summer. She said several of her regular central girls would not return to the Ponce next season and that there was no reason why a local person should not be employed. If Jenny could work the antiquated West Palm Beach board she could have one of the positions at the Ponce. She was instructed to hold herself in readiness a few days before the mid-December opening.

JENNY RECEIVED THIS glad news shortly before her birthday in July. She walked on clouds. She was not going to be merely outside the Ponce; she would now be inside, where she could see everything, all the time. The news was partial compensation for the conviction that Tip, enlarging his camp out in the Glades, had forgotten her birthday and would not come in for that day.

She prepared to give herself the birthday present of going across the lake. As she dressed she looked out at her tree. Even this late, many blossoms remained on it, while the ground under it was a thick red carpet. The poinciana had come back strongly since the hurricane, growing so that now it reached to the second story of the house. The twisted tree, with its stiff, spreading top, and feathery foliage, grew like a part of her, the same as the yellow building it inspired across the Great Divide.

Jenny stepped out of her front door and onto the porch. Her white pique rainy-day skirt swished like the palmetto footmat she trod. Supposed to be worn only in bad weather so that your skirts did not sweep the wet ground, it was short-ened almost to the tops of her white canvas oxfords. Worn on a dazzling bright day like this, the skirt was daring, even considered indecent.

Much the same could be said for the thinness of her dainty

white nainsook shirtwaist which lifted to a high boned lace choker collar. She obtained the courage to wear both these advanced garments because a magazine article had stated they were coming to be accepted in the north as the latest style for everyday wear. Care must be taken not to show the limb above the shoe top.

Jenny walked down the street to the lake, and then north. Her gait was brisk even in the sticky Florida summer heat. The steady near-tropical temperature in the high eighties bothered her very little. She seemed attuned to it. When beads of perspiration stood out on the faces of others, her skin remained dry. It was helped by the wide sailor hat that shaded her face.

Her black eyes took in the sights with interest. Many more houses and places of business had been built. There was over a mile of shelled streets. The town had a population of nearly two thousand.

Jenny saw Emma Duncan a block away, in the metro-politan section of town, the line of red brick buildings on Narcissus Avenue. She would pass her there, in front of the hitching posts against which men lounged. The wide-hipped wife of the marshal stood talking with a woman Jenny didn't know, a newcomer to town.

Jenny let them both get a good look at her costume before she said politely and demurely, "Good afternoon."

Emma criticized Jenny from head to foot, with her look and manner, forcing Jenny to stop to be examined further. Jenny didn't mind, not even when Emma decided:

"That's a wrong, brazen costume, Jenny. You're out in your shape."

The woman with Emma stared, and though she said nothing, her head nodded slightly in agreement.

Jenny felt no need to defend herself. She thought, if it is true I am out in my shape, at least my shape is good, and not great bunches of rolling blobs of fat, failing to be well contained in a spreading corset and causing wet patches of perspiration to appear here and there on the vast contours of a body all too loosely female.

She knew it was wrong of her, but she could not resist the temptation to kick the hem of her rainy-day skirt at Emma and her friend, to reveal, right out there on Narcissus Avenue, with the men loungers watching, a quick sight of an inch or two of white cotton stocking.

As she went on, leaving the two women behind her, she heard Emma exclaim distinctly, "Well! I never! I never in all my born days! There ought to be a law! I'm not sure there isn't a law."

The men gawked, as much amused over the decided opinion of the marshal's wife as they were interested in Jenny's shapely ankle.

She made her way on in the shade of the overhanging corrugated tin sidewalk roof that extended to the curb. Bicycle racks held wheels, some of them slim, light, stripped-down racing models. Along the street one of these flashed by, the rider bent low over the downward curved handlebars. Store proprietors and clerks practiced their racing around two square blocks. As they passed their stores they slowed down to look in for a customer. If they had one they stopped, put their wheels in a rack and attended to business. Afterward, they came out to ride again.

Jenny hurried to cross the lake, walking over the bridge

instead of waiting for Mr. Varney's ferry which was not at its dock on this side. In many ways she liked the Ponce better in summer than at any other time. For then she had it all to herself, or almost, having to share it only with the gardeners and a few watchmen. She examined the poincianas and saw that their blossoms looked slightly pale. If she saw the gardeners, she would speak to them about that.

As she mounted the steps of the main entrance, she pretended that she was Mrs. William Rhinelander Stewart, who had just descended from her Afrimobile after winning ten thousand dollars at Bradley's, and was now going to her suite to have the assistance of her maid in changing her gown for dinner.

Grandly Mrs. William Rhinelander Stewart took the stairs, gracefully holding the skirt of her exquisite gown so that she might walk freely. All those in the green chairs on the broad veranda stopped rocking to watch, and to admire, and to whisper as Mrs. William Rhinelander Stewart arrived among them. She did not hesitate, to invite more of their stares or adulation; she needed none of either, but was far above them. She swept right on toward the front doors, which the doorman swung wide for her.

Jenny found herself facing the tightly closed front doors of the Ponce. Lost in her pretense, she had almost bumped into them.

She laughed at herself. The sound of her voice echoed hollowly against the wall of the hotel and the high ceiling of the empty veranda. She whirled and skipped away from the doors. She danced about the piazza, gliding between the big pillars. Among them she played a game of hide-and-go-seek, skipping nimbly to catch herself. She kept it up for a long time, dancing faster and faster, waltzing and whirling, until finally she collapsed, exhausted, against one of the great round pillars.

She clung to it for support. She saw its white surface close to her eyes. It was sumptuous, good, inviting and attractive. It was like her own body, seen with shameful secrecy and admired in private. She wanted to be as pure as the whiteness of this Ponce column. She felt a sudden yearning for it, and put her cheek against it. Slowly her arms stole about it, hugging and partially encircling it. Her eyes half closed as she embraced it.

Jenny jerked her cheek away from the pillar when she was startled into guilty discovery by a voice exclaiming, "Jumping catfish!"

At first she thought it was one of the gardeners or watchmen who had come upon her. She whirled.

It was Tip.

He stood there with an incredulous, amazed expression on his face.

They stared at each other. His dark hair was tousled from his running a hand through it, which now made it look as though it stood on end from surprise at what he had just observed. As if he couldn't believe his own words, he said, "I saw what you did."

Jenny had left the pillar. She jumped away from it, instinctively trying to deny her act and do everything she could to erase any impression that she had made it. Completely she disassociated herself from her conspirator, the column.

Color was in her face now, flushed into it with anger. Her eyes blazed. Sharp glints, little flecks appeared in them that looked like sparks of fire. One hand went to her throat, where she nervously and unconsciously fingered the lace there; the other was at her side, holding her purse; those fingers not engaged in clasping it twitched and opened and closed as though wishing to get at something.

Exasperated by his discovery, she stamped her foot on the Ponce veranda and flared, "What do you mean by spying on me?"

Tip might not have heard. Her indignation did not reach him, or if it did, failed to impress him. He was still obsessed with what he had come upon. "I tell you," he repeated, as though trying to convince her, "I saw what you did."

Annoyed by his repetition, she demanded, "What?"

"Why," he said, "you hugged that pillar." He stared at the pillar, accusing it now, for an instant, instead of her, but soon turned back to her.

"I didn't!"

"You did and I saw you."

"I—" She bit her lip, catching it between her teeth. She turned her head away, as though she could ignore all this that he was saying, and by merely looking elsewhere be in another place, divorced from his opinion. She seemed to decide quickly that this was impossible and adopted another course. She turned back to him and in a level tone told him, "All right, I did."

Now that she made her admission he gave his full comment. "You being interested and sort of crazy about the hotel, is all right maybe, and one thing. It's like the way I feel about the Glades. But doing what you did, hugging that pillar—that's like something funny and queer, Jenny, and straight out unnatural."

She didn't reply. For a moment he didn't seem to know

what he should say further. The impact of their difference touched them both at the same time.

"I didn't forget your birthday," he said. "I came in from the Glades and when you weren't home I brought my present over here. I knew this was where I'd find you." He held out a flat square package.

It was the first time she noticed what he carried.

Her anger melted. Chastened, she took the box, and after a glance at him, opened it.

Inside lay a pair of black stockings, silk to the calf and lisle above that.

He had remembered, from long ago, his promise to give her a pair of silk stockings.

"Oh, Tip!" Contrite and shamed, she wept.

He came to her and put his arms about her. She clung to him, crying, "I'm sorry I snapped at you—I'd rather hug you than any hotel."

"It's all right."

They held each other. "It's just," sobbed Jenny, "that I need something to take the place of what we haven't got. Sometimes the Ponce does that."

"I know."

"That's what it is. And that's why I hope you won't mind when I tell you what I've done."

After he heard it he admitted, "I suppose you got to have something to take up your time." His greatest objection came upon learning that she would have to live in the hotel. "Why is that?"

"It's a rule. Because sometimes you're on duty at night and they want the centrals where they can find them at all hours."

"With me gone all week like I plan," he agreed, "I guess it's better than you being alone in the house all the time. And maybe it's better than coming over like this." Dubiously, he went on, "Living apart ain't exactly the way we planned things, Jenny. Maybe we'd both better give up——"

"It's only for part of the year, Tip."

He accepted that, but said, "I expect not much turns out the way you think it will."

WITH SOME TREPIDATION, for she had never held a job before, Jenny kept her appointment with Miss Morris two days before the Ponce opened. She found her sitting on a couch placed near the long hotel switchboard in the rear of the rotunda. One section was being operated by a lone central. Miss Morris, even more billowy in the bosom than Jenny remembered, greeted her in friendly fashion. "I had you over a little before the first meeting of all the girls," she said, "to be sure you can handle the work. You don't mind giving me a demonstration?"

Suddenly afraid that after all she might fail, Jenny cautioned, "You understand it's a magneto board I learned on."

"I'm sure you won't have any trouble." She rose and led the way to the end section at which the girl sat. Miss Morris waited until the girl completed a call and then told her, "Helen, this is Mrs. Totten." To Jenny she introduced, "Miss Dodd, one of our best operators."

Helen Dodd and Jenny nodded to each other. Helen was a pretty girl about her own age, with ash-blond hair and a quick smile. She left the board and now Jenny took her place.

She was nervous, after not expecting to be, when she sat at the hotel switchboard. A white light flashed, but she did nothing. Helen Dodd called her attention to the signal.

Jenny plugged in, received the number to be called, another in the hotel, and found it without difficulty. She rang it, missing the crank to which she was accustomed.

The next call went more easily. She was amazed at the effort saved here. A few more calls came through that were no real test for speed. Then a number bunched up. While the other two watched and listened, Jenny handled them smoothly, now with complete assurance and deftness. She kept her voice low, distinctly articulated and well modulated.

"That will do," said Miss Morris.

Jenny, with a smile at Helen, changed places with her.

"You're better than some of my regular girls," Miss Morris said. She examined Jenny. "Probably because you want to be here so much."

Jenny blinked her appreciation of this friendly and understanding spirit. "Thank you," she said fervently, "for giving me the chance."

"I think you know the salary—twenty dollars per month with room and board."

Other girls had been drifting in, until now there were nine of them in addition to Helen Dodd. Miss Morris introduced Jenny and instructed them all to sit down. Jenny, conscious that she was the object of some curious stares, sat tensely and listened carefully to all that was said, acutely aware that she was entering a life of which she had dreamed. She caught a new term, "operator," used for telephone centrals. She felt that she was keeping right up to the minute in the world. That was always the proud way of the Ponce.

Miss Morris explained that all eleven of them would rotate in the hours and duties, including that of being the extra girl. They were required to be prompt, efficient and neat in their appearance. They were in no circumstances to associate with guests. They would take their meals in the dining-room of the second officers, being classed between the first officers and the "ordinaries," who were waiters and chamber-maids.

Jenny felt a thrill at that. It was like being a little better than most of the employees. And it was one of the few things she hadn't known about the Ponce. She felt humble in her ignorance.

The girls, Miss Morris continued, would room two to-gether. The odd girl would room with her. She paired them off according to their requests after being here a few days to learn preferences. Because Jenny knew only Helen Dodd, they were chosen as roommates. Helen flashed her quick smile at Jenny, who beamed back.

After being dismissed by Miss Morris, the two girls went up to the room assigned to them. They rode, with the others, in one of the rear elevators. The rope that slid through slots in the floor and roof of the elevator lifted them slowly and majestically only to the fifth floor. To the sixth dormer floor they had to walk up a flight of stairs. Side by side on these Jenny told Helen, "I hope you didn't want anybody else."

"I'm glad we're together," Helen told her. "I've been here three seasons and I was getting tired of some of the others." She glanced sideway at Jenny. "You're new—and different."

Their room was a small one in the original section of the hotel. It had a single window which overlooked the lake. Under the sloping ceiling at either side of the window stood one bed. There was barely room for two dressers and two straight-backed chairs. Jenny was not disappointed that they would wash by means of a bowl and pitcher. It did not seem at all like going back to the cabbage house. This was the Ponce. Private bathrooms and running water could hardly be expected for employees on the top floor. Only it would be strange to sleep here instead of with Tip.

Jenny liked her work at the hotel even more than she had ever dreamed. It was one of her few expectations to be exceeded by reality. Never before had she fully realized the Sybaritic luxury and genteel splendor of the Ponce. She thrilled at seeing, and associating with, famous society leaders and business tycoons. She spoke over the telephone with renowned people. She actually talked with Colonel John Jacob Astor, Mrs. George Jay Gould, Admiral Dewey and Charles D. Gates, better known as "Bet-a-Million Gates" because he was supposed to have once bet a million dollars on the single turn of a card. There was even nobility with whom to converse, such as the Duke and Duchess of Manchester and Countess Boni de Castellane.

She learned that there could be immense wealth without refinement, and came to recognize, instantly, the difference between the two. She also knew the two when combined, and found, to her dismay, how rarely this occurred. She saw the Florida sun pale the blue intensity of diamonds adorning the magnificent bosoms of dowagers. She was amused, with a greater snobbishness than any genuine social leader could possess, at elderly wives of newly crowned Texas cattle kings or Chicago pork packers who had leaped directly from the washtub to Palm Beach. She laughed with others at social climbers who asked bellmen or wheel-chair men to identify certain people and after being misinformed, courted the wrong persons until the mistake was learned with chagrin.

Jenny was so eager to take in all these sights, absorbing them greedily, that she was ready to substitute for other girls, working extra hours. She never tired of the endless display of humanity, clothes, manners, and jewels. She gloried in her position and felt herself privileged to have it.

It was Helen who first pointed out an admirer Jenny had among others working at the hotel. Tom Currey, a medium-sized youth of twenty who was an assistant room clerk at the main desk, developed a blind adoration for Jenny. The fact that she was older than he and had a husband seemed to escape him entirely; she didn't look older, and never having seen Tip, he didn't exist for Tom. Jenny was touched by his callow attentions. She gave him her best smile in exchange for using him for several purposes.

She had tried to down all sense of perturbation at what would happen when Cleve Thornton came to the hotel and saw her. She wasn't so sure now that being an employee would stop him from still paying attention to her. Helen had confessed that sometimes she went out, discreetly, with young men staying at the Ponce. Jenny knew some of the other girls did the same, even one who had a husband in the North. Miss Morris either did not know, or chose to close her eyes.

To be prepared for the arrival of Cleve Thornton, Jenny asked Tom about him. She didn't know whether she felt glad or disappointed when he told her that Cleve had made no reservation this year and the hotel was booked full for the entire season.

"He couldn't come even if he decided to?" Jenny asked.

"I suppose he could. We always keep a few suites for really important people."

"Is he important enough?"

"I guess he is, because he's so rich. Not that he has the brains to make money himself; he has others do it for him. He's a liquorhead."

"Does he really drink a lot?"

"Like a fish. He can't live without it." Suspiciously, in his worship of her, he asked, "Why're you asking about him?"

"Oh, I'm just interested in everything at the Ponce."

"Are you going to the Cake Walk with me tonight like I asked?"

"If it's all right why I'd like to; yes, Tom."

"It's all right. They let a few of us sneak in and watch from the back every week."

She went with him that evening to the main dining-room, entering it from the kitchens. Jenny had heard much about the Cake Walks, and now she saw one. The tables had been cleared and piled out of the way at one side of the vast room. The chairs were lined up as in a theater, facing the other side of the room. Most of the hotel guests occupied them, dressed in their finery, glittering with jewels and dripping furs, even though the evening was warm. They listened to the orchestra playing before the formal entertainment began.

In front of the crowd, out on the open floor, four judges, prominent guests staying at the hotel, sat before a table. On the table was set a huge white cake. This was the prize. The best performing team of the evening won the cake. Other prizes of sizable sums of money were also given by the judges of the evening.

Avidly Jenny took in everything as she stood in the back of the room, watching while a colored quartet came out of the kitchen and offered a number of selections, including, *Oh, Dem Golden Slippers, In the Good Old Summer Time,*

Ain't Dat Scan'lous, and ended with *Ta-Ra-Ra-Boom-De-Ré.*
The latter put the crowd in a good humor, everybody joining
in. Jenny didn't know if she should sing along with the hotel
guests, but did so when Tom nudged her and she looked at
him to see that he was singing.

The band played a roll on the drums, the doors of the
kitchen were opened wide and in marched six Negro couples,
all dressed flamboyantly except for one. Some of the men
wore red satin trousers and green coats. The women sported
vivid chiffon dresses. All were heavily made up. The last
couple received special applause from the crowd. It consisted of Choo Choo with the fattest colored woman Jenny
had ever seen; she must have weighed at least three hundred
pounds, and her flesh jiggled like great pillows of loose dark
dough.

Even so, Choo Choo outdid her. He wore no costume
except his regular wheel-chair knickerbockers. But in his hand
he carried his bell, which he clanged like a train; in his mouth
he had his whistle, which he blew like an engine; and attached to his belt in back was a lighted bull's-eye lantern
with a red glass in it.

The couples pranced high, including Choo Choo's partner.
Choo Choo shuffled, his feet never leaving the floor. They
marched around the room several times, accompanied by the
orchestra, and finally came to a stop at one end of the room.
The presiding judge then called out: "First couple!"

The band struck up again and the first couple danced the
Cake Walk. This consisted of strutting and striking extravagant postures, in time with the music. The man, who wore
a high silk hat and carried a cane, threw one and then the

other and finally both together, into the air, and caught them each time they descended. The couple danced for some time, perspiring to do their best, and received loud applause when they retired to the other end of the room.

More couples performed, grimacing, swinging their partners, prancing, bowing and scraping grotesquely. The walkers were nearly professional in their performances. Famous cake walk songs were played to inspire them, including *Georgia Camp Meeting,* and *De Cake Walk Queen.*

Last came Choo Choo and his ample partner. Choo Choo did not strut or dance or kick. He merely was himself, a train. He shuffled into the depot, came to a stop and his partner, pretending to be a passenger, got on by the process of lining up in back of him and putting one hand lackadaisically on his shoulder. She jiggled all her bulbous parts in time to the music as the train gave a loud whistle and started off. The train had to pull hard to move her bulk. She rocked as the train rang its bell and went around a curve. She hung on while the train negotiated a hill, climbing up and up, chugging loudly.

The other cake walkers had worn wide grins and smiles while they performed, but Choo Choo and his partner kept straight, sober faces. When the train came to the passengers' station it stopped and she got off. The train, blowing steam above the sound of the band, went on, circling the room, and then came back to pick up the passenger again. Off they went on another trip, engine chugging, bell ringing, whistle blowing, red light burning, passenger jiggling before and behind. As a finale the orchestra played, while everybody sang the chorus:

> "I've been working on the railroad
> All the livelong day;
> I've been working on the railroad,
> Just to pass the time away."

Deafening applause greeted Choo Choo and his partner when their act was over. Jenny beat her palms together until they hurt. There was no doubt about who would win first prize. The train and its passenger were chosen and announced with loud acclaim from all. They went forward to claim the cake, going through their act again, the train stopping before it, the passenger taking the cake aboard to hold it high in one hand and then they chugged off.

Laughing with Jenny, Tom exclaimed, "They take the cake!"

IN THE MIDDLE of January Tip arranged to come in from the Glades on a day Jenny went over to look after the house. They kissed, but their greeting was almost formal. After glancing at each other quickly, they felt strange. Each lived his own life now and they had to get to know each other again. They didn't have time that day to accomplish it.

"You like it over there?" he asked.

"Oh, yes." She didn't want to sound too enthusiastic.

"Nobody been bothering you?"

"One of the young desk clerks thinks I'm the love of his life, but he'll get over it."

He studied her. "You haven't got a freckle left."

Her skin was clear and translucent. "That's from being inside so much."

"And wearing a hat all the time," he reminded. While her complexion had become almost alabaster white, his had deepened in color, so that he looked nearly like an Indian. The contrast between the two of them was startling. Tip continued, "My camp is filled all week. The cook I hired is working out fine. The accounts bother me some."

"We're both having to do with Ponce people," she said.

"They want me to catch gators and crocs again."

Concerned, she demanded, "You aren't?"

"Some of them saw me do it before. They've told their friends."

"You said you wouldn't."

"They offer to pay me more than ever."

"Tell me!"

He answered evasively. "You see all my arms and legs on me."

"You haven't told me yet," she persisted.

"I'm not doing it," he said, "even though they keep after me."

She saw Grace, who gave her usual report on the local gossip about her. "It's scandalous and a disgrace," she related, "a married woman working when she doesn't have to. It will come to no good end."

Jenny felt troubled that they were saying such things.

"Emma," said Grace, "is sure you mean to desert Tip. You're going to try to catch a millionaire. Of course you'll never do it, even though she admits you've got the face and figure."

"I might surprise her," Jenny commented.

"Miss Potter has her large nose in it. One minute she guiltily takes responsibility for starting you off on your mad career. The next she says it isn't her fault and that she tried to discourage you. But you wouldn't listen."

This made Jenny so angry that her troubled mood left her, and she felt no sense of wrong at being over at the Ponce.

Back at the hotel Tom greeted her, "Well, he's come."

Instantly she knew whom he meant.

"Arrived without any warning at all," Tom said. "Probably too drunk to think of it. He just came in his private car attached to the afternoon train without bothering to make a reservation."

That, Jenny decided, was quite a way to do things. Her eyes danced at the thought of what it must be to lead such a life.

She saw him the next day and had the opportunity to show herself to him. Most of the unmarried, and many of the married men, when they had the chance, eyed the switchboard operators. Cleve Thornton was no exception. Jenny was on duty when he came to peek. But when his glance went down the line of three girls, she averted and partially bowed her head so that he would not see her.

She could not do that every time he might glance in her direction. She knew that they must meet and have something to say to each other. It seemed inevitable, and she felt perversely drawn to it. She wished to have it happen and get it over with. But she did not invite or seek it out.

The fourth day after he arrived she came face to face with him as she left the switchboard, following her afternoon stint.

He discovered and greeted her with the same words he addressed to her exactly ten years ago. "Well, well . . ." He glanced from her to the switchboard, taking in her connection with it. "Mrs. Totten. I should say Jenny—I think I know you well enough—it's good to see you again. Especially here."

Jenny knew that the other operators were watching when they could take one eye from their work. Helen was one of these. Miss Morris was not about. Jenny acknowledged Cleve Thornton's remark with the cold tone of a reprimand. "Mr. Thornton."

"Still as beautiful as ever."

"I'm an employee of the hotel, Mr. Thornton."

"So you are."

"I'm not supposed to talk to you this way."

"What way?" He laughed. "You ought to know by now that rules are made to be broken. I've spent most of my life breaking them."

"Please don't break any with me." She could have walked on then and failed to understand why she didn't.

"Even if the Ponce disapproves," he said, "you can't really mind my speaking to you."

She was taking him too seriously. He made her feel absurd and on the defensive. She wanted to laugh, too. Instead, she reminded him, "I'm a married woman, Mr. Thornton."

"Many pretty women are."

She made an exasperated sound and started to turn from him. He took a quick step in front of her, preventing her from leaving, and asked, "How's Tip?"

She answered that with another reminder. "He believes what you told him."

Now he mocked her solemnity. "I don't think I'll hunt this year. Not with you here. Do you think Tip will come in and shoot me?"

Jenny could not keep her own eyes from twinkling at the point their exchange had reached. "He might," she said.

"You know, I meant what I told him when I said it. Then I had another look at you."

"Good-by, Mr. Thornton."

His smile at her as she left told her he had not by any means given up his pursuit.

She managed to avoid him for twenty-four hours, largely because of her late periods of duty, but she could not prolong it beyond the second day. He caught her again as she left the board at noon.

"Jenny," he said, "I know you're going to lunch. Can't we have it together?"

"Here at the Ponce, Mr. Thornton?"

He acknowledged that this was impossible by saying, "Oh, there are other places. Runyon's Island up the lake; it's very cozy there. Or any place you say. Where they have music. We'll dance again. I've never forgotten how well we dance together and I'll wager you haven't, either."

She made her voice cold when she said, "No, thank you."

"I'm only asking as a friend of the family, Jenny." He enjoyed this tantalizing banter. "Sort of like a favor to Tip."

"I'm sure he would appreciate it."

He laughed again. "Then come on."

"I can't, Mr. Thornton; you know that."

"You haven't said you don't want to."

Her eyes flashed. "Then I say that now."

"You know," he told her slowly, "something tells me you don't mean that, not all the way."

This time when she turned from him with an exasperated sound, she did not let him stop her from leaving.

Excitedly, Helen and the other operators wanted to know about his interest in her. Jenny told Helen alone something of it. Her roommate rolled her eyes and shook her head, exclaiming, "Twenty million dollars! And you're telling it no."

"But Helen——"

"I forgot. You've already got one husband. And you couldn't use two. I guess that's against the law."

"Yes," said Jenny, "that's against the law."

"I don't suppose," Helen said, "you'd want to turn the twenty million over to me, would you?"

"He's yours."

"The only trouble is," Helen lamented, "I haven't got your face. Or your form."

Cleve Thornton didn't drop his attentions, but he was left little time for them when there arrived, as though following him, the Madison family consisting of father, mother and daughter. Elizabeth Madison, the daughter, was a New York debutante of two seasons back. Her escapades since then were notorious. Once she had eloped with a young man definitely not of her family's choice, for he was virtually penniless. The couple had been apprehended before they could find anyone to marry them, and matters were set straight. Or, it was whispered, almost straight.

Next Lizzy, as she was known even in the social gossip columns, where she was something of a darling, had become engaged to the son of reputedly rich people. When it was discovered that no real wealth was to be found in his direction, however, the engagement was abruptly terminated by her parents.

By this time it was plain that Lizzy's mission in life was to marry money.

She had the background and regal nerve to pursue her career openly. Jenny recognized Lizzy as the prime example of a type represented by dozens in the hotel. She was tall and beautiful in a hard way. She was spoiled and could be vicious. She would stop at nothing to get what she wanted. She had little restraint and said and did almost anything that seemed to come to her mind. She liked to show off, and her means of doing this, the evening she arrived at the Ponce, was the talk of the place for a week.

It was known that a few daring women now smoked cigarettes, in private, or, if they were really bold, in Bradley's. The gambling club was the first and only public place in which it was countenanced. It was unthinkable that a woman would smoke anywhere else.

Lizzy chose the main dining-room of the Ponce to flaunt her disregard for this convention. Her parents rested from the train trip in their suite, so she dined alone that evening, occupying a small table in the center of the room not far from where Cleve Thornton dined with a large party. Every corner was crowded. The orchestra played softly. The black doorman received hundreds of men's hats, remembering each owner faithfully without using any mark. All was in the usual perfect Ponce order until Lizzy Madison was seen to take a box of Egyptian Deities from her handbag.

At first those seated near her weren't actually sure that it was a box of cigarettes that she produced. When they saw that it was, they fell silent with shock, watching her. Others near them noticed that people were looking at Lizzy, and they followed suit. A hush fell in the great room, broken only by Cleve's sudden laugh of appreciation.

Waiters stopped their work to stare, open-mouthed, at Lizzy. People stood up to crane their necks. Virtually everyone present watched while Lizzy coolly took a cigarette from the box. She didn't try to hide what she did, dangling the offensive cigarette between her lips for all to see.

She brought forth a box of matches, lighting one without a sign of nervousness. She might have been alone in the privacy of her bedchamber practicing a shameless vice instead of at the center of over a thousand eyes. She held the match up until the flame was full and then applied it to the end of the cigarette. She puffed, took the cigarette from her mouth and blew out smoke. She put it to her lips again and puffed with evident enjoyment.

She paid absolutely no attention to the sensation her act made throughout the room. She seemed oblivious to the shocked comments, the backs turned to her and people nearby who rose and stalked indignantly from the room, their meals unfinished. Only Cleve was delighted.

Everyone agreed that the Ponce handled the matter firmly and discreetly. The headwaiter, who had watched all this with fascinated horror, was said to have turned slightly pale under his black skin. When he had sufficiently recovered he signaled to several assistants. Quickly, each of these men seized a screen and carried it in Lizzy's direction. They acted as if going to put out a fire, which was almost the case.

The headwaiter, following rapidly, directed them in placing the screens completely about Lizzy's table, shutting her off from view. At this point Cleve deserted the party he was with and walked over to the screens, disappearing into them. From behind the barricade Lizzy was heard to laugh in her high, shrill voice. Smoke emitted thickly into the air.

Jenny watched when it became evident that Cleve was Lizzy's next choice to replenish her family's fortunes. She learned more about Lizzy from one of the assistant housekeepers. Mazy Demarest had a room of her own just down the hall from that of Jenny and Helen. She was a thin, pinched-faced little Irish hunchback who, by sheer spirit and spunk, had worked herself up from being a maid to her present position of overseeing the maids on the third floor of the original part of the hotel. After long experience with the wealthy, she had little respect for them. Looking up from her bare four feet of height, her neck craned slightly to one side because of her deformity, she said:

"Most of them are as twisted as my back." A sad expression

came to her face; then it became bright again and filled with the glow of the physically handicapped who appreciate the world more than those fully and well formed. "They don't know what they want, and care less."

"Do you know Lizzy Madison?" Jenny asked.

"That one!" Mazy cried. "Isn't she on my floor? Didn't I have her last year? Haven't I known her at Saratoga, too?"

Jenny asked, "What about her?"

"What about her?" Mazy shrilled. "It's no thing for a lady to say, or for a body like you to listen to, but there's only one thing that Lizzy Madison is, and that's a hussy."

Jenny was startled at this strong word from the lips of the little hunchback.

"She has no morals," Mazy went on. "That is a thing I can tell you."

"She——"

"More than once, and I have the means of knowing it."

"Do you think she and Cleve Thornton——"

"If the worthless thing isn't, it's only because her parents have the knowing of why it would be the biggest mistake in the catching of him."

Late one night Jenny was on duty alone at the switchboard. All was quiet in the hotel except for the soft music coming from the palm room, a slight chatter reaching her from the grill, and an occasional couple or party returning from Bradley's. She listened to the latter boasting of winnings or bemoaning losses.

A few minutes after one o'clock Lizzy Madison came in through the front doors on the arm of Cleve Thornton.

Jenny had to recognize what a handsome couple they made. With a pang of envy she took in the sight of Lizzy's glittering dress. It was blue-green, with a slight train and daringly cut. She didn't bother to lift the train as she walked, but let it drag, waggling behind her across the thick rotunda carpet. She was less sober than her companion, or at least showed more the effects of drinking.

Cleve saw Jenny, who had turned around to look at them. Dragging Lizzy, who protested, he came over to her at the switchboard.

Jenny turned away from them. Cleve came around so that he could see her face again, still pulling Lizzy. He stared at Jenny.

"Hello, hello girl!" he exclaimed.

Jenny saw Lizzy glare at her, examining this common creature who drew her companion's attention.

Dropping her eyes and then lifting them again, Jenny said politely, in the tone of an employee to a guest, "Mr. Thornton." At the same time she watched Lizzy out of the corner of her eye.

Lizzy pulled at his arm. "Come on, Cleve."

Cleve clung to his ground like a rock. "I'll bet," he told Lizzy, "you don't know her."

Lizzy shot Jenny a venomous look and replied, "I'll bet I don't want to know her." She pulled hard at Cleve, and this time moved him, forcing him to leave with her, walking away down the corridor. Once Cleve managed to turn and wave broadly at Jenny, yelling, "Good-by, hello girl!"

In spite of herself, Jenny smiled. She had a sense of triumph in the recollection that Lizzy was the second woman who had pulled Cleve Thornton away from her.

"LIZZY," ONE OF the hotel jokes became at the approach of the George Washington Birthday Ball in February, "is taking Cleve."

Jenny had to content herself with watching the preparations for the ball. For years she had been hearing about these grand events and reading detailed, rapturous descriptions of them in newspaper accounts. They were so hugely attended that the octagonal ballroom had become too small to hold the crowd, and for the past several seasons the ball had been held in the cleared, much larger dining-room.

The ball was the climax of the Palm Beach season. People came all the way from New York, Boston, Chicago and Philadelphia to attend it, remaining for that one night and returning the next day. The most stylish of the people who had stayed the season at the Ponce also departed the day following the ball, or soon after.

Jenny asked Tom if, as at the Cake Walks, any employees were allowed to look on at the ball. Tom replied that it wasn't exactly the same thing. The management would severely frown on any of them trying to see the ball. For one thing, that night millions of dollars' worth of jewels were on display around the necks, in the hair and on the wrists and fingers of the wealthy guests. Special detectives were brought down from the North to augment the hotel guards.

"Haven't you ever even looked in?" Jenny asked.

Tom admitted, "Maybe last year I sneaked in through the kitchen for a minute."

"You did?" Genuine admiration was in her voice.

Encouraged by this rare accolade from her, Tom went on, "I hid behind some palms and nobody saw me."

"You're awfully daring, Tom. It takes a lot of courage to do things like that."

"Well, I don't know." Her praise was now so extravagant that it made him suspicious.

"I'd like to do that this year," she proposed. "With you."

He groaned. "I thought something like that was coming."

"But maybe you wouldn't want to risk it again." Her words contained a challenge to his manhood.

"It isn't that, but——"

"I wouldn't blame you any if you didn't."

"It's just that——"

"We wouldn't have to stay long. Just a peek, that's all I'd want."

Tom searched desperately for an excuse to put her off. "I'm not sure they'll have palms near the kitchen entrance this year," he temporized.

"Have they every year?"

"I guess so, but——"

"Then they probably will this year."

"But——"

"You'll do it, won't you, Tom?"

He gazed at her, considering, and finally said with resignation, "It looks as if I'd do anything for you, even if I know it's crazy before I start."

Jenny was never quite sure how that plan of peeking in

briefly at the Washington Ball, expanded into a far greater and more daring venture. It started with her speculation on how wonderful it must be if you were one of the fortunate persons actually to attend the ball. She had the bold, fantastic conception of not merely looking in on it, but of stepping out a few more feet and actually dancing at it.

When she mentioned this to Helen as they lay awake in the night talking back and forth between their beds, she did not take the project seriously. She knew she had been right to regard it no more realistically when Helen merely grunted. They both considered the idea as a beautiful dream.

It was in this spirit that Helen brought it up when Mazy visited them in their room for a gabfest. At the mention of Jenny going to the ball the little hunchback looked sharply at her.

"And why not?" she cried.

"What do you mean?" asked Jenny.

"And why shouldn't you go to the ball?" demanded Mazy.

Jenny, sitting on her bed, straightened, stirred by Mazy's brave words. Then she sank back, shaking her head. "It couldn't be."

"She'd be fired," Helen stated.

Mazy was not stumped. "What is life for," she asked, "if not to do exciting things with risk in them? Is there anyone to know that better than I, who can't do the things you might?"

The other two girls looked at her, offering their silent commiseration for the shape that had been given to her.

Mazy told Jenny flatly, "If I had a straight back and the looks of you, I would be at the ball."

Again Jenny was spurred by Mazy's spirited declaration,

but only briefly. "No," she said. "Why, I wouldn't even have a gown grand enough to wear."

Mazy brushed that aside as being the smallest of the difficulties. "You need nerve more than a gown. As for a gown, the rich don't know how many they have. I'm taking more to the cleaning and sewing rooms now than would fill a store. If you were to have the gumption to go, I would get you the gown, the best there is and all things to go with it."

Jenny gave a laugh that had a little hysteria in it. "And what if its owner saw me in it?"

"You'd tell her it was made in Paris for yourself. It would be all in the way you said it."

Jenny went still. She regarded Mazy as though hypnotized by her. "I think," she breathed, "I could do that."

"You'll go?" cried Mazy.

Automatically, not knowing altogether what she did, Jenny nodded, slowly.

Helen shrieked, "You're both insane! You'd never be able to do it."

"And the reasons why?" demanded Mazy.

"For—for one thing," Helen stuttered, "she would have to get an escort. Tom's the only one and he would never do it."

"Men," Mazy said contemptuously, "can be made by pretty girls to do anything at all. Not that I'm one ever to have done what I say. But I am one to have seen it."

Helen stared at Jenny. "Are you really going to do it?"

Jenny sat on her bed, trembling a little now that fuller realization came to her of what she meant to do. She glanced at Mazy for courage and made her decision. "I'm going to be at the ball."

"A girl with good spunk!" approved Mazy.

187

Helen reminded excitedly, "It will probably mean losing your position."

Jenny considered that for only a passing instant. Recklessly she declared, "But I'll have been at the Ponce ball."

Mazy turned to Helen. "Are you with us or against us?"

Helen considered. Even being connected with such a plan would be dangerous for any employee who wished to continue working at the Ponce. She took a far more serious view of what the other two meant to do than they did. Looking at them, they gazed back as if she were on trial.

Finally, she smiled. She laughed. "I'll help. I'll do anything I can, even if it means my position, too."

They all laughed then, bound together in the excitement of a venturesome conspiracy. The two straight-backed girls put their arms about the hump on the back of the third, and they held each other, all three laughing and planning and swearing secrecy.

THEY DIVIDED THE project into three parts. Mazy would furnish the clothes. Helen would arrange for Jenny to be off duty the night of the ball. Jenny herself would persuade Tom to escort her. There remained but four days before the twenty-second. They would have to work fast.

When the time came for Jenny to do her part, she was dubious. "I wouldn't want to get Tom fired."

"He'd get another place for himself," Helen assured her. "And no great harm done to anyone."

"The likes of him," Mazy declared, "ought to be grateful to be at the side of one such as you at the ball. Likely it'd be the only thing he'll have to tell his grandchildren about."

Jenny strolled with Tom that evening along Main Street. They followed the railroad tracks past Bradley's, beyond the yellow barracks for white and colored hotel help, up to the Breakers and then back again. On the barely lighted thoroughfare it was doubtful if anyone from across the lake would recognize them.

Tom was a respectful and timid admirer. His boldest gesture had been to try to take her arm, and even this she had not permitted him. Tonight, when awkwardly he made motions in this direction again, she allowed it. When she felt his hand tremble at the intimacy she decided on a frontal attack. "Tom—about our looking in at the ball."

"Maybe," he said hopefully, "we'll give that up."

"I was expecting you to do even more than keep your promise."

"*More?*" He looked at her blankly.

"I know how well you look in tails," she flattered him, "from seeing you in them behind the desk. You would look fine at the ball."

"*At* it!" he cried.

Casually, she suggested, "I thought we might as well go all the way and get dressed up for it."

Involuntarily, as he caught her full meaning, he nearly jerked his hand away from her arm. "Great snakes!" he exclaimed. His hand seemed to think better of its privileged place and remained, though now listlessly.

"It would be all right," she assured him. She had to swallow to convince herself of her own words.

"All right?" he remanded. "Great golden snakes alive! You're talking about us going to the Washington Ball and you say it will be all right."

"Let me tell you——"

"Nothing you can tell me will do any good. I won't do it. Not even for you."

She waited a moment, to show her hurt, before she took cruel advantage of him by reminding, "Do you remember when you said you would do anything for me, anything at all, no matter what I asked?"

"I remember, but——"

"You didn't mean it."

"I meant it. But a thing like this. Why, it——"

"I know," said Jenny. "They would dismiss us if they knew. But they won't know."

"Oh, won't they? What's to prevent them from seeing us?"

"I'll tell you. We've got it all worked out."

" 'We'?" Tom cried in alarm. "Who else is in on this?"

"No one else is going with us," she assured him.

"But others know about it?"

"Only Helen, and Mazy Demarest—it's really her idea."

"That hunchback believes in pixies—and this. But you can't make me believe in it."

"You haven't given me a chance to show you how it will work."

"Because it would never work."

"We wouldn't try to sneak in when the ball starts, or for a long time after it was under way; not before midnight. Maybe a little after twelve. By that time everybody has been drinking some, haven't they?"

"What if they have?"

"I mean, they aren't noticing everything that goes on. And there're nearly two thousand people at the balls now, aren't there?"

"Supposing there are?"

"Two more won't be noticed. We'll just be lost in the crowd."

"Maybe you'd be lost, and I don't think you would be, either," he said. "But I wouldn't. Do you realize that everybody in the Ponce asks me for their keys at least once a day? They know my face. They'd recognize me in half a second."

"We've thought of that, too."

"It isn't a *masked* ball, you know."

"But it can be, a little, that is. You're going to wear a disguise."

"A what?"

"We all thought a mustache would be best. Have you ever worn one as part of a costume and seen how much it changed your appearance?"

"Maybe I have, but that doesn't mean——"

"And then if you part your hair differently—not in the middle, like you have it, but on the side, the way some of the men are doing it now—why, hardly anybody would ever know you."

"Supposing they wouldn't . . ." Tom considered but found no attractions at all to favor the plan. "No, sir; nothing doing; I'm not going to do it."

She pressed his hand against her side. "We wouldn't have to stay long," she said. "Maybe a few times dancing around the hall. We'd just slip into the crowd from the kitchen while a dance was on, and then out again."

"Even that——"

"We could see how safe it was and then decide how long to stay. We wouldn't even go in unless it looked all right."

"But——"

"No one would ever notice us, especially with your mustache."

"Still . . ." He had some complaint left. "If I hadn't seen you turning down that Thornton fellow, I'd think you wanted to be at the ball to get next to him."

"I couldn't do that even if I wanted to." She squeezed his hand again with her arm. "Tom," she whispered, "do it—for me."

Tempted by her closeness beyond his powers of resistance, he gave a whimper of resignation. "Do you know what Charlie, the mail clerk, told me when I first pointed you out to him?"

"What did he say?"

"He said you're too good-looking, and you'd get me in trouble."

"If he's as wrong about the second part of that as he is about the first, we won't get into any trouble."

"I'd say it was just the other way about."

"Don't worry, Tom."

"That's about all I'll be doing."

Helen reported success with her arrangements. But it had been achieved only at the risk of having to let Miss Morris know about the plan. Jenny had been scheduled for duty that night. In order to convince the supervisor that it was necessary to make a shift and permit Helen to substitute for her, she had to be told.

"I thought," Helen said, "it would be all off right then. But she chuckled and laughed until I thought she couldn't stop. She said if there was anything she could do to help, to let us know."

"Has she got any jewels?" Jenny inquired. The only thing that worried her about her clothes was not having any proper jewelry to wear beyond a tiny gold crucifix on a thin gold chain. And though this had belonged to her mother, and she treasured it above all else, she felt that at the Ponce ball she ought to have something more brilliant.

"Nonsene to that," Mazy said. "You're enough of a jewel yourself. You don't want anything to outshine you. Wear your crucifix only and try to be as innocent as it will make you look. Let the others doodab themselves with diamonds and pearls and tiaras; they need them to call attention away from their ugliness."

On the morning of the day before the ball, all the phone

girls knew of what Jenny and Tom meant to do. By that afternoon word had passed among the bellmen, half the maids, the porters, engineers, waiters, elevator operators and most of the rest of the staff. But such was the delight they all felt in two of their members having the brazenness to do such a thing, that it was a secret well kept from any who might have disapproved and interfered.

Jenny was given encouraging looks and whispered words of good wishes. Tom experienced the same treatment. It scared him. He sought out Jenny to complain, "Everybody knows about it. Everybody in the whole place."

"No one will tell," she assured him.

"But I thought you were going to keep it a secret."

"This way," she pointed out, "maybe we'll be helped, if there's any trouble. Have you got your mustache?"

"It's all ready. I've practiced with it and got it to stay on straight. It changes me, all right. And I can part my hair on the side. With enough pomade, it will stay down."

"That's fine. Now you know where we'll meet and when?"

He repeated, as though they were instructions carefully learned by rote. "At midnight sharp in the laundry entrance of the kitchen corridor leading from the maids' and valets' dining-room. The door to the laundry will be left open. The first one to get there is to go in and close the door and wait for the other. I'm to get there first if I can. And both of us will use the back stairs."

"If you pass anyone," Jenny further advised, "or anyone sees you, just keep on going without saying anything."

Tom shivered. "I wish it was over."

On the evening of the ball, Jenny was so excited that she couldn't eat her dinner. The vast activity that had been going on in the Ponce for a week alone was enough to stir the soul. It was still more exhilarating because the preparations being made on every hand were not solely for others. They were for her as well.

Now that the great night was here, she became frightened. Half a dozen times during the past four days she had wanted to call it off and even hoped that Tom would back out. Each time Mazy or Helen, or both of them, were there to shame her faltering.

She could barely wait to get to her room after the evening meal. Though she had until midnight to get ready, at eight o'clock she felt it was nearly time to start. Both Mazy and Helen would help her. Helen had to report to the switchboard at twelve and shortly before that would leave. Mazy would stay with her until the moment she entered the ballroom.

She waited nervously with Helen in their room. Mazy would not arrive with the dress and the rest of the clothes until ten o'clock or after. It was thought best not to have them in their room until the last minute. And until that hour Mazy would be helping guests with their preparations to attend the ball. It began at ten.

They went to the window and saw below, by craning their necks, evidences of the evening's event. The yachts and houseboats clustered in front of the hotel were ablaze. Small boats, with strings of colored lights on them, passed to and fro over the water. Extra illumination had been installed on the pier. The hotel itself was so lighted that a great glow diffused from it. Wheel chairs flitted back and forth on the walks, their lanterns making them look like fireflies. At the edges of the walks burned hundreds of altar candles, suspended in their little glass cups from metal rods thrust into the ground. The scene was one of lively and luxurious beauty.

Seeing it disturbed Jenny. She was so agitated that she couldn't stay still for an instant. She walked up and down their tiny room, moving from one corner to the other. She peered out into the hall so frequently to see if Mazy was coming that Helen told her to stop it and advised her to lie down and rest.

Jenny tried stretching out on her bed. She didn't stay there two minutes. She got up, restless again.

At nine o'clock Helen exclaimed, "For goodness' sake, go take your bath now. Maybe that will settle you."

"Do you think so?"

"I hope so."

In wrapper, with her towel over her arm and carrying her soapdish, Jenny made her way down the hall to the bath. She ran the water in the tub as fast as it would go for fear she wouldn't be through in time, disrupting the schedule. The water wasn't any too hot because hundreds of other people were also taking baths around this time. With so many drawing on the supply, it was a wonder that it reached the top floor even lukewarm. On this night the hotel boilers were run full blast, nearly to the bursting point.

Jenny had washed her hair in the afternoon. She tied her towel about her head to keep it from getting damp, and, slipping off her wrapper, she stepped into the tub. She sank gratefully into the water which seemed to relax her. She lay back for a moment without doing any more.

She felt depressed and wondered if it was worth taking the risk she planned. She thought it would be better just to lie here in this soft warm water and forget the whole thing. The sense of the wealthy society leaders of the nation, all going through their preparations on the floors beneath her, scared her anew.

She thought of Tip. She hadn't had much time to consider him. She had no need to wonder how he would like what she was doing; she knew he would dislike it intensely. But there was no real harm in it. And Tip seemed far away out in the Everglades.

She looked down at her naked body lying half awash in the water. That it was desirable, she knew. It seemed to say to her that it belonged at the Ponce ball. It would be as beautiful as any there. Daring décolletage was the rage that season and Jenny hoped the dress Mazy would bring might be cut low enough to show a little of her breasts. Certainly they were worthy of making at least a suggestion of themselves known to the world. They could live up to any gown ever fashioned.

Lying there, Jenny remembered how as a child she had thought the brown dots on her chest were shameful blemishes. She recalled hoping that they wouldn't grow any larger or become more prominent than they were. At the mistake of her childhood, Jenny began to giggle. She couldn't stop herself for long moments, but kept on uncontrollably. Suddenly everything seemed not half as important as she had worked herself into believing.

She sat up in her bath and reached over the edge of the tub for her soap in the dish on the floor. She made lather, spreading it over herself. She sang lightly as the film of soap, manufacturing little bubbles that floated off into the air, slid over her body.

WHEN JENNY RETURNED to their room she told Helen, "It came over me that I could go to the ball as well as anybody else."

"This is quite a time," Helen observed dryly, "for you to decide that." She now became more distraught than Jenny, waiting impatiently for Mazy to arrive, while Jenny remained quiet, even amused at the other girl's excitement.

It was ten-thirty before Mazy appeared. She carried enough boxes to equal her size. With her, carrying more, was one of the Ponce hairdressers, an Amazon of a woman called Big Alice because of her size. "I brought her to help with your hair," Mazy said.

"I'd heard about what you're doing," Big Alice said, "and was going to come anyway."

The four scurried to deposit the boxes on the beds and chairs, the door was closed and they tore off the box lids.

"I want to see the dress," Jenny said.

"That you shall!" cried Mazy. "It is not only the best, but it is the safest thing that could be found. It comes from a girl who is sick and cannot go to the ball. The poor thing, slim as you and near the exact size, is loaning her gown."

"Does she know it?" asked Helen.

"Little will the not knowing hurt her," said Mazy as she took the lid off the largest box and drew out the gown. She held it up.

Jenny caught her breath.

The little dress was made of rich, creamy repoussé lace. Its skirt was full and sweeping, with alternate bands of inserted inch-wide delicate pink satin ribbons. The eighteen-inch girdle, of pale blue, looked so narrow that it seemed no mature female could possibly fit in it. Short puffed sleeves left the arms bare. Most of all, the bodice was deeply décolleté, cut square to reveal the largest expanse of bosom possible.

They all looked at it, uttering ecstatic cries of admiration. And each pair of eyes went from the size of the gown's waist to that of Jenny's. "She can get into it," declared Mazy.

Their fingers flew to find out by dressing Jenny from the skin out.

No modesty was thought of or considered as they got off her wrapper and helped her to pull on the full drawers that dropped nearly to her knees. They were fashioned of silk with lace trimming and inserts. Jenny gasped when she saw them, and gasped again when they were on her, for the beautiful fabric felt wicked against her skin. Over her head went a short chemise, also of silk. Nearly everything was of silk, even the stockings, which were silk all the way. She pulled these over her fingers; they were the first pair like that she had ever seen.

The straight front corset, pinched in at the waist, was squeezed on Jenny. Helen, given the duty of pulling the laces, exerted herself to the point where they almost broke. Jenny, hanging on to a bedpost, breathed with some difficulty when Mazy said she thought they were tight enough. The hunchback slipped a tape measure about Jenny's waist and reported triumphantly, "Exactly eighteen it is!"

Her attendants were less frenzied when they knew that the

gown fitted. They worked much more slowly and carefully. Mazy had brought a wide selection of accessories. They took a long time holding these up, discussing them and deciding which were best.

A corset cover was next. After that was tied into position, Jenny was seated and the stockings carefully pulled on and fastened to the rosebud supporters dropping from the corset. A number of pairs of shoes were brought out and considered; flush blue satin slippers, to match the gown's girdle, appeared magically on her feet. She stood up to step into a single petticoat.

"Shouldn't I have another?" Jenny wanted to know.

"One's enough," Mazy ruled.

The gown was then dropped over her head. Mazy and Helen fussed with the dress while Big Alice worked at her hair. "You'll never have any need for a hair curler," Big Alice told Jenny, "with the waves you have." She studied Jenny's head. "I think it best to keep it simple."

"As I said!" reminded Mazy.

Mazy kept jealous track of the work Big Alice accomplished. She approved of Big Alice minimizing the prevailing pompadour style and permitting Jenny's natural waves to show as they would. When Big Alice brought forth three artificial gardenias that looked so real they might have been just picked in the Ponce gardens, it was Mazy who made the final decision as to how many should go in Jenny's hair. "One!" she ordered.

"I think two," said Big Alice, "one on each side——"

"One!" Mazy cried fiercely.

Jenny didn't looked into the dresser mirror until everything was done. While Helen held a hand-mirror for her she ran a powder chamois over her face and then tucked it into her bodice, deep down. With a finger she spread coral salve on her lips, advised and helped by Big Alice. She took up her mother's gold crucifix and chain and Mazy, reaching high, fastened it for her in back.

Big Alice raised the only question about the overall effect and in this Helen backed her up. Critically, Big Alice said, "She ought to have a bracelet or something on her arms."

"Nothing," said Mazy.

"I think," said Helen, "ribbon bands at her wrists——"

"*Nothing*," Mazy repeated decisively. She gazed at Jenny with her large burning eyes. "She has a body to be proud of, not to hide. Let her show all of it she can. Let her not cover it up with another single ribbon. Look at her! Look at the beautiful thing and tell me if she should not be as bare as the public will stand for!"

They looked, and silently agreed.

Jenny turned to see herself.

She wondered if she could be the exquisite creature who stared back at her from the glass. Coolly, she examined herself and knew instantly that Mazy was right. She saw the slow sure swell of her breasts and the sight more than matched all her hopes. She felt a shameful delight at the exposure of herself.

She lifted a hand and visualized a glittering bracelet or ribbon at her wrist. She saw that anything like that would detract and draw attention from her natural charms. She fingered the crucifix at her throat and, running her eyes up and down the reflection of herself, she was content. Lost in the sight of herself, she reached forward and took up her bottle of Violette France and applied it to her ear lobes.

She was ready.

It was almost time. Helen looked down at her watch fastened to her shirtwaist. It was nearly twelve. She gave Jenny a hasty kiss. "Good luck," she said.

Big Alice left with Helen when she departed for the switchboard, also offering her good wishes. Mazy took entire charge of her.

The little hunchback gave her a last examination. She straightened a ruffle that was already perfect and stepped back to appraise her handiwork.

Impulsively, Jenny threw her arms about her and cried, "Thank you, Mazy! For everything you've done." Without knowing it, she found herself patting the hunch on her poor back.

Mazy endured the caress a moment and then drew herself away, crying, "You'll be spoiling yourself!"

She opened the door, and peered into the hall. No one was in sight. She led Jenny out and down to the stairway.

Here they descended without being seen. Below the sixth floor few ever used the stairs, and no one was on them tonight. They went down floor by floor until they reached the third. The route had been carefully worked out. On the third floor they swiftly negotiated the corridor between the rooms in the middle rear wing of the Ponce. A man and a woman dressed for the ball came out of one of the chambers. They passed them without comment or glance.

At the end of the corridor they took the stairway to the first floor. From there it was only a few steps to the laundry entrance. The door of this was closed, but unlocked. They opened it and went in.

A low light burned here. Jenny saw the shaking Tom clad in his tails. She tried not to smile at his appearance. The dark brown mustache that adorned his upper lip made him look almost like a man. This, and his new haircomb, changed him drastically. Jenny was sincere when she said, "Tom, I would hardly know you."

He stared at her, entranced. He couldn't speak. The sight of her nearly made him stop trembling. When he finally spoke, his voice shook. Hoarsely he pled, "Let's not do it."

Mazy, at the sight and sound of him, lifted her skirt and fumbled in a pocket of her petticoat. She brought forth a tiny bottle of whisky. She uncorked it and handed it to Tom, saying, "This will make you feel braver."

Tom took a swallow. He coughed. Before he could object further, Mazy ordered them both, "Follow me, directly. Stop for nothing."

Like disciplined soldiers, they followed the hunchback as she went briskly out the door. They went down the corridor and turned left, entering the vast Ponce kitchens. Here many cooks and chefs were in a frenzy of preparation for the ball supper. It was doubtful if more than a few of them noticed the odd assortment of three people—hunchback, beautiful girl, frightened young man—who raced down the side of the room. A few who saw blinked as though viewing an apparition. No one paid further attention.

Mazy stopped them behind a tall cabinet near the door leading into the ballroom. "Go," she said, "quickly, before anyone here comes to investigate." As they both hesitated she hissed, "Hurry!" She pushed them forward.

Before they knew it they were through the swinging doors. They found themselves standing behind banked potted palms shutting off the kitchen entrances. Beyond, through the palms, spread the ballroom where hundreds of couples whirled.

TOM STOOD FROZEN. He couldn't move of his own volition.

Desperately, Jenny made him take her in the attitude of a dance. She forced him to go forward. They glided out between the palms, joining the throng of dancers. After one startled glimpse about, Jenny looked up, smiling with easy outward content, into her partner's agonized face.

That one quick glance, and subsequent ones stolen as they circled the room, showed Jenny the glory of the entrancing scene.

The decoration motif this year was red and white bunting draped over the arches, wound about the pillars and carried along the walls of the immense room. Festoons of tropical foliage appeared all about. Long strings of varicolored electric globes were strung profusely. At the far end of the room the combined orchestras of the Ponce and the Breakers played on a raised platform. Every seat around the chamber was taken. Hundreds of other people stood about while still more danced.

Jenny beamed into Tom's face, trying to get him to look less glum and frightened. She said, in a simulated society manner, "Aren't the decorations novel this season?"

Tom tried to answer. His teeth merely chattered. He nodded his head in agreement.

Jenny gave up and took in the scene further. Her eyes

sparkled at the sights. She saw Mrs. Oliver Belmont in ivory with black jet trimming. Mrs. Charles Delmonico wore a white lace gown. Mrs. Thomas Waterbury had a magnificent gown of black spangled net, and wore a diamond sunburst in addition to emeralds and pearls. Jenny hoped to catch at least a glimpse of Mary Lily and Mr. Flagler.

She had more than a glimpse of them. There they were, seated at one side of the ballroom, surveying the scene like royalty. Mr. Flagler looked older than when she had first seen him, while Mary Lily, in her gorgeous misty blue gown, appeared to be younger, perhaps by contrast. Jenny kept her eyes on them as she circled the room.

She did not have to look about for another. He found her. Cleve Thornton, with Lizzy, spied her and danced over. He seemed highly tickled to see her here and cried, "Why, you're the belle of the ball!"

"Some people," Lizzy observed, "have come in where they don't belong."

Cleve spoke again, but Lizzy, momentarily taking over the lead of the dance, maneuvered him away.

Tom had nearly jumped out of his shoes at the encounter. Hoarsely, he pleaded, "We'd better get out."

"Just dance away from them," Jenny whispered.

This they couldn't do. In spite of Lizzy's obvious objections, Cleve again danced toward them. The two couples raced around the hall, dodging between others. Jenny became aware that another interest was being taken in them, perhaps caused by the first. The second one unnerved her.

Here and there about the room were standing men who were strangers to the Ponce. By now Jenny knew a hotel detective when she saw one; even clad in full evening dress as were these men, something about their manner marked them. Two of them, not of the hotel, but brought down from the North, had their eyes on her and her partner.

Tom didn't notice. If he had, she was sure he would bolt. She watched to make sure. It became certain when the two men walked along the side of the room, following them. It was then that Jenny realized the men had no means of knowing who they were. They did not recognize them as hotel employees who had sneaked into the ball. They were suspicious of them as persons not checked at the entrance.

Jenny's heart leaped into her throat as the dance music showed signs of coming to an end and the two detectives started for them. Using the last few notes of the music, Jenny now almost pushed Tom as close to Cleve and Lizzy as she could manage. She didn't know exactly why she did this, except that she felt Cleve might save them in some way. They were standing within ten feet of the other couple when the detectives arrived on the scene.

In a low, courteous, but firm voice, one of the men asked, "Would you be kind enough to identify yourselves?"

Tom looked blank and still more frightened.

Jenny played for time. "What do you mean?" She tried to sound haughty, but her voice shook.

"We can't place you among the guests," the second man said, "and wish to know who you are."

The state of affairs penetrated to Tom. "I knew they would catch us," he moaned.

The detectives exchanged glances. The first one said, "You had better come along with us."

Tom was ready to go, but Jenny stood her ground. "No," she said.

"We don't want to make a scene, miss," the second man said. He put his hand on her arm.

Jenny had been watching Cleve take in the scene, and now he arrived with Lizzy. He knew, without explanation, what the detectives were about and told them, "Go away."

"But Mr. Thornton——"

"Go away," Cleve said again.

They went away, glancing back.

Nastily, Lizzy commented, "You should have let her be arrested."

The music started again.

Cleve moved toward Jenny. As he had at the railroad depot, he took her hands and placed them in dancing position.

Lizzy boiled over. "Are you ditching me?" she demanded.

Cleve nodded his head toward Tom, who stood like a pillar, the color drained from his face. To Lizzy he suggested, "See if he is alive."

He danced off with Jenny, who looked back to see Lizzy flouncing away. Tom, jostled by the dancers, came to with a start. He looked about and then ran for the kitchen entrance.

Jenny didn't say anything for a moment. It had happened too quickly, too perfectly, for her to take it in at once.

Cleve didn't speak. The dance was a waltz, as had been their first. They whirled in exact unison, looking at each other. They were mutually conscious of the good looks of each other. Jenny was serene in the conviction that she and Cleve made an even more handsome couple than he and Lizzy.

"Thank you," she said.

"You headed to me for rescue."

She could not deny that, or minimize it by saying it was done in desperation.

He appeared to want to say nothing more, but merely to hold and dance with her. His silence continued for so long that she was constrained to say, "I don't think you should have left Miss Madison that way."

"Oh, yes," he said, "you do."

"Do you think she will tell on me?"

"Wild horses couldn't stop her."

"Do you believe she knew who my partner was?"

"If she didn't, she'll find out."

"Oh." Jenny looked away, as though to find Lizzy.

"Tell me," he said, "how you did it."

She outlined it candidly, through the appropriation of the dress to the present moment.

It was an episode he could appreciate, something that appealed to him.

The music stopped. A ragtime selection, the newest thing in dances, began. Because she shouldn't be with him any more at all, to say nothing of never having danced to such music, Jenny said, "I can't——"

"We can."

They ragtimed, he showing her how for a short time, and then their bodies moved in faultless rhythm. She realized, as though for the first time and in a dream, that she was dancing at the George Washington Birthday Ball in the Royal Poinciana with Cleve Thornton, one of the richest young men in the country. She felt as though she were betraying Tip. She wondered if she had been as guileless as she believed in not thinking of Cleve when she worked herself into the ball. She couldn't tell. She couldn't tell anything except that she was

208

glad to be here and that she enjoyed it more than any event at which she had ever been in her life. Tip, she felt, would not blame her for that. Maybe not too much. She would tell him all about how it happened.

Her gaze, as though going back to her own world for a moment, caught sight of Mazy peering out through massed palms. When she passed the place again, Mazy was gone.

After this dance, supper was served. Cleve offered his arm, but she held back. "I shouldn't stay any longer."

"Of course you should. I haven't been paid back fully for saving you from jail."

"It will cause too much attention."

"Not any more than you've caused so far."

"What do you mean?"

"Haven't you noticed practically everybody has been looking at you?"

She shrank back, and her glance darted about.

"Oh, they've stopped for the most part. But they know you're here."

"I've got to go."

"You might as well be hung for a sheep as a lamb. And we may find some way to save you from the gallows."

He led her toward the buffet tables. She was hesitant and abashed until she actually saw some people staring and speaking as though about her. She tried to ignore them, holding up her head. Cleve brought her a plate and a glass of champagne. He drank a stronger brew in quantity.

The champagne emboldened her to ask, "Do you have to drink so much?"

He waggled a finger at her. "Someone has been telling you I am a drunkard."

"You told me."

"Then it must be true."

Tonight she could laugh with him at that. "Three genera tions from shirtsleeves to shirtsleeves," he said. "I'm the third; I'm the return to shirtsleeves."

She glanced at his faultless evening clothes, worn with easy grace. "I haven't noticed them."

"I'm still working hard toward them."

She danced with him again, knowing it was wrong. He didn't balance or keep time as well as before. But the less sober he became the better seemed his manners. He noticed that the Flaglers had risen preparatory to departure from the ball.

"That," Cleve decided, "is the way to save you." He stopped dancing, took her hand and started to lead her over to intercept them.

She stopped, protesting in a horrified voice, "Oh, *no!*"

He pulled her forward so that she had to go with him. "Let me do the talking," he advised. "If you've got to say something don't tell any lies. Old man Flagler has a rat-trap mind that catches the littlest fib in man or beast."

He took her right up to the Flaglers, stopping them. They greeted each other and then Cleve introduced his companion.

"Mrs. Flagler, may I present Mrs. Jenny Totten? And Mr. Flagler."

Both the Flaglers murmured gracious acknowledgment to a mute Jenny. They had been staring at her, especially Mary Lily.

"Mrs. Totten," Cleve now announced, "is one of your best telephone operators. And certainly your most beautiful."

The Flaglers stared again. High above Jenny Mr. Flagler's

great white brows contracted ominously. Before he could speak a word of disapproval, Mary Lily exclaimed to Jenny, "But you're the one who looked through the gates!"

Jenny, who had been standing in acute misery, grasped at the friendly recollection. Dumbly, she nodded.

"You know each other?" Cleve pounced on this. "You're old friends?" He went on outrageously, "Mrs. Totten knows now, after I severely lectured her, that she should not have broken the rules of the Ponce and attended the ball. But she is Cinderella. And Cinderella is afraid, because she didn't drive back in her pumpkin coach before the horses turned to mice again, that she will lose her position."

Mary Lily smiled and turned to her husband. "We can't let that happen," she suggested.

Flagler's brows relaxed. He made deep sounds in his throat that after a time turned out to be a chuckle. "Certainly not," he agreed.

Jenny pleaded, "And those who helped me?"

"And those who helped you," Mary Lily assured her.

Flagler peered closer at Jenny, bending down to do so, and said, "I'll have to give instructions for all the centrals to be as pretty as you."

Jenny found her voice again. "Please," she stammered. "I can't tell you how grateful I am, not for myself, but for . . ." She choked to a stop.

Mary Lily put an exquisitely gloved hand on her arm. "It's all right, my dear."

As the Flaglers passed on, and Jenny turned to Cleve, he winked at her, just as he had winked back in St. Augustine.

This reminded her, as he took her to the liquid refreshments again and then danced with her once more, to tell him impulsively and mischievously, "Did you know that we had met before the railroad depot?"

"We met a million years ago," he claimed.

She related the St. Augustine incident.

"You see?" he cried. "We have a basis."

"A basis?" she questioned. "For what?"

"For you taking a ride with me on Choo Choo's train."

She shook her head. "This is only for now, tonight."

"More than that," he said. "You see, I know about you."

"What do you know?"

"All about your infatuation for the hotel. And in the Glades I saw how you've drifted away from Tip. I recognize those signs; they are the things I'm expert on."

Jenny stopped dancing abruptly. "I'm leaving," she said. She glanced about. "Do I go back through the kitchen, or will you take me out the front way?"

Gravely, Cleve considered the problem. "Anybody," he said, "can leave by the front way. Why not be distinctive?"

"Then it's through the kitchen?" she asked.

"With me."

"You'd better not."

"With me. And we'll let them see us go."

They were seen, for Cleve made a point of marching the length of the ballroom with Jenny, straight toward the kitchen doors and out, following a waiter with a loaded tray of dirty dishes. Jenny felt a hundred eyes on them. She knew she should not indulge in exultation at this flaunting of convention, but she could not prevent herself from feeling much else. She leaned on it, to carry her along.

Through the kitchens they went back along the route by which she had come to the ball. Instead of climbing the stairs they mounted in one of the elevators. At the fifth floor she would have had him leave her, but he insisted on walking up to the sixth floor and accompanying her to her room. At the door here she turned, to say good-by to him by asking, "You aren't going to drink any more tonight?"

"Not much," he told her. "And my first drink is this." His arms went swiftly about her and then he was kissing her.

Caught off guard, Jenny felt a stinging, momentary sweetness before she pushed him away, releasing herself.

Aghast at the realization that another man than her husband had held her in his arms and kissed her, Jenny watched Cleve turn and make his way down the hall. He weaved unsteadily, holding himself at an angle.

TIP SAT AT the head of the long table in his new camp dining-room, which consisted of screened sides all around and a thatched roof. It had proved popular with his hunters. He had quite an establishment now. It made more money than he had ever anticipated.

Idly he listened to the lunch talk of his customers. Mostly it was about hunting and fishing. They bandied their successes and failures back and forth, boasting and taunting. It was always the same, even with the new batch of men who had come out after the Washington's Birthday Ball, all strangers to him until a few days ago.

The talk veered to business. Usually the leading subject among these men, they discussed high finance, mergers and corners of the stock market which here only rated second place. In connection with all of these a good deal of ill feeling was expressed against President Theodore Roosevelt. Sardonically he was referred to as the trust-buster. "I tell you!" one man declared belligerently. "He'll ruin the country." Vincent O'Brien was a big, blustering Chicago meat packer with a skin as pink as the pigs he sold.

"He sounds like a traitor to the constitution," another said. "I don't see why all men aren't free and equal to organize any kind of business they want." This was Howard Gaylord, a dapper little jeweler from New York.

"What Roosevelt doesn't realize," said a third man, "is that large private business has been responsible for building this country. In many ways it has made it what it is. Certainly it has hurried its shaping and development, for without it long years would have elapsed before many things were accomplished."

"Look at Flagler here," O'Brien pointed out. "What would Florida amount to without him? Why, the Crackers would still be climbing the coconut trees for food."

The talk shifted to Flagler. It was decided that his marriage to Mary Lily had worked out well, even though she was much younger. The theme became more general about women. One man pronounced, "They can raise hell with a man."

"A pretty one is worst. She's always thinking about how much better she could have done than you—or seeing if she can still do better."

"Thank God I'm not married to a beautiful woman," declared O'Brien.

"Like the phone operator at the Ponce that Thornton is chasing."

"I understand she's married locally," said Gaylord. "I wonder if her husband knows what's going on."

Tip went still and white. He held himself tensely and warily, as he did when facing dangerous game. The talk went on, pursuing the same dreadful subject.

"At least they say she isn't a trollop. Thornton will have to marry her to get her."

"Every woman's a trollop if she looks at another man while she's married to one already."

"Well, maybe you're right."

"It looks as if this one knows what she wants. If women can be said ever to know what they really want."

"There's no doubt about what Thornton wants in life."

"Liquor and women."

"In his case the usual order is reversed."

"They say this woman has made it nearly the other way around with him. She's a beauty."

"I saw her at the ball with him. She outshone every other woman in the place."

That dire accolade made Tip sure. For an instant he had hoped it might be another of the switchboard centrals about whom they spoke. Now no doubt remained that it was Jenny.

He pushed back his chair. The sudden movement, before the meal was ended, made some of the men look in his direction.

O'Brien demanded, "What's the matter with you, Tip? A minute ago you got white as a sheet under that tanned hide of yours, and now you're as red as a turkey cock."

Tip got to his feet. Half-dazed, he glared down the table. All the men now attended him. As though angry with them, he muttered, "You'll have to do your own guiding for the rest of the day."

They glanced at him sharply.

"But what——"

"Wait a minute——"

Hardly knowing what he said, Tip told them, "I've got to go to town."

Gaylord protested, "But this afternoon we were heading for——"

Not wanting to discuss it further, Tip informed them, "You heard what I said."

"This is an outrage!" O'Brien cried.

Tip couldn't restrain himself from saying, "So is Thornton, taking up with my wife."

They stared. O'Brien's face became deep pink. Others got red and apologetic. There were a few exclamations. Most of the men were silent.

Gaylord followed Tip out when he went to tell the cook and his other help about where he was going. The man laid a hand on Tip's arm and said sympathetically, "Beat the stuffing out of him. He's been deserving it for a long time."

Tip shook him off.

He didn't take the wagon and horses. He couldn't tell when he would be back, and the conveyance was needed here. He could make almost as good time by walking. He strode off, hitting a fierce pace.

L ATE THAT AFTERNOON Tip came upon what he sought. He found them at a remote place on the Lake Trail, and placed himself squarely in front of Choo Choo's wheelchair in which they rode. Choo Choo slowed down and came to an abrupt stop, sizzling slightly, A frightened expression came across his black face. He knew trouble when he saw it.

Jenny's hand went to her throat. She breathed, "Tip——"

Cleve was equal even to this. Pleasantly, almost jovially, he greeted, "Hello, old fellow."

Tightly, Tip said, "I figured you wrong."

"At least," Cleve told him, "I'm glad to see you haven't brought a gun along."

"I don't need a gun for you."

Jenny now cried, "Tip!"

"If she won't keep away from you," he said, "I mean to keep you away from her."

"Tip," Jenny pleaded, "it isn't the way it looks. This is the first time I've been with him like this."

"Except for the ball," he reminded.

"That wasn't the way you've probably heard. It——"

"We'll have that out later," he interrupted. "Then you can decide between me and Thornton here or the Ponce or whatever it is you want. Right now him and me have got something else."

Cleve began, "Wait a minute, old fellow——"

"I won't wait a minute!" Tip cried. "Get out of that go-cart before I take you out!"

Cleve seemed pleased when he saw Tip's full intention. "You mean we're going to fight?" he asked.

"If you can," said Tip.

Jenny intervened. "You can't! You can't! Not here! Not at all!"

Tip addressed Thornton. "Are you getting out?"

Cleve turned to Jenny. "Life," he said, "is exciting with you."

He started to get out of the wheel-chair, but she held him back by catching his arm. "You can't fight."

"I have been challenged," he said.

He got out of the chair and started to take off his coat. "You'll lick me, of course," he told Tip. "That's why I want to propose something."

Taking off his own coat, Tip asked contemptuously, "What?"

"If I fight you on your terms, afterwards you will fight me on mine."

"I can lick a Thornton any way."

"That's agreed, old fellow?"

Scornfully, Tip corroborated, "It's agreed. Put up your fists."

"No!" cried Jenny. "No!"

Tip dropped his coat by the side of the trail. Cleve handed his to Choo Choo, who rolled his eyes and mournfully tolled his bell.

As if the bell were a signal to start the fight, the two men lunged at each other. Cleve fought better than Jenny or Tip expected him to. He used his fists scientifically and moved his feet with agility as though he had had the benefit of boxing lessons.

Even so, Tip hit him almost at will. Cleve was able to defend himself to a degree, warding off some of the blows. Although he was rocked by several haymakers, he stood up to them, remaining on his feet. Blood appeared at the corner of his mouth.

Jenny sprang out of the chair, crying, "Stop it! Stop it!" She tried to intervene, but they paid no attention. When she thrust herself between them, Tip took her by the shoulder and set her aside, ordering, "Get out of the way!"

The men flailed at each other again. Soon Cleve forgot the science of boxing. Breathing hard, he alternated between holding his arms in front of his face when Tip's blows landed, and swinging wildly. One of his swings, by accident, caught Tip on the eye. He blinked and a trickle of red ran from the cut.

"Choo Choo!" Jenny appealed to him frantically. "Stop them!"

Choo Choo sat on the seat of his Afrimobile. He rolled his eyes in wider arcs. In her right senses Jenny would never have called on him. The Negro would no more put a hand on either of the battling white men than he would have touched her. He blew steam and rang his bell furiously. As if to further express his perturbation, he pedaled his vehicle back and forth.

All through the fight a slight smile remained on Cleve's face. He was not afraid of being hurt. He seemed amused over the prospect. Tip caught him on the jaw with a solid blow. Cleve staggered back, nearly went down, but caught his balance.

He returned to the battle with a wider smile.

Tip swung. Cleve's hands went up to protect himself. But this time he was not fast enough.

He went back and down, crashing full length at the edge of the path. He remained there, smiling up through blood spreading all over the lower part of his face.

Choo Choo stopped pedaling, to sizzle on a low note.

Jenny stared, sickened and horrified.

The blood ran from Cleve's nose and mouth. He took a white handkerchief from his trouser pocket and dabbed at his face. The cloth brightened with vivid red stains. "Something of a mess," he said.

He sat up as Choo Choo went to him, carrying a bottle kept behind the wheel-chair cushions. Cleve reached for it eagerly. He took a long gulp of whisky, then a shorter one. As Choo Choo took back the bottle Jenny saw that the handkerchief was saturated with blood. She went to Cleve's coat and took another from the breast pocket and gave it to him. He nodded his thanks and dabbed with that. The profuse part of the bleeding stopped. He struggled to his feet and Jenny helped him.

"It looks," Tip said, "as if I should have let him lick me. Then maybe you'd be attending me instead of him."

Jenny didn't reply.

Cleve observed, "From the way my nose and other sections feel, I rather wish you'd followed out that idea." He regarded Tip. "At least I gave you an eye."

The cut near Tip's eye had stopped its slight bleeding, but the eye itself was rapidly discoloring.

"Does that tell you," Tip demanded, "better than I did in the Glades?"

Cleve shook his head. "Oh, we've got to try it my way next."

"What's your way?"

"You can beat me in a fistfight," Cleve said, "but you can't in a drinking bout."

Tip's forehead creased with question.

Jenny understood before he did what Cleve proposed, and cried, "No! You've fought enough——"

"You mean," Tip asked Cleve, "you want to see which of us can drink the most?"

"I want to see," Cleve corrected, "who can drink the other one under the table. And I'll be starting with a slight handicap."

"But more practice," Tip pointed out.

Jenny said, "You can't, you can't."

"A drinking contest," Tip mused. He looked at Cleve, at Jenny and then at both, as though wishing to study them together.

"You agreed," Cleve reminded pleasantly, "to try it my way after I tried yours."

"Thornton," Tip told him, "I think I can lick you at that, too."

"Jenny," Cleve proposed, "can be the judge."

"I won't be any judge," Jenny stated flatly. "I won't have a thing to do with this. I don't want to see it." To Tip she pleaded, "I only want to go away from here and tell you how this all came about. Please, Tip, let me do that."

She saw, even while she asked, the refusal in his narrowed

eyes. She had never thought him capable of the rage that showed in him. She was tormented by it.

"You started something," he told her, "or at least let it start. You better see the end of it."

The two men paid little further attention to her as they made their plans.

"We can't very well hold it at the Ponce," Cleve decided. "That's a little too public. I suggest Bradley's. You will both be my guests there for dinner."

"What are you trying to do, Thornton?" Tip demanded. "Get out of it? You know it's against the rules for Florida residents to get in there."

Cleve chuckled. "Leave that to me. Both of you can dine there with me if you don't enter the gambling room."

That part now was accepted at least tentatively by Tip. He had another objection. "What about a dress suit for me?"

Cleve looked him up and down. "I have two, and we're about the same size."

This time it was Tip who laughed grimly. "All right, Thornton," he agreed. "I'll wear your suit and I'll drink you under the table."

"Good!" Cleve said. He turned to Jenny. "You'll come with us. If you don't, we might get in a fight again."

Jenny had thought of that herself. It might be worse for her not to go with them than to be there to at least keep them from hurting each other. She tried to prevent them beginning, asking Cleve, "Please don't do it."

"We've got to, you see," Cleve told her. "I must have my chance to beat him."

She appealed to Tip with her gaze.

He looked away stonily.

"You'll referee?" asked Cleve.

"I won't referee anything," she told him, stricken. "But I'll go with you, to try to shame you out of it. Both of you."

THEY RODE BACK to the Ponce squeezed in the wheel-chair. Jenny sat in the middle. Because of the bloodied and slightly battered state of the two men, Choo Choo didn't chug up to the main entrance. He rolled them to an entrance on the ground floor, near the rotunda. Inside, by the elevator, they would meet in an hour.

In her room, moving mechanically, Jenny dressed in her own simple evening gown. She wished that Helen was not on duty, and Mazy not busy with her chambermaids, so that she could talk with them. She was nearly frantic. She had a quick impulse to go to Mr. Flagler or Denbaugh or Bemerill and ask them to stop it. Her hand, puffing her hair, became still in her decision to do this. She wondered why she hadn't thought of it before.

Then she knew she couldn't. This was her affair. It was she who had brought this about, or at least caused it. It was she who must settle it, if she could.

She didn't see how. Perhaps if she made herself beautiful enough they would be embarrassed to drink too much in her presence. Looking at her drawn face in the mirror, she decided that she wasn't that beautiful.

Jenny arrived at the rendezvous before the two men came. She wanted to be sure to be on hand to take advantage of every opportunity to stop them from the shameful drinking contest.

When they arrived, she saw that meanwhile they had made a start. Tip looked strangely and stiffly distinguished in Cleve's tails. His shoulders bulged out the coat, and his hands and legs stuck out noticeably, but otherwise the clothes fitted him as though made for him. He had even been able to get his feet into a pair of Cleve's evening pumps. His skin looked nearly black next to the stiff white wing collar in which his neck squirmed. Liquor was on his breath. His darkened eye made him look owlish.

Cleve, his cuts cleaned up, his face puffed only a little, was delighted with Tip.

"You've both been drinking already," Jenny accused.

Cleve reported, "We're about neck and neck. I think he's going to give me a run for my money."

Jenny made an exasperated sound to which they paid no heed.

They went outside where Choo Choo waited for them. It was now dark. The hotel windows shone with lights, those on the grounds also burned and the lanterns hung beneath the Afrimobiles had been lighted.

As they rolled toward the Beach Club, Jenny was struck with the bitter irony of her seeing it in the present circumstances. She tried to talk to Tip again, and to Cleve, but they were resolved about their project.

Choo Choo pedaled them up to the entrance of Bradley's, under the porte-cochère, which was small, being only for Afrimobiles, and discreetly unostentatious. A single small light burned in its ceiling; from a short distance away it was difficult to make out the identity of anyone seen here. They descended from the wheel-chair and, after giving Choo Choo instructions to wait, they approached the rather narrow white wooden door. Its upper panel was of frosted glass in which were the clear letters, "B. C."

Here stood a tall, husky, keen-eyed white doorman, clad like themselves in full evening dress. He greeted Cleve deferentially, swinging the door wide for him and his party.

They passed into a small cream-colored lobby with a green carpet on the floor. It amounted only to a tiny foyer. Two doors led off it. Both had upper parts of glass panels. The one in the left corner was painted black and had printed on it in gold letters, "Entrance For Club Members Only." The one in the right corner was glazed and on it clear letters stated, "Office of the President and Board of Governors." In the lobby, seated behind a plain flat-topped desk, was a dapper, pink-cheeked little man whose small sharp eyes crinkled at the sight of Cleve. He said immediately, "I see you've brought some friends and want to break the rules." He seemed to know who Tip and Jenny were, or at least sense some thing of their identities.

Cleve introduced him as "Mr. Secretary," and explained his guests frankly. The secretary warned, "Only in the café or dining-room."

"Agreed," Cleve told him.

The Secretary took hold of the doorknob of the left-hand door and was about to open it when his gaze, still traveling over Cleve and Tip, examined their cuts and bruises. He stayed his hand, looking questioningly at Cleve, who laughed and said, "A slight discussion."

The Secretary suggested, "You don't mean to——"

"No, no," Cleve assured him, "we're great friends now." He put his arm around Tip's shoulders.

Tip threw him off.

"The Colonel wouldn't like it," the Secretary cautioned Cleve. "It would mean your membership card."

"Don't worry," Cleve told him.

The Secretary finally pulled open the door and they stepped inside.

A long, cream-colored paneled corridor led to the right. Off this was the formal dining-room, which looked out on the depot and the T of the Ponce, now shut off by green curtains. At the end of the corridor an arched entrance, set at an angle, led into the octagonal gambling room. To the left of where they stood extended the long café, with bare wooden tables. Green carpets were on all the floors. Potted palms stood about in profusion. From behind a large group of these string music emanated.

There were not many people about yet. An air of aristocratic ease permeated the rooms, whose green and white décor represented the racing silks of the owner, Colonel Bradley. Softly, above the music, came the sounds of muted clicks and the modulated voices of a number of men repeating some ritual that sounded almost like holy worship. These sounds puzzled Jenny until it struck her that they were made by the roulette wheels with their balls jumping about in them, and the dealers calling out instructions and results to the players.

Cleve was greeted unctuously by the French headwaiter, to whom he said, "A good table in the dining-room, shortly, Antoine. We'll have a snort or two before."

Antoine bowed. Cleve led them into the café, where a waiter held a chair for Jenny at a select table. They sat down and Cleve asked Jenny what she would like to drink.

"Nothing," she said.

"Your world will seem rosier," Cleve urged.

"Nothing."

Cleve looked at Tip. "We'll keep to the same?"

"I can drink anything you can, Thornton."

"Quantity," Cleve smiled, "is the question." He turned to the waiter. "Three double Scotches. Neat. Each."

The waiter stared.

"Lined up right here," Cleve instructed him. He poked his finger three times on the tabletop in front of his place and reached over and rapped it stiffly three times in front of Tip. "And if you tell the Colonel, I won't give you five dollars."

The waiter bowed without offering anything further of his opinion and hurried away.

Jenny and Tip sat estranged, their gaze never meeting.

"Of course, you know how this place is operated," Cleve told them. "It has a regular charter from the state as a social club. The by-laws say it's organized to conduct certain games of amusement. The rule I like best is the one to keep people from smoking in the roulette room and making it stuffy; this one reads, 'Gentlemen are requested not to smoke in the ballroom.' That office door you saw in the lobby is eyewash. The Colonel has his real office back of the gambling rooms; he's the President and Board of Governors. You know about him."

Tip found his voice to speak, for him, volubly, as though he didn't want Cleve to best him in any way.

"He contributes to both sides in an election," he said. "Then, no matter who wins, he's in with them. He's anxious to give to any charity that comes along, because that makes friends with the church groups, keeping off their criticism. He's more than willing to lend money to local interests. That keeps them from kicking about his gambling. He's got practically everybody so they don't even admit there is such a thing as the Beach Club and if they do, they whisper about it."

"A very clever man, the Colonel," Cleve chuckled. "A little stiff-necked in some respects, but a real sport. You'll probably see him around before the evening's over. In fact, you're bound to."

Jenny wondered what Cleve meant by this.

Their drinks arrived and were placed exactly as Cleve had instructed.

Cleve picked up one of his.

Tip took one of his.

Cleve proposed, "Bottoms up?"

"Bottoms up."

They drank, emptying the glasses.

Cleve took up a second glass.

Tip lifted another.

They drank again, following the same procedure.

Jenny said to both, "You can't——"

"Oh, this isn't serious drinking," Cleve assured her. "We'll get down to that later. I want you to enjoy yourselves now." He picked up his third drink and held it toward Tip, who now also took his third.

They drank.

Tip blinked.

"Feel that?" Cleve inquired solicitiously. "I'll give you a chance to get in form. That's all before dinner." He rose, and they got to their feet.

They made their way out of the café and down the corridor. More people were now coming in the Beach Club. Despite the perturbation that possessed her, Jenny recognized them as the smartest guests at the Ponce. She noted a number of men with ladies not their wives, and some ladies with men not their husbands. Several large gay parties entered and headed for one of the three rooms, to drink, to dine or to gamble.

Instead of turning into the dining-room, Cleve led them on down the corridor to the gambling room. "You can peek," he told them.

They peered through the arched doorway into the famous gambling room. Eight roulette tables were placed around the room at each point of the octangle. Only half of the tables were now running; later all would be in play. Men and women stood about, placing their chips on the marked green baize tables. The dealers deftly pulled in the chips with their little black wooden rakes, or paid out chips precisely to winners.

Cleve said, "You see the latticework over the doorway on the other side of the room above the arch there? Behind that is a steel plate and in the plate is a hole. And behind the hole is a man with a rifle. He's watching every move made in the room. If anybody tried to hold it up he would shoot."

Jenny lost interest in this. There was no use in appealing to Tip. Of Cleve she pleaded, "Don't you and Tip drink any more. Please. For my sake."

His eyes were bright when he looked at her closely. "I would like to please you, but I can't."

They went into the dining-room and were shown to their table by Antoine, who himself took their order. This consisted of his listing the items of the menu being served. He concluded, "And for wines——"

"For wines," Cleve interjected, "with the exception of madame, who will have——"

"No wine," Jenny in turn interrupted Cleve.

Antoine's eyes bulged. "Nothing, madame?"

"No wine."

Antoine appealed to Cleve by spreading his hands.

"No wine, she said," Cleve told him.

"And you, monsieur," the headwaiter said to Cleve, "for you and the other gentleman, you were about to say——"

"For us, instead of your regular wines, we will have a bottle of whisky."

Antoine drew back, blanching. "Monsieur Thornton!" he reprimanded.

"And don't tell the Colonel," Cleve instructed him, "or I won't give you ten dollars."

"It is not the Colonel," Antoine protested, "or what you say you wish to give me. It is that you know better than this, monsieur."

"A bottle," Cleve insisted, "of good Scotch."

Antoine drew himself up. "Monsieur," he said, "I have made this to be one the best restaurants in the world. It is so recognized by cosmopolitans. It is comparable with anything in Europe. You cannot ruin excellent dishes with such a thing as whisky."

Cleve put a finger in the middle of the snow-white tablecloth. "Put the bottle here. Now," he ordered.

Antoine seemed to collapse like a deflated balloon. He resigned himself. "As you wish," he said coldly. He muttered in French, *"Les Américains ils sont comme les cochons."*

"I heard that," Cleve said pleasantly.

"I am glad you did, monsieur." Antoine wheeled and departed.

Tip wanted to know, "What did that frog say?"

"He said Americans are pigs."

Jenny felt an unnatural desire to laugh and keep on laughing, hysterically.

The whisky, with two glasses, appeared almost instantly, brought not by Antoine, but by a waiter. Cleve and Tip had a drink.

They had a drink, sometimes several, between courses of the exquisite meal that was served by the pop-eyed waiter.

Jenny did not attempt to enjoy the food, which consisted of canapés of caviar, cold consommé in cups, pompano à la cragin, Parisienne potatoes, pheasant breasts with bread sauce, terrapin, pâté de foies gras, aspic, toasted crackers, deviled cheese, Macedoine of fruit, cake, coffee and finally a cordial served to her. Off in a corner of the dining-room she saw Antoine regarding this with triumph. Most of the food had choked Jenny as she sat, forced to watch the two men drink, but she sipped at the cordial.

The bottle of whisky was nearly empty. Tip's eyes had a slight glaze to them. Cleve, peering at him, predicted, "I thinks it's going to be under this table."

Tip spoke thickly. "I'm still on top of it."

Cleve laughed. "I'd like to see that. It would liven up the place." He looked around.

Other diners had been noticing their drinking. They frowned at the whisky bottle on the table. Someone audibly whispered something about the Colonel. Dowagers looked at Jenny, recognizing her as one of the Ponce telephone operators, and they put on their bulldog expressions.

Cleve poured the last from the bottle. They drank it, and he said, "Let's try another table."

They rose. Tip had to grasp the back of his chair to keep his balance. Cleve, who merely leaned over at a slight angle, chuckled. Jenny, her face burning, walked ahead of them out to the corridor. She wanted to keep on walking right out of the Beach Club and keep going forever.

Instead, as they joined her in the corridor, both of them weaving unsteadily, she pleaded, "That's enough. Don't drink any more, either of you."

"Where's the table?" Tip wanted to know.

Cleve took his arm. "Let me help you, old fellow——"

"Don't touch me." Tip withdrew his arm.

They returned to the café, to the same table as before. Another waiter appeared to take their order.

"Think you're up to three doubles again, old fellow?" Cleve asked.

"I'm up to anything you're up to."

Cleve repeated their order of before.

The waiter examined them. He nodded his head and went away.

The drinks did not arrive. In place of them, Jenny learned what Cleve meant when he said they were sure to see Colonel Bradley.

A tall, dignified, straight-backed man, clad in faultless evening dress, appeared at the side of their table. Colonel Edward R. Bradley had icy blue eyes, thin lips and a severe expression. It was said that he preferred horses to men because he knew men so well. Now, frostily, he regarded the three of them. His gaze passed over Jenny briefly. It hung for an instant on Tip, who stared back at him mistily. It came to rest on Cleve.

"Oh-oh," Cleve said, and warned his companions, "teacher."

"Mr. Thornton," the Colonel stated in an even, unemotional tone, "you know very well the Beach Club does not countenance the kind of drinking you have been doing."

"Colonel," Cleve told him, "you're a betting man."

"I will bet on anything," the Colonel admitted.

"Well, we're just trying to settle a little bet."

"Kindly do not settle it here in the way you are doing. You will either have to stop drinking—in fact, I have instructed the waiters to serve you no more—or leave."

"We've got to keep on drinking to settle our bet."

"Then your presence is no longer welcome."

"You're kicking us out?"

"You will please leave. Immediately."

"Just——"

"Mr. Thornton, I don't know why I do not request your membership card. I have asked for others on less provocation." He turned to Jenny and gave her a slight stiff bow. "I am sorry."

His ramrod back straightened, he turned and marched away.

Jenny sat horrified, yet entranced. In his icy glance the famous Colonel Bradley had seemed to appreciate her position, even though he didn't understand it. He had apologized to her. Nothing could have been more correct or gentlemanly.

She seized upon a greater thing. Now the drinking bout would be brought to a close. She thanked the Colonel, and thanked him again.

Tip appeared to think along the same lines. Muddily, he accused Cleve, "Fixed it so we can't go on, didn't you?"

"Oh, no," said Cleve. "We can go on, all right."

"Colonel," Tip pointed out, "said we couldn't."

"We'll simply go elsewhere, old fellow," said Cleve.

"Where go?" asked Tip. He twisted his words.

To Jenny's consternation, Cleve said, "I think Banyan Street is about the best place."

"Whisky Street," corrected Tip. "That's what called now, Whisky Street."

"Whisky Street it is," Cleve repeated, delighted. "I would say that is most appropriate."

J ENNY FELT NUMB as Choo Choo pedaled them across the bridge. She listened to the Negro acting like a train, for he loved making the noises of a locomotive on the bridge more than anywhere else. Here he chugged on the footwalk right alongside the railroad tracks.

Jenny knew she couldn't persuade the men to abandon their reckless contest. She might bring them to their senses about where they were going. "Do you know where you're taking me?" she demanded.

"Won't hurt you a bit," Cleve assured her. "The Four Hundred come here regularly."

Jenny knew that most Banyan Street denizens encouraged the habit of Palm Beach winter visitors to come slumming among them. It meant added revenue and gave them a chance to see the other half. Reputable West Palm Beach people, however, had a stricter sense of propriety than the Four Hundred. Jenny was sure that if Tip had been himself he would never take her to Banyan Street.

She stared at him hopefully as he sat up straight. He took deep breaths and shook his head in the night air to clear it partially. He said nothing about their destination, but leaned slightly over Jenny and informed Cleve, "I'll take drink for drink with you, Thornton, and the least man goes down." He spoke with little blurring of his words, his voice strong, steady and even confident.

237

Cleve, on the other hand, now slumped. The large amount of alcohol he had consumed was belated in its effect on him. When it took hold, it did so strongly.

"What good will all this do?" Jenny cried. "What will it prove?"

She was not answered.

They came to Banyan Street. Choo Choo rolled his train up it triumphantly tootling. On both sides of the street the establishments were brightly lighted. Some of the pool halls had their entire fronts open. The half-doors on the bars swung busily. The tinkle of mechanical pianos in the bar-dancehalls made a chorus.

Street loungers noticed the wheel-chair pedaled by the giant Negro and occupied by the two men in tails between whom sat the beautiful young woman. Banyan Street people called out, not derisively, but in welcome. Cleve acknowledged this recognition by bowing right and left.

He consulted Tip. "Have you any preference about the place?"

"Any place where they have liquor you can't hold," Tip replied.

"Then I think," said Cleve, "the Plaisance."

"Choo!" came from behind them. The train had heard and pedaled toward this destination. The present Plaisance was a gaudy new building which replaced the former Doolittle Cottage that had been destroyed by fire. It comprised a violently decorated dancehall, bar, skin-game gambling cubicles and accouterments of general sin. It even had a small stage at one end of the main room where, at intervals, a traveling troupe entertained.

They descended from the wheel-chair under the metal sign

of the Plaisance. It was made of tin with the name of the establishment cut out; behind it an electric globe etched this metal stencil in the night.

The place was crowded when they entered. Whispered word of their presence went through the people like wildfire. Heads turned to regard them. They were greeted with grins of hospitality. A man yelled, "Swells!"

As they took chairs at a table an argument broke out in a group at the bar. A man, looking at them, said audibly, "They aren't swells. That's Tip Totten and his wife."

Another said, "And that's Cleve Thornton with them; he's——"

The discussion was drowned in the sudden starting of the mechanical piano.

Jenny was beyond caring about being the center of public attention. She knew she should leave both Tip and Cleve and no more be a party to what they were doing. But she could not bring herself to go. She had to see the outcome, if only to prevent them, should she be able, from fighting again.

A waiter with a dirty apron tied about his middle sidled up to them, holding a tin tray and he stood silently, waiting their order.

Cleve didn't seem to notice. He sat staring.

"Let's get down to business," Tip told him.

Cleve came to with a start. "Oh," he said vaguely, "yes. Yes, indeed."

Tip looked at him. "I've got a proposition to make to you, Thornton."

"Anything you want, old fellow."

"Let's end this quick, fast and big."

Jenny looked at Tip hopefully, but at his next words her heart sank.

"We'll take double whiskies at five-minute intervals," Tip proposed.

"Excellent idea, old fellow." Cleve spoke with an effort.

Tip turned to the waiter. "Keep them coming."

For the first time the waiter took an interest. "Drink contest?" he inquired.

"Mind your own business," Tip ordered, "and start them coming."

The waiter began to serve them as requested, but he didn't mind his own business. His whispered word went around the place rapidly. People at other tables and at the bar turned to watch. Soon the whole room looked on, at first silently, then taking sides, coming up closer and cheering on the contestants. The mechanical piano played *I'm On The Water Wagon Now*.

Jenny went pale as the men downed drink after drink. She gripped the edge of the table with white knuckles. She tried to take her mind off the battle, at least temporarily, by looking at the crowd. She noticed, for the first time, some of the girls. They were clad in garish evening gowns, cut low, and they were painted heavily. Through the thick cosmetics she could see that some of them were ugly and gross, while others were pretty and soft. Men stood with their arms about them, or they had their own arms about the men.

Jenny wished Marshal Duncan would appear to put a stop to the drinking bout, and then doubted if he could. Once she tried to stop it herself. It was at a point where decision was in sight.

Tip sat close to the table, the gleaming white front of his

boiled shirt pressed against the edge to help support him. His elbows also rested on the table. His eyes were glazed again, but they were held steadily on his opponent. He paid no attention to the people crowding his chair or their shouts. Sweat stood out on his forehead and bathed his dark brown face.

Cleve sat more slumped than ever. His countenance was set in a smile, indicating nerve greater than his physical capabilities. Only his spirit sustained him as another double whisky, and then another, went down his throat. They were coming at closer intervals than five minutes now. Once he gagged. He grinned apologetically, swallowed several times and sank still lower in his chair. Neither he nor Tip said a word. They kept to the hard work of drinking, steadily, seriously. They had no energy left for talk.

Jenny could stand it no longer. She jumped to her feet and cried wildly, "Stop it! Stop it! Oh, stop them! Somebody stop them!"

Tip and Cleve paid no attention. They lifted still another drink to their lips.

"Let'm alone!" a man said.

"They're doing fine!" another advised.

Jenny covered her face with her hands. She took them away almost immediately, for a shout came from the crowd.

She looked, to see Cleve sliding from his chair. He started to go gradually at first. Then he collapsed completely, disappearing under the table.

The crowd yelled. Men pummeled Tip on the back. He thrust them off roughly, staggered to his feet and lurched away toward the rear regions of the Plaisance.

No one approached Cleve, to help until Jenny went to

him. She pulled at his sodden body, but couldn't budge him. His eyes were closed in utter insensibility.

Finally, men's hands reached down and lifted him up. His head hung back, and Jenny wondered if he was dead. "He's all right," one of the men assured her. "Just out. Where does he go?"

She looked about wildly but didn't see Tip, and so led the men through the doors to the wheel-chair. It relieved her to find that Choo Choo was not at all disturbed by the sight of Cleve being carried to his chair. The Negro took it as a matter of course, as though quite accustomed to it. Cleve, then, if this was a regular occurrence, would not die.

He was put in the chair. Choo Choo arranged him comfortably in one corner, fussing and clucking over him like a mother hen with a lone chick.

The men who had carried Cleve out went back into the Plaisance, leaving Jenny standing uncertainly. The music of Banyan Street, with many songs making a confused discord, beat in her brain. She felt as if she had taken drink for drink with the two men, and her head whirled.

Suddenly she became aware that Tip stood beside her, and she looked up to see his face. He was pale beneath his deep color, as though he had been sick. His hair was tousled and wet from being held under a faucet; his face still had drops of water on it. He stood, wavering only a little, and gazed at Cleve seated in the wheel-chair, being attended by Choo Choo. His voice shook when he told Jenny:

"I'm saying you shouldn't have played along with him, you being a married woman, married to me. I ain't saying there's been anything wrong between you and him, but——"

For the first time, in a searing blaze of release, Jenny felt

242

clear anger. "Oh, you're not saying there's been anything wrong!"

"All I'm saying is that if it's come to a choice to be made, you got to make it now."

Roused further by his ultimatum, she cried, "Well, maybe there is a choice to be made!"

"Like I say, if there is, then you make it." Jerking a thumb at Cleve, he said, "He's one thing. I'm another. You got to decide which side of the lake you want to be. You can go back across with him or come home with me now and give up everything over there, cut it all off, get away from the hotel and all it's meant to you."

The frightening alternatives of this increased her anger. His lesser demand alone might have appeased her rage. But in stating that she abandon the hotel as well, he asked for something she couldn't give.

"Not the Ponce!" she cried.

"That as much as him and what he is. In some ways the Ponce is the biggest part."

Her resentment rose. "You haven't any right to——"

"I got every right, and I want to know now, all the way, and for good."

She stared at him. She turned and looked at the insensible figure in the wheel-chair and an unaccountable pity came to her. It was one more spur to make impossible the decision Tip called for.

She gave no answer.

"I take it," he said, "you ain't coming with me?"

She looked at him again. His eyes burned at her. She was filled still with her anger, mixed now with distraught confusion. If only, she thought, he didn't ask that I give up the Ponce. That held her fast, rooting her to the spot.

He turned on his heel and strode off down Banyan Street. At the nearest corner he left the street and as he disappeared Jenny, as though outside of herself, cried in her mind:

Oh, Tip, I don't want to do this to you, to us! But I can't help it! I can't! You ask for too much!

TIP APPEARED AT his camp early the following morning. Still clad in full evening dress, he had walked all night through the Glades. Never had the animals, the crawling things and the wild flying creatures seen such a sight.

The hunters at the camp were nearly as amazed. Tip spiked their comments by looking at them with his black eye and informing them gruffly, "Mind your own affairs."

He divested himself of tails, boiled shirt, trousers and soggy pumps, depositing them in a heap. "Throw them in the pond," he ordered the Negro cook. When the cook hesitated, Tip made a movement toward his gun rack.

The evening clothes went into the water and were carried off down into the Glades. It became a minor legend that a big crane found and donned them, and was often seen dressed for all solemn occasions.

The wealthy hunters, after Tip was dressed again in camp clothes, regarded him uneasily. Gaylord looked as if he wanted to ask Tip a question but didn't dare. Tip answered the man's unspoken curiosity. "I did what you said."

"Good," Gaylord replied. He began to explain to the other men, "I advised Tip to beat up——"

"Any of you," Tip interrupted harshly, "still want to go on a live gator hunt?"

The men gazed at him. His tone was so unlike him that

they were held by it. They saw how much he was affected by what had happened. His manner repelled most of them, but O'Brien blustered, "Sure, I want to go."

Tip looked around.

Gaylord nodded and said, "Count me in."

They were the only two.

"When do we leave?" O'Brien demanded.

"Right now," Tip told him.

Two hours later, down along a stream some miles to the southwest, Tip gave the men the same chance he once presented to Thornton. The three of them were hunched down, crouching behind clumps of tall grass on the shore. O'Brien held the short lengths of rope, Gaylord the long. Behind the grass an eleven-foot alligator lay sleeping, unsuspecting that men were ready to pounce on it.

"This is your last chance to back out," Tip whispered to his companions.

Gaylord shook his head, half-smiling. O'Brien's pink skin had grown a little white, but he replied defensively, "Not me."

The man spoke loudly enough to rouse the gator, so Tip did not wait an instant more. He sprang up and led them at a run.

They surprised the gator so that they were on it before it was fully awake. It had barely time to move. Tip didn't bother to go through the usual procedure of first getting a rope around the beast's body. He saw his chance to grasp the shut snout and took it.

O'Brien had flung himself on the body, sprawling his great weight over it, and Gaylord held on in back of him. The gator lay quiet, only switching a little the end of its long tail.

The two hunters were disappointed.

"He doesn't fight," said Gaylord.

"Is this all there is to it?" demanded O'Brien.

"We ain't got him yet," Tip replied, "and maybe we won't if you don't tie this snout I'm holding shut before he gets over his surprise."

"I can leave holding the body?" O'Brien inquired.

"Hurry up," Tip told him.

O'Brien lifted himself off the broad black back and came forward to the long head. Tip tensed for the alligator to start fighting. It didn't. It seemed a particularly apathetic reptile. Tip found himself disappointed, too. He had wanted to fight something else, giving vent to the still charged feelings within him.

O'Brien began to tie the snout. Tip, watching carefully, was reminded of the time Jenny tied the snout of the crocodile. It brought her back to him vividly, and brought Thornton, also, and all of last night. In place of the Chicago meat packer's pudgy red hands Tip saw those of Jenny. He couldn't stand the sight and turned his face away.

The next thing he knew the gator had made a wild, convulsive lunge. If it hadn't struggled before, it now began to fight in various ways all at once. It heaved part way up. It curled its great tail and flung it, throwing off the small Gaylord, who was bowled to one side and landed, bruised and dazed, some yards away.

The rope around the snout, which O'Brien hadn't yet made secure, slipped away. The gator's jaws, jerked sideways out of Tip's hold, were free. They opened. Twisted toward O'Brien, they closed, narrowly missing him when they boomed shut. O'Brien fell back, white as a sheet, and then scrambled to his feet, running some distance away.

247

The alligator now bit furiously at the air. Tip had been too concerned about not letting O'Brien get caught to think of himself. Thus it was that the giant reptile found a mark and sank its jagged teeth into Tip's right leg, just below the knee.

At first he felt no real pain. There was only a sudden dull ache as though from a tight, powerful squeezing. At the same time he knew the big teeth had penetrated his flesh deeply. He could feel his own warm blood flowing down his leg.

He was thrown diagonally away from the long head of the gator, which simply lay there with its jaws clamped on his leg. Tip didn't struggle for fear his captor might become active again. He was stunned, incredulous that this thing could be happening. When he realized that it was, he looked for Gaylord and O'Brien. He saw the former, sitting on the ground, still dazed as a result of the knocking about he had received from the gator's tail.

Tip's voice shook when he told the man, "Get the rifle."

"Rifle?" Gaylord asked.

"In the boat."

Gaylord got to his feet. Standing up, he could see the boats. He turned to Tip. "There isn't any rifle."

Roughly, Tip ordered, "Get the rifle from the boat!"

"I tell you we didn't bring any."

The cruel fact dawned on Tip. In his fury and preoccupation with another matter, he had been careless in fitting out the expedition.

At that moment he felt the full shock of pain. He looked at the alligator, at its great length again quiescent, at the jaws about his leg. Panic seized him momentarily, but he quickly steeled himself. He wondered if he had brought a hatchet. Swiftly he thought back. He had not.

He looked at Gaylord. "Where's O'Brien?"

Gaylord responded, "In one of the boats."

Bitterly Tip asked, "Funk?"

"Blue. What——"

"You can find a pole—wait a minute—get an oar and come back here. Stick it between his jaws to pry them open—try to get O'Brien to help."

Gaylord hurried away. Even before he left, the gator started what Tip had been dreading. It began to edge slowly backward, dragging him toward the water, where it would drown its prey.

Tip, prepared for this move, resisted as well as he could. He used his other foot and his arms to brace himself, digging them into the ground. It had little effect, tearing his flesh even more; the blood now flowed profusely and the pain stabbed through him unmercifully. Once the reptile partially loosened its hold and got a better grip, farther down on the fatter part of Tip's leg. After that Tip resisted hardly at all, and even actually helped himself along to relieve the pull of the sharp teeth.

He was dragged into the grass. Water lay there, and Tip knew that if the gator ever reached it with him, that would be the end. He yelled for Gaylord.

The man came back alone. He carried one of the oars. With relief, Tip saw that at least he was going to try. The man stared at the scene, at the blood showing on Tip's trousers and on the ground. "My God!" he panted. "My God!"

At Tip's instruction, Gaylord thrust the blade of the oar

into the alligator's jaws where they stuck out beyond their hold on his leg. The gator stopped. Gaylord pried, twisting the head of the gator so that the teeth on one side sank deeper into Tip's leg, making him cry out. Gaylord hesitated, but Tip yelled for him to keep on.

The beast seemed to pay little attention, until abruptly its jaws opened wider. They released Tip's leg and snapped at the oar. The teeth crunched on the wood, which it instantly spat out to yawn at Gaylord, who dropped the oar and sprang away.

Free, Tip tried to move. He made the mistake of endeavoring to get to his feet instead of rolling away. His injured leg would not hold him. Sitting up, he made a ready target when the gator turned its attention back to him. Angrily it sprang to seize him on the upper part of his right arm. The long teeth crunched to the bone.

Sickened, Tip looked up at Gaylord. Now the man was as white as O'Brien. He made a half-hearted movement toward the oar. He was relieved when Tip gasped, "No. If he lets loose up here maybe he'll grab my head."

Gaylord backed still farther away, stricken with terror.

"Get the ropes!" cried Tip. "Put one around him and hold him back!"

Gaylord only continued to back away. He was in a blue funk himself.

"Damn you!" Tip tried to rouse him. "Get the rope and help me!"

Gaylord stood frozen with fear. Tip saw that he could not count further on the man. It was doubtful if Gaylord could have held the heavy gator alone in any case, and there was nothing here about which to fasten a rope.

Tip looked at the creature that held him in its terrible grasp. The greenish-gray eyes, like those of a cat, were passionless. Man and beast regarded each other. The blotched hide of the alligator was dried in the sun, yet musky. On the end of its snout were two dreadful twin holes, the nostrils.

Tip groped for his hunting knife in its sheath at his belt as the gator began to move again. Only with effort could he keep from shrieking at the excruciating pain. He hoped his knife was still in its place. His hand felt for it, his breath coming in long, difficult gasps. He thought his heart would burst out of his chest, or fail him completely. Never in his life had he experienced such fear.

The fingers of his left hand found the hard handle of the knife and drew it out. He didn't think the blade could penetrate the armored head of the gator to its brain, and didn't want to try. He wouldn't even molest the eyes for fear the beast would go for his own head. He wanted to try the side of the belly where he could reach.

The alligator continued that slow backward movement, dragging him inexorably toward the water, now not many feet away. Once the animal stopped and chewed on his arm, as though savoring it, sending streams of such acute pain through his entire body that he nearly fainted.

Holding the knife with its sharp point downward, Tip saw the side of the whitish belly. He tried for it, but his hand was jerked away by the erratic pulling. He tried again, this time reaching it with the weapon.

Then he knew how weak he had become from loss of blood, which now saturated him. The unprotected skin-plates of the stomach of the alligator were tough, but ordinarily he could penetrate and cut them with his sharp blade. Now he made no impression on them.

He was pulled almost to the water's edge before he had another chance. The gator's tail entered the water; in another minute the creature would be entirely in its active element, where it could move, not awkwardly as upon land, but like lightning, for the kill.

Tip realized that this was his last chance to thrust his knife into that scaly belly and tear it open. Calling upon his final reserve of strength, he stabbed, only nicking the hide.

The gator moved once more, farther into the water. Tip stabbed again, frantically. By great good luck he hit the exact spot already nicked. The point of his knife disappeared into the bulging stomach of the alligator. He thrust it in farther, up to the hilt. Then, desperately, he ripped.

He opened the entire length of the gator's side belly. The great beast shivered with shock. The slit widened, and from it poured cold, slimy blood that flowed over Tip's hand and made his skin crawl. There followed entwined entrails. The stomach itself had been reached, and from it cascaded a sickening mass of partially digested fish, frogs, snakes and one discernible rabbit. The stench choked Tip.

All movement of the alligator stopped. It no longer pulled backward. Collapsing with Tip's torn arm still in its jaws, the expiring beast shuddered all down its length. Its eyes closed as though being shut forcibly.

Tip was able after a moment to lift the upper jaw and draw out his mangled arm. From it blood gushed in steady streams.

He tried to lift himself and failed. He grew rapidly weaker. "Gaylord!" he cried in tones that sounded to him like a shout, although he merely whispered. He thought he saw the man and heard him speak before he was shocked into realizing that his eyesight was growing dim. He wondered if he were dying. He was sure of it just before he lost consciousness.

IN THE AFTERNOON of that day, Jenny rode with Cleve in Choo Choo's wheel-chair. Cleve looked haggard after the events of the previous night. He listened, more seriously than Jenny had ever known him to do, when she told him that she felt she ought to go to Tip and have a further discussion with him. Perhaps in the heat of their difference they had been hasty with each other.

Cleve advised, "Wait until you've thought it out more."

Jenny allowed herself to be persuaded because she didn't know how she would be received by Tip, and because she drew back from facing West Palm and the knowing looks and censuring remarks she would receive if she went there.

"Don't be suspicious of my motives," Cleve told her. "As far as you're concerned they're far better than anyone believes. I've had a year to think about you."

"I can't believe that."

"I can. I'm sick of society girls like Lizzy who are only after money, and chorus girls after the same thing. I want something I've never had—a loving wife."

"What about the one who divorced you?"

"She was my wife, but not loving. I could have stopped the drink with her, maybe, if she had been."

"You can stop now."

"No, make no mistake about that. I want to tell you how it is with me on that. I've tried everything."

"Have you ever tried to stop drinking?"

"I've stopped," he said. "But that didn't work."

"Why not?"

"Because it started to kill me. I had the shakes so I couldn't hold a spoon in my hand. I began to starve to death. And when a cure threatens to kill the patient it isn't any good." He twisted his neck around to consult Choo Choo. "Isn't that right, train?"

The train didn't in the least know what he was talking about, but agreed readily by ringing its bell, blowing its whistle, letting off steam and saying, "Choo."

"I even took the Keeley Cure," Steve said. "That's also called the Gold Cure because they inject bichloride of gold in your veins. You go to live near a Keeley Institute and four times a day for three weeks you get the injections. You also drink some medicine they give you. Both give you a distaste for alcohol so you never want to swallow it again. At least they do to most people, but not to me. It only made me more thirsty." He turned to her and spoke more seriously than she had ever heard him. "I'm a toper and I'll always be one. I'll probably drink myself to death. I'm being honest with you, Jenny, just as I know you would be honest in not loving me."

"How can you expect me to?"

"I couldn't, for a long time. Probably not until—well, have you thought I might be able to give you children, as I know you want?"

She looked away, saying nothing. She faced the fact, denied until now, that this thought had entered her own head, slipping in and out again like an electric thrust that stung and enlivened the brain. She couldn't keep her pulse from beating a little faster.

"It wouldn't be a bad bargain for either of us," he proposed. "I'd be getting the best of it."

Jenny found herself at an unmarked fork on a tortuous road. "I don't know, Cleve, I don't know!"

Pulled one way by the thought of Tip, another by the thing Cleve might give her, Jenny was torn and devastated, unable to commit herself, resenting the call that she must.

Cleve asked, "How would you like to see my private car?"

"I'd like to, but—" Her dubiousness was involuntary, but plain.

He laughed. "Eddie, the steward, will be there to chaperon us. I wish you'd believe I'm not thinking about you like that."

"It isn't easy, because you did at first."

"This is now. I'm offering everything good about myself I can. A poor thing, Jenny, but my own."

"You know too well how to get around a woman."

"Especially when I mean it."

Choo Choo delivered them at the car. Only half a dozen remained after the exodus following the Washington Ball. Eddie, the Negro steward, handed Jenny up the steps and into the vestibule. Jenny could not restrain her curiosity about seeing the inside of a private car. She had always wanted to.

Cleve showed her into the observation room. It was finished in English oak and had art glass cathedral windows, with an Empire ceiling illuminated with gold leaf. Set crossways was a deep upholstered fringed couch dripping with pillows. Before this was an ottoman and several hand-buffed black leather chairs. Jenny had never seen such luxury.

Down the corridor leading along one side of the car he led her to the three large private rooms. One of them had a shining brass bed in it, and at this magnificence she caught her breath. Without embarrassment, Cleve showed her the fully equipped bathroom, whose window was of stained glass. She was amazed to see on a train a bathtub, a white metal washstand with mirrors above it and a fancy flush commode enclosed in white-painted wicker that covered it most elegantly, making it look more like a chair than what it was.

Farther on was the dining-room with a large oblong table, sideboard, china cabinet and writing desk with bookcase above. This room, too, was finished in golden oak and had an English Wilton carpet. Silk and velour drapes were at the windows. Jenny fingered them.

At the far end of the car were the kitchen and Eddie's quarters, to which he had repaired. Jenny returned with Cleve to the observation room. Here, when they sat on the couch, Jenny thought she would keep on sinking into its softness and never stop. Eddie appeared with a drink for Cleve and a glass of orange juice for her.

They sipped these. Jenny asked, "Why did you bring me here?"

"To show you a little more of what I'm offering."

Jenny pictured herself riding to New York with him while sitting on this soft couch. She had never been to New York. There would be the mansion on Fifth Avenue. She could be mistress of such a place. She would direct servants. She would have carriages, perhaps one of those new automobiles everybody talked about. And clothes! She would go to Paris for them.

There would be nurses for her children. Her children. Aunt Erminia would visit her then. She thought of her aunt's shock, then surprise, then breathless pleasure if this came about.

As though reading her mind, Cleve said, "It wouldn't all be easy for you, Jenny. Some people would never accept you; the kind that resents anyone else climbing up because it makes them seem less grand. You'd be snubbed. But I think we could carry most. We could get them to forgive your beauty. Especially here, with Mary Lily Flagler behind you."

Jenny wondered if she could come to the Ponce at all. Perhaps neither Tip nor Cleve would allow her the hotel. In that circumstance, what did she want?

"Have you thought," Cleve went on, "that it could be a mistake for both you and Tip to try any more?"

"If I could believe that . . ."

"You'll see that it's right. I know how you feel, Jenny. Such a break seems like the end of the world, or a great turning over. It is, of course. But once it's decided it isn't as formidable as it looks now. Not as much as you think."

"I don't know what to do," she said miserably.

"My lawyers would take care of everything. I'm sure Tip wouldn't make it difficult. You would have to do almost nothing, sign a few papers, that's all."

He didn't speak the dread word, divorce. But it screamed in Jenny's head. Singing there also was a refrain: My children, my children.

"What do you say, Jenny?"

She put her fingers to her temples. "Let me think, let me feel, some more."

"I don't want to hurry you," he importuned. "But the Ponce is closing soon, and I'll be leaving."

"I can't tell, Cleve, I can't!"

He said no more, but gulped at his drink.

She looked out the window at the huge yellow hotel close by. That, somehow, was what caused her trouble. For the first time Jenny felt a resentment of the Ponce because it was bound so closely with her present torture.

In the silence she was startled at the sound of a telephone ringing. She looked about, at the same time remembering the special lines run to some of the private cars.

Cleve put down his drink and took his feet off the ottoman. "Oh, yes," he said, "we have all modern inconveniences here, even your favorite instrument hitched up to the hotel."

He rose and went over to the phone which Jenny now saw for the first time fastened to the wall at the other side of the observation room. Cleve took the receiver off the hook and spoke into the long mouthpiece. "Yes?" he asked, and after listening for a moment, said, "I see . . . Yes, she's here." He turned to Jenny. "It's for you."

Jenny knew, as she went to take the receiver, that it must be Helen at the board who had found her here, and that it must be something important for her to be found.

She didn't know who spoke at the other end of the wire until he said his name. "This is Douglas, Jenny."

Alarm shot through her. "Yes, Douglas?"

"You'd better come at once. There has been an accident."

She cried, "What is it? Is Tip——"

She could sense Douglas hesitating over the wire.

259

"Tell me!" she implored.

"I expect I had better. He was chewed up by an alligator and brought in——"

"He's dead!"

"Now wait a minute. He isn't dead. He's a good deal chewed up, and it's true he may not live, but——"

"I'll be right over."

"I'm at my office now to get some medicine and more bandages. I'll go back to your house and see you there."

Jenny hung up, staring for an instant at the phone instrument.

She felt as though she had been flung into an abyss, and that she deserved it. While she had been debating about deserting Tip, he lay at the point of death. She was sure she was responsible. Because of her he didn't care what happened to him.

That accusation brought unquestioned decision.

Cleve asked, "What is it?"

She turned to him. "You know how Tip wasn't supposed to catch gators, not alive. But he did. One . . ."

"Can I help?"

"By un—understanding," she stuttered, "that I'm going to him."

He made his comment a question, to know more. "Yes, Jenny?"

"To stay."

He resigned himself as though he had expected this. Gently, he said, "If you ever change your mind, I'll be around."

DOUGLAS WAS WAITING for her on the porch when she arrived, breathless. She was thankful for no one else being there; he must have shooed others away or they remained away by their own volition. Douglas said nothing of this; he didn't mention not having seen her for some time or any of the things he undoubtedly must have heard about her. He saw how agitated and shaken she was and forced her down into a chair. "Now take it easy," he instructed. "Nothing is ever as bad as it seems at first."

"But it's bad?"

"It's bad. Getting excited about it won't help. Instead, it will hurt."

They regarded each other, she trying to read more about Tip, he judging her in order to tell how much to reveal to her. His eyebrows had bushed out, partially gray; although only middle-aged, he was already slightly stooped.

"Let me know," she pleaded. "Everything. Because what I'm thinking must be worse than it is."

"I'm sure of that," he said. He told her what the men from the Ponce had reported after they brought Tip in on the wagon. "At least I got those miserable people to tell me what happened," Douglas concluded. "I don't know of any other man than Tip who could have done what he did. When I got him he didn't have much blood left in him. It's a good thing it was a gator instead of a crocodile."

Jenny's eyes flew toward the second story of the house. "Now——"

"I've had him under an opiate since noon."

"Noon!" she cried.

"They brought him in shortly before."

She accused, "Why didn't you——"

"I wanted to see what chances he had."

"What are they?"

"Physically, about fifty-fifty. If his wounds heal properly, he could come out of it with a stiff arm and not much else. That would be something of a miracle."

"It's better than I thought."

"Don't count on it, because it isn't all, Jenny."

"You haven't told me——"

"I haven't mentioned the other part. It isn't physical. That, as I say, is about an even chance, which could go one way or the other. I think you know what the other part is."

Jenny asked slowly, "You mean he doesn't want to live?"

"That's the part that is going to count if he is ever to get well," he said. "So you must know and understand this more than the other. Spiritually, right now, he hasn't the slightest chance to live. He wants to die."

"I made him do the gator hunting again. He thought I didn't want him any more. I'm to blame if he——"

"Stop that!" Douglas spoke sharply. "Who's to blame for what isn't the question now."

She swallowed and asked, "If it's so that he wanted to die, and that he did the gator hunting on account of it, why did he fight and kill it? Why didn't he just let it——"

"Pure instinctive self-preservation, I expect," Douglas theorized, "that he couldn't stop to think about. Anger at the gator, too. His desire to die probably was never actually conscious. It only existed in the back of his mind."

Impatiently, she asked, "Can I see him?"

"Presently. I want you to realize that two things are necessary to save him. The first is, at least for a time, nearly continual nursing. The second, and greater thing, is making him want to live. And there is only one person who can make him do that. You are the single one who can save him."

She whispered, "How can I do that?"

"I don't know. I wish I did. Perhaps by showing him that you still want him."

"I can do that," she said. "But I don't know if it will be enough. Oh, Douglas, help me—at least tell me what you think about what's happened between us."

"From what I know," he answered slowly, "I'll tell you this: You remember I once said some people meet their problems right, and others don't. You and Tip haven't met yours right. You've both fought it too hard, and it's bigger than you, so it licked you. Don't ask me whose fault it is because it's both, in degrees no one can judge."

Silently she thanked him for his plain-spoken words.

"Beyond that," he continued, "I can only do the physical part, and find someone to help you nurse him."

"I don't want anyone else."

"You can't do it alone."

"I won't have anyone else."

"You haven't seen him—you don't know, Jenny. His dressings will have to be changed every few hours."

"I'll do it."

"Day and night."

"I'll do that."

"You aren't able."

"I am."

"I can't let you——"

"I won't let anyone else in the house."

"That isn't sensible."

"I want to do it that way. You speak of degrees of blame. I'm taking the biggest."

The physician gave her a long look. "I'll let you try."

"Can we go up now?"

"Are you positive you have the stomach for this?"

Jenny stood up. "I've got to save him."

Douglas picked up his bag and the cardboard box of medical supplies he had brought. "I'll show you what must be done."

They entered the house and climbed the stairs.

They went into Tip's room quietly. Douglas had already partially arranged it as a hospital room. A table had been moved in and placed close on one side of the bed near its head. The room had been cleared of all except what was necessary to attend a patient.

Tip lay on his back on the bed. Only his head showed above the sheet that covered him. Through the deep color of his lifelong tan, gray appeared. His cheeks were sunken. His eyes were closed. Mercifully, he remained under the effect of the drug administered to him. He moaned occasionally and moved feebly.

Under the sheet Jenny could make out the lumpish shapes of his bandages. One of them was stained with a spot of red where the blood welled up.

"I forgot to tell you," Douglas said to Jenny, "we will need hot water. I have some on the stove. Will you get a pitcher of it? Be sure the container is clean."

Jenny went back downstairs. She hurried to scour a pitcher and fill it from the large pot on the stove. Her hands trembled as she worked. She shook so that she could hardly hold the pitcher.

To keep from dropping it she put it down on the kitchen table. She leaned against the wall. In her weakness even that was not enough to support her. Slipping down, she sank slowly to the floor. Her legs crumpled under her; she sat there, gripped by fear, her senses numbed.

She must not give way like this. She had to fight. She had to get back her love for Tip that in a nightmare she had thought of discarding.

She climbed to her feet and pulled herself together again. She knew more about what she had to face. Resolutely, hurrying to make up for lost time, she carried the pitcher upstairs.

Douglas had Tip partially uncovered. His right arm was bare. The sight made Jenny feel faint. Raw ugly gashes completely covered the upper arm, cut to the bone. Actual large teeth marks could be seen.

"Fill the basin," Douglas ordered.

She was glad for the respite from the sight. As she poured the water she summoned all her strength, preparing herself for anything to be seen on Tip's body.

Douglas showed her how to mix an antiseptic solution in the water, saturate a dressing in it and apply it to the wounds. It took a number of large ones, well wrapped in place, to cover those on the arm.

He proceeded to do the same with Tip's leg. Once again

Jenny sickened and fought for control of her reeling senses. She was pale when they were finished. But she had prepared and placed the last dressing, and Douglas had approved.

They left the room and returned downstairs to the porch.

"There isn't anything more to be done for the present," he told her. "I'll come back this evening. I want to see you do all of it before I leave him alone with you."

"I'll expect you." She had only one misgiving. "If he wakes up?"

"Give him one of the tablets in the small bottle on the table. Don't try to feed him anything yet. Eat something yourself."

She shook her head.

"I'll bring you some supplies," he said. Then he left.

Alone, Jenny felt helpless. Douglas had told her to do no more for Tip unless he showed signs of needing it. She wanted to do something. She had to occupy herself.

She decided to clean the house. It needed cleaning, for she had not been over for some weeks. Dust was on everything. She scrubbed the floors and dusted the furniture, working furiously. In the middle of it she was sure that Tip had died. She rushed upstairs, to see him lying as before. He seemed hardly to breathe. She watched him for a long time and then returned to the cleaning.

Grace and John Doolittle arrived. Their faces were grave, and his could not keep out of its expression his disapproval of Jenny. Uncomfortably and nervously he slapped the great gourd that was his stomach. Grace, embracing her, had none of this. "What can we do?" she asked.

"Nothing," Jenny responded dully. "Except keep people away. At least until tomorrow."

They promised to do this and in turn exacted word from

her that she would call on them for any need. They left, with the mayor muttering in more friendly fashion, "Good you've come."

She was tired when Douglas returned that evening, but careful not to let him see this. Tip's room had been straightened and made neat. This the doctor did see and nodded satisfaction.

He watched while she changed the dressings. She was sure and exact. She did not flinch from the touch or sight of any of the awful cuts and gashes. When blood welled she sopped at it immediately, stopping it with a fresh bandage. She bound them on securely and painstakingly.

When they left the room, Douglas said, "That part is all right. Now it's a question of your strength. You aren't fooling me right now. You're to go in your room and lie down, even if you don't sleep. I'll let you do without food tonight, or until you get hungry, but not without some rest."

"I don't——"

"Get in there. I'll wake you up later, when I leave."

She obeyed. On her bed, she was sure she would never sleep. She didn't know when she did.

It was late when Douglas shook her by the shoulder. She sat up, asking, "What time is it?"

"Midnight."

She got hastily to her feet. "You should have——"

"I've changed his bandages," he said. "I'm leaving him in your care until morning. Change them again around three, and then at six and nine. I'll be in again by then. I won't tell you to rest any more because I know you won't."

She didn't. Her eyes were sprung wide awake for the rest of the night. She was on the alert every second. She took a

267

rocker into Tip's room and sat there. She left on only the light in the hall, which reflected in the room. She followed instructions to the letter. Her only time of alarm came when he began to be restless and throw himself about on the bed. She managed to get him to swallow one of the tablets. After a time, he quieted.

DOUGLAS MADE HER serve him breakfast and eat some of it herself when he came in the morning. He told her, "He's no worse or better. That's as far as his injuries are concerned. I'm going to let him come to partial consciousness today, even though he is in some pain, to see how he is otherwise."

Alone again, Jenny suffered or was grateful when people began to call, to inquire about Tip's condition.

Mr. Varney arrived early, acutely worried. He had heard the whole story about the Ponce hunters deserting Tip in the gator fight. He chomped his toothless jaws together with fury. He looked about at Jenny's arrangements, poking his nose into everything, and informed her, "I'll bring you groceries."

"You can't let the ferry stand idle while you do that," she protested.

"I can and will," he said. "And if any Ponce men ride with me, as a few of them do, I'll throw them overboard."

In the middle of the morning Grace brought a bowl of steaming chicken broth. "This isn't only for Tip," she said. "I won't stay because you won't let me do anything, but I refuse to leave until you've swallowed some of this."

Jenny managed to down a cup of the broth. While she consumed it, with one ear cocked for any sound from upstairs, she asked Grace, "What are they saying about me?"

"Everything unkind they can think of."

"Can't they see——"

"They won't believe yet that you gave up twenty million dollars to come back to Tip."

"You know——"

"Bulletins arrived from across the Great Divide at pretty regular intervals, Jenny."

"I've got more to think about now than what the town believes."

"And better," advised Grace.

Doc and Cap Jim Bethune came to wish Tip well and also to rage over the actions of the Ponce hunters. The marshal and Emma made no effort to hide the fact that curiosity and censure of Jenny brought them; their solicitude was for Tip alone.

At noon, Helen and Mazy came over from the Ponce, thoughtfully bringing Jenny's clothes. "I'll be at the house-cleaning," the hunchback declared.

"No, Mazy," Jenny told her. "Thank you, but I want to do it myself."

"You haven't the strength I can tell the doing of all here will take."

"If I haven't, I'll find it."

The hunchback gave her a long and penetrating glance. "You looked into your heart, the right place to find yourself."

"He——"

"His car went out last night."

Jenny asked Helen, "I hope Miss Morris wasn't put out too much."

"It hasn't mattered," Helen replied, "because it's so near

the end of the season. She says your place will be kept for you next year."

Jenny shook her head. "Tell her to get somebody else."

"But you——"

"I won't be back."

"Well—we'll miss you."

In the afternoon Tip's eyes came slowly open. Shock was in them. They were dull. More was there. He looked at Jenny without recognition, or as if she was a being about whom he didn't care. She spoke his name, but he didn't reply.

She tried to feed him some of Grace's broth. He wouldn't take it. The liquid spilled from his mouth, down his chin and onto the bedclothes. He turned his face away.

He murmured, trying to speak. He tried to lift both hands and put them outside the covers. The right would not work. The left struggled out, reaching for something.

"What is it, Tip?" she whispered. "What do you want?"

He groped, murmuring unintelligibly. She took his hand, and he suffered it to be held, but listlessly, unaware of who touched him.

Douglas shook his head when Jenny related this to him. "If he knew it was you, and wanted you, we could have hope," he said.

For some days Tip knew nothing. He was out of his head with delirium. Continually he reached out, muttering a want he knew nothing of himself. Jenny held his hand by the hour, hoping her touch might help him.

A week after being brought in from the Glades, Tip came back clearly to consciousness. That morning he was truly awake and himself. He was in pain, but he knew what had happened to him and what he saw in the room.

He showed no interest at seeing Jenny. His gaze was entirely apathetic. He had no interest in anything else. Jenny spoke to him as brightly as she could.

"You're going to get well, Tip. I'm not just saying this. Douglas says you are."

He looked down at his form on the bed. His eyes went from his bandaged arm to his leg, both showing under the sheet. He glanced up at her again. Disagreement with what she told him was plain in his expression. He might have said aloud, "I'm not going to get well," and added, "I don't want to. I don't mean to, and you can't make me."

"I've come back to you, Tip. Everything else is over and we're together again."

He spoke his first actual words, murmuring them in so low a tone that Jenny couldn't hear at first. After asking him to repeat them, she bent low to listen.

The words struck her like a blow in the face.

"You're only here because you feel sorry for me."

She jerked back, crying, "No! I'm here because I love you, Tip. More than anything else in the world! Because I found that out."

His head rolled weakly on the pillow, denying what she said.

"But it's true!" she implored. "The other is finished. It never really started. I was so wrong, Tip; oh, darling, I was so wrong!"

He stared at the ceiling, unable to believe her.

She pleaded for his acceptance of her, reiterating. "I'm here because I love you, Tip."

He spoke again, barely whispering. "We had love. It wasn't enough. We can't have anything now."

"We can!" she declared with all the depth of her being. For one thing, we can have each other more than we've had ately. We'll be together more. I'm going to keep your accounts for you—you've never liked that—and I'll go to the camp and stay there part of the time, in the old cabin, with you. I an arrange the business end with the Ponce better."

He was smiling, bitterly. Weakly, he said, "Never hunt again."

"You will! Of course you will!"

He rolled his head. He would accept nothing of what she aid. It was only then that she fully realized how deeply she ad hurt him and became desperate to find a way to ease the mortal wound.

WHEN DOUGLAS SAW her after that he said "You look worse than he does. You're both killing yourselves You've got to let me——"

"No," she said.

"I'll get——"

"I don't want anyone else to touch him."

"You can't keep on this way."

"Have I done everything right?"

"Yes, but——"

"Could anyone else have done more?"

"No," he admitted.

"Then until I can't satisfy you, let me alone," she pleaded

"You haven't had any sleep for days, not proper sleep."

"I get some. I don't need much."

"Jenny, I'm not going to let you——"

"You are," she told him. "You said if anyone could give him an interest in life, I had to do it. I don't want anybody else wasting his time. I want all of it. I'm going to make him live. He's already getting better in body."

Skeptically, Douglas asked, "Is he?"

"Come and see."

He followed her upstairs and into the sickroom. While Tip showed no sign of caring one way or the other, Jenny exposed his wounds. She had seen the healing process, welcoming it with a grateful thrill. The clean gaps in the flesh showed the first signs of beginning to close. No feared infection had set in.

Douglas looked at her. She knew it was partially for Tip's benefit that he said, "You've done this, Jenny, with your constant attention. You've put him days ahead of when he had any right to have this happen."

If Tip heard, he paid no heed, gave no sign. He was not concerned with the healing of his wounds or the fact that his wife was nursing his body back to life again.

Douglas lectured him, "You've got to fight, man. You're going to be able to keep at your guiding and some of your hunting. Except for gators and crocs. You touch one of them varmints again and I won't have anything more to do with you. I'll let you die then for sure."

Tip's lips twisted into a grimace that seemed to say he was going to die right now.

"Come on and live," the doctor urged.

Tip turned his face to the wall.

"That's no way to do," Douglas scolded. "Not when Jenny has worked over you the way she has. You've got to get well for her sake."

Tip's gaze turned back to Jenny. He looked at her, but it was queerly.

Douglas spoke harshly. "People have come back together again after more estrangement than you've had, a lot more."

Tip gazed at the ceiling. More than one thing had conspired to crush him, so that his body lacked the strength to give to his mind the power to see things whole.

Downstairs again, Douglas told Jenny, "His body is getting well as far as it can go by itself. His stubborn spirit is sicker than I believed it could be, or any man's could be. He takes things hard, as he always has. It will undo the work of the body, everything you've done. It will kill him."

In anguish, Jenny pleaded, "Don't say that. There must still be some hope."

"I don't know what, even though you need only one point of penetration to rouse him, no matter what it is. Unless . . ."

She glanced at him expectantly. "Unless what?"

"I've got a long report to read about something I can't altogether believe yet myself."

"What is it?"

He looked at her. "I won't tell you any more now. I shouldn't have mentioned this much. I'll get at studying it right away."

"But——"

"Be patient, Jenny. It would do no good, and perhaps harm, to mention it to you now, if there isn't anything to it in the end. I'll let you know in a few days."

She tried to contain herself. She had the diversion of having Grace warn her, "A delegation is going to call tomorrow afternoon. They want to see if everything Douglas has been telling them is true."

"I don't care——"

"You might, later," advised Grace. "If you can stand it, let them come."

"They won't see Tip."

"It's you they want to look over. I'll see that they don't hang on."

Grace came with Emma, Miss Potter and three other ladies. Jenny entertained them in the parlor, serving tea and cake prepared at a cost in time and strength from caring for Tip that she had been loath to give.

The ladies appreciated the sacrifice. After their first murmured inquiries about Tip they settled down to chattering about everything except the one subject that was the object of their visit. But there was no need to mention this. They had only to look at Jenny.

She was thin and gaunt. Her cheeks were sunken. Her facial bones stood out prominently. Her eyes had drawn back into her head in deep hollow sockets. Most of all, the ladies observed, she no longer cared about her appearance. In anyone else this would have been slovenly. In Jenny Totten it meant a different thing entirely. On it they feasted their eyes until Grace stood up and said:

"I think we've stayed long enough."

Miss Potter patted Jenny's hand and said, "I'm sure everything is going to be all right with both of you."

Emma shook hands warmly, and spoke the only forthright words connected with the purpose of her presence. Sincerely, even though a little stiffly, she said, "We are all happy and glad to have you back, Jenny."

"Please call on us for anything you want," another woman chirped.

"At any time," still another added.

Grace looked back as they left and gave a grimacing nod.

Jenny found herself touched at this acceptance of herself. Tears sprang to her eyes at being forgiven and taken back. She had crossed the Great Divide one way and returned, a still more difficult feat.

This, combined with what Douglas came to reveal to her that evening, made her day complete. Carefully and at length he outlined the mysterious thing he had only intimated before. When she took it in, incredulously, she wanted to rush to Tip at once. But Douglas cautioned, "Wait until tomorrow. You're excited now. Drink it in a little more yourself. And don't forget," he cautioned, "it isn't positive, only very probable."

She didn't have to wait until the next day. That night, as she arranged her nursing equipment on the table, she turned for an instant and caught Tip looking at her. His gaze jerked away immediately.

Jenny's heart pounded with elation. It was the first time he had shown any positive interest in anything.

She went about her duties of preparing things for the night, prolonging them. She kept her back to him as much as possible, giving him a chance to look at her more if he wanted, and to think.

She heard him clear his throat. He had not done that before; he didn't care enough about living to assert himself even to that extent.

When he spoke, of his own accord, without being questioned or addressed as had been his procedure, Jenny did not turn at once. She couldn't. His voice was choked with emotion, to show that his strong will to die had at last been broken. He could feel.

"It's my fault," he said in a strangled tone, "making you work like this—nursing me . . ."

She whirled and went to her knees beside the bed. "It isn't anybody's fault!" she cried.

Her arms went out to him, and she held him while she placed her cheek against his, and he suffered her and welcomed her by reaching for her.

"I shouldn't have had you out to the camp with Thornton," he said. "That was a mistake. I was to blame."

"Nobody's to blame." She had learned that nothing was accomplished by blaming. "And he isn't half the man you are right now. He isn't a quarter of the fighter. He isn't a part of the drinker, and that's what he does best. He couldn't kill an alligator that had him in its jaws."

She was crying, and she knew that he wept, too. His sparse tears mingled with her profuse ones, running down their cheeks.

They hardly knew what they said.

"I don't feel like any of the things you said I am."

"We'll build you up."

"You can stand some building yourself."

"We'll both be fine again."

"You got your freckles back."

"I'll have lots of them, to stay this time." She choked, "We may be able to have something else, Tip." She told him what Douglas had imparted to her. It had been discovered that what you ate had something to do with the ability to have children. In Ohio they had been accustomed to having lots of dairy products and vegetables. Not having them here threw their systems off. Douglas was almost sure this had been their trouble all along. But now milk, eggs, cheese and vegetables were more available. "Tip, do you understand?" Jenny pleaded. "It may not be too late for us."

His eyes gleamed briefly. "Even if it doesn't turn out that way—we've got each other, that being enough."

"We've found that out."

Tip indicated the window. Through the pane the branches of the royal poinciana could be seen faintly. The flame tree had grown to fill the space outside. "Did you notice," he asked, "how your poinciana has come up so that you can't see the Ponce any more from the window?"

Jenny nodded, unable to speak. Now the tree offered its greatest service to her. Its leaping flames, soon to come in its blooming, would consume the hotel forever. She wept, softly and happily.